novum pro

WHISPERS OF DEMONIZED SOULS

Antonia Kattos

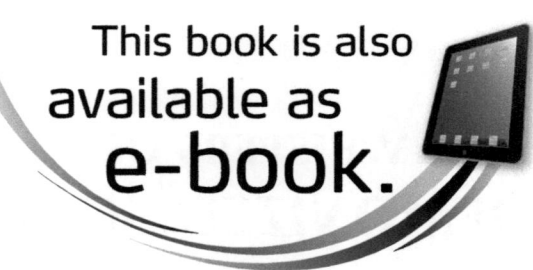

www.novum-publishing.co.uk

All rights of distribution, including film, radio, television, photomechanical reproduction, sound carrier, electronic media and reprint in extracts, are reserved.

Printed in the European Union, using environmentally-friendly, chlorine-free and acid-free paper.

© 2016 novum publishing

ISBN 978-3-99048-290-2
Editor: Louise Darvid
Cover photo:
original painting by Irene Kattos
Cover design, layout & typesetting: novum publishing

www.novum-publishing.co.uk

PROLOGUE

PROLOGUE

1. Knowing...

I was sitting on a blue hospital chair. My grandpa was in his hospital room; his condition was something I never liked to speak of. It was our weekly visit; he'd been in a coma for more than three months after the car accident. He never spoke, he never moved, just lay there lifelessly, the slow movement of his chest was the only indication there was still a soul in his body.

We were allowed to go inside one at a time. I never went inside; I didn't want to see him like that. Maybe it was because of the strong bond I had with my grandfather that I could not accept his condition. I didn't want to think of him like that. I was waiting outside curled up on a chair, covered with a blanket, reading "A Midsummer Night's Dream". It was distracting enough, enough for me not to think.

It was October in Wisconsin; St. George was dressed in white exactly like every other year. I was waiting for my parents for hours, it was getting dark outside, but I didn't mind. This was hard on my dad, his father was in an extremely bad state of health and even though my dad never admitted it, he was very pessimistic about it. Everybody was. I refused to be anywhere near my family, I would isolate myself from everybody else; I would just hide in a corner and do anything that would take my mind off of things.

It was the only way for me to bear it.

That day though, for some reason I just walked to the glass; the blanket still around my shoulders and the book in hand; I stared at him, I hadn't seen him in a while. He looked emaciated, his cheeks had sunk, his eyes were deep in their sockets, and he looked pale, dead almost. He was connected to beeping machines and an oxygen mask was over his mouth and nose. His chest rose slowly and dropped back down smoothly – he was still there. There was a soul in this functionless body – my only hope.

"Life is a very fragile thing, April..."

I gasped in surprise; there was someone next to me. Where had he come from? I turned my head to the side, an old man, a stranger. I stared at him in wonder. "No one seems to realize that until it's too late..." The man continued in a very soft and gentle voice, turning his head to view my grandfather briefly. The brown of my eyes met the blue of his.

He stared at me intensely. I had never seen a blue so deep in my entire life... His face was folded with wrinkles, his talc-white hair came all the way down to his shoulders, but his eyes seemed so young, out of place on his weathered body. They were bright and shining and deep, a beautiful blue unlike anything I'd ever seen; almost not human...

"April, Josephine, Smith," he murmured to himself, turning to look back at my grandfather. My name; how did he know my name? My heart raced immediately and banged against my ribs. He turned around and leaned in my ear, tucking a strand of hair behind it. I froze; the blood in my veins was running cold. He whispered in a calming, soft melody. "Only *you* can stop *The Whispers*..." he breathed. His eyes glimmered under the bright light of the hospital waiting room. The book fell out of my hands responsively, crushing on the hard tile with a loud thud; I was petrified on spot, scared now. "*You should be just scared of yourself, not of anybody else...*" he musically murmured in my ear and pulled away.

I stared at the floor, trying to find words to reply. I looked up again.

He was gone.

PART 1
"The Difference between Illusion and Reality"

2. Lime to neon green

Saturday. Night.
Voices.
"*Follow...*" the voices demanded. Deep and unidentified. Hypnotizing. Maybe hinted to sound dark. But not very. Almost neutral. With no emotion.
"*Move...*" There was no echo; it seemed as if the voices were one. I was in bed, but awake, still turning from side to side, trying to find the perfect position to sleep. I kept my eyes shut.
My eyes fluttered open at the sound of it.
I *had* to move.
Everything else zeroed. Anything else in my mind lost significance, was erased, deleted. I lost the ability to wonder, to question, to find, to think. I couldn't fear or feel anything, right there, at that moment, when I was staring at the ceiling, in the darkness of my room. The only thing I was aware of was the obligation.
"*Walk...*" the voice said sternly. I didn't process anything, just obeyed. Unemotionally and mechanically, I slowly slid out of my bed covers. It was late. My parents were completely unconscious. Being as quiet as possible was my first priority. I pushed my feet into my shoes, slowly, quietly.
"*Walk...*" the voice repeated as I turned to pace down the hallway. I walked silently, every step I made had a lot of effort in it. My face was utterly blank and my eyes wide open – unblinking. My arms rested motionless to my sides. All I could think of was the obligation, the request of the voice. And all I could do was obey.
I stopped at the staircase, unsure of where to go. My face expressed no feeling and so did my body, I stood there absolutely motionless, waiting for the voice to tell me, to guide me in the dark.
"*Follow...*" the voice said, and for the first time the word came out expressing something. Approval.

With the same care and silence I walked down the stairs one at a time. My eyes stared at something, somewhere far away. I walked slowly, hypnotized by the voice. *"Come..."* The tone of it was impelling, made me want to follow even more. I walked to the door, and stopped, outstretching my hand to the doorknob, ready to twist it. *"Open it..."* the voice ordered me again. I obeyed – my eyes were vacant, empty.

I cautiously pulled the door open and a wave of cold wind slapped my face. I didn't feel it though, I could feel nothing. I was completely hypnotized. I closed the door behind me as noiselessly as I could. *"Walk away... Far away..."* said the voice, harsh but soft at the same time. I walked down the porch, mechanically; no sentiment was mirrored in my face. It must've been cold... though, I'm not sure... I couldn't feel anything at that moment.

I wasn't sleepwalking, this was different. It was like someone had invaded my mind, in every single thought, in every single breath I took. Something in me urged to find that voice, to follow, to leave everything I knew behind. I forgot who I was, where I was, what I was doing – nothing registered, I realized nothing.

I didn't even feel fear of walking in the woods in complete darkness, with the wind being strong and cold, and my feet sinking in snow... I kept on going, walked away... far away... My breathing was steady and a little cloud formed every time I exhaled.

The breeze carried snowflakes in it, made the trees bend and shriek. The smell of fresh pine travelled around me, I could listen to the lake nearby, to the waves breaking onto the shore. I was somehow alert, but not fully. The cold was severe, and after I'd walked what I now assume was a mile, my feet got numb and it wasn't tiredness, it was the snow.

I collapsed, clenching my jaws because of the extreme conditions, although I wasn't able to feel anything, my body responded to the cold, I was just wearing a long sleeved shirt, and was wet to the bone. I was shivering from head to toe. *"Keep going! Don't stop!"* the voice was yelling, I could discern concern and anxiety. My eyes flared. I crawled on four, battling with hypothermia.

I didn't feel pain despite the struggle. I knew something was wrong with me but didn't know what exactly. Nothing would stop me from moving on, the voice's words echoed in my head. *"Keep going!" "Don't stop!"* I had to. I had to keep on going, move into the unknown of the forest, the part of the woods I'd never dared to explore.

"Come on! We can't afford losing you! Do you understand?!" The voice expressed one thing intensively – agony. Why was it so agonized? Why would my loss affect it whatsoever? But I didn't even question anything at that time, I just knew I couldn't stop, I wasn't allowed to stop. A while passed, to me though, it seemed like forever, a wave of icy wind peeled my skin off, immobilized me. I could feel my heart in my chest, beating so fast and hard it shook my entire ribcage. I was so cold, so cold I was unable to move, my system was shutting down.

"Come on, come on... you're almost there!" The voice tried to sound reassuring, persuasive, but the concern was still there, hinting each and every word. I wanted to get up, to make myself move, but was completely unable. I looked up, only now did I realize I was climbing a hill, the terrain was uneven, rocks and projections stuck out. I must've travelled a decent distance from my house. I instinctively searched for light, I stared at the sky, but there was no moon, it was a moonless night. The stars provided light but it was trivial, insufficient, I was lost in the gloom.

Every move demanded so much energy – energy I did not have, even lifting my chest to breathe was a challenge. Every move caused me excruciating pain. I was slow, extremely slow, but I had to follow the voice's instructions, I had to move! It felt like my limbs weren't a part of my body anymore, I was so numb, and so cold my lips had turned purple. I somehow managed to extend an arm in front, to sink my fingers into the mud and drag myself forward. *"Yes! Yes! Climb up. Come on!"* the voice yelled, trying to push me, to help me.

I was quivering, my jaws vibrated. I kept on going though, pulled my functionless body forward with my hands, gripping on to the frozen mud. I started getting my senses back. I felt pain, unbearable pain, and I don't know how or what made me clench my teeth and move on. It would be impossible to any ordinary person. I just kept on repeating the voice's words in my disorientated mind. *"You're almost there!" I'm almost there*, I thought to myself, over and over again. I'd covered a long distance, and this was a part of the forest I didn't recognize even though I'd been running in these woods ever since I was a little girl. For the first time that night I felt fear. I felt something.

What was I doing? Why was I even listening to voices? Was I paranoid? Crazy? There was a decent chance I was mad. But I wasn't.

I dragged myself forward. I was filthy, covered in mud, snow and greenery. The forest remained soundless, I could only hear myself, the dragging sound as I pushed myself in front planting my fingers in the dirt. My jaws vibrated uncontrollably, I was shaking. I suddenly stopped, unable to tolerate the iciness anymore. I slowly pulled my hand out of the soil. I stared at it. It was red and I couldn't feel it. At all. Every part of me was shaking, blinking was hard, a great challenge.

"Don't you stop... Please, **we** *need you..."* The voice was soft now, it had turned into a melody. A pleading melody. I couldn't move, I could follow any more. "I can't..." I weakly whispered, my eyelids falling shut. I couldn't do it, I wanted to move so badly but just couldn't.

I allowed my head to fall, my body to recoil, thinking that these were going to be my last moments. I was exhausted. I awaited death, I'd been exposed to the cold for too long, my body temperature had dropped dramatically, my body wasn't responding. I was admitting defeat. Suddenly, I heard footsteps, heavy footsteps. I opened my eyes, lifting my head slightly. I couldn't run away if someone was coming for me. I realized that, I realized I was trapped.

Then, I saw him. A young man, my age, pushing the snow covered bushes away. He extended his muscular arms towards me and grabbed me. He pulled me up. I hadn't realized I'd managed to climb the cliff. I didn't react to his foreign touch, I was too weak to.

He set me on my feet. Assuming I was stable enough, he let go of me and I smacked to the ground at once. "Woah, okay, you're not walking tonight..." he murmured picking me up in his arms. I buried my face in his chest, touching my lips and nose on his shockingly warm body. A sound of relief left my mouth, the warmth soothed my pain.

Who was he? What did he want from me? What was he doing in the woods at night?

I didn't bother questioning at that time, I was just so glad I wasn't going to freeze to death. I was just so glad someone had found me even though I didn't know his intentions. I found his heartbeat reassuring. His warmth soothing. He was well built, very muscular, his torso was rock hard. I could feel every sharp line of his body. Maybe that was why I had this feeling of security.

I opened my icy palms and touched them on his abdomen, a sound of relief escaped from my lips. "Little human..." I heard him commenting. Little human? *Human*?

He walked, his feet steady, his breathing even, and his arms securely around me. Where was he taking me? Fear started making its appearance. What was he planning to do with me? Even if I needed to run away I was incapable of it. If he wanted to harm me I had no strength to defend myself and I was so unable to flee. It scared me. The fact that I couldn't do *anything* scared me. I relied on a stranger, a total stranger, and for someone like me, who never trusted anyone generally, it was a scary feeling, having to trust and rely on someone because of the circumstances.

I eagerly pressed my body against his absorbing the warmth, warmth I so desperately needed. His body radiated heat, lifesaving heat. I could breathe, I could breathe without any pain. My heart was still beating unnaturally fast but slower than before, before he had found me. Why did he even bother saving me? How had he managed to find me? Questions. Countless questions started forming in my head.

And suddenly, I realized something. Something that made my closed eyelids fly open. The voice. Where was the voice? Why wasn't it talking to me? Why couldn't I hear it anymore? I panicked and I started fighting his grip.

"What is it?" he enquired. He sounded confused.

"I have to leave! I have to go!" I squeaked. I was detectably nervous.

"Where?" he questioned sounding puzzled.

"The voice... I have to follow the voice..." I was murmuring at myself in that sudden rush of panic I was under.

"Oh, I can take you there..." he answered.

What? He could hear the voice too? I turned to look at him, shocked.

His eyes. In spite of the fact it was so dark, and even though the light was so poor I could see. They were green, but a green so unnatural. A green so... not human. The color of lime in the center and as you moved outwards neon green. The shock in my eyes must've been so obvious... Who was he? Or perhaps it would be better to say: *What* was he? Every joint in me tightened at that question and my heart raced immediately.

"Do you trust me?" he questioned. I swallowed hard while the picture of his eyes registered. What was he? I kept on asking myself over and over again, in fear of this... creature. Goosebumps travelled down my body and it wasn't the cold... My breath had caught responsively, because of his intimidating green eyes.

I nodded, unable to swallow.

"I'm glad," he said and turned his head in front, lifting me up in his arms again. "Because if you didn't trust me I'd have to do this the hard way..." he muttered. I swallowed. The hard way?

He walked remaining silent. I'm not sure if what I felt was fear. I think my curiosity was greater. My interest and fear mixed together, creating an emotion I can hardly describe. I felt safe. For some inexplicable reason I felt safe being with a creature I couldn't name. A creature I couldn't label as "harmless" or "dangerous" and it was that that terrified me. On the other hand, I was so interested in knowing what he was; I wanted to determine whether he was harmless or dangerous for me. And in what way. A part of me screamed to run and another ordered me to stay.

My body was tight, it had instinctively tightened. He detected that. "*We* won't harm you," he reassured me, though I found no comfort in his words.

"Stop! Stop!" I said; my voice had returned, I could feel my lips; the words came out panicky.

"What?" he asked just sighing a little bit.

"I can walk. I can now," I said, and pulled away, managing to jump out of his arms and smash into the snow with a thud. I figured out I couldn't do it; I couldn't trust him to carry me around.

He pulled me from my arm, setting me to my feet, lifting me with such ease as if I weighed as light as a feather. It was all so awkward, all so weird. "Walk. In front of me, don't you run away," he demanded and I obeyed. I hated it, knowing that he was behind me, that this creature might be planning to attack me and that I was unable to escape, that I was in such a frail position...

I wasn't very happy about leaving his warmth but I felt better like this. I felt better being cold than to have him touching me. I preferred that. I breathed heavily and it wasn't the wintry setting; it was because of him. I couldn't help it. I was nervous. What did he want? Why was he following me so protectively?

I felt my heart beating wildly in my chest. Then I saw it. A glow. A blinding glow, just in front of me; a perfect sphere. The beautiful white light illuminated my surroundings. My breath caught in amazement. And suddenly my amazement gave way to fright; terror actually. I stared at the sphere as it rotated on spot, as it circled and circled unstoppably and realized that whatever was going on was completely unnatural. So eerie and mysterious.

I heard someone approaching, slowly and steadily. He stood beside me and only now did I realize how much bigger he was in comparison with me though I, myself, was a quite tall girl. He turned to look at me with those creepy, unearthly but yet attractive green eyes. His face once again mirrored no emotion, but wasn't absolutely blank.

I glanced at the glowing sphere once again, it was slightly bigger than a car even though it sent out a pleasant wave of heat; I assumed being too close to it would be dangerous, the snow near it had melted forming little streams of water.

"What is this?" I asked in a mesmerized whisper, my eyes were out of their sockets. He turned to look at me again and I turned to look at him as well, the bewilderment was more than apparent in my gaze.

"If I were you I would try to make a run for it. Although there's no point in that. It's futile trying to run away from something inevitable..." he said, his tone – enigmatic.

There was a long pause. A moment of silence.

"You are the *Chosen*," he said, his voice turned somehow melodic. I just stared at him. Confused, so totally confused.

Lost...

3. Lost

I stared at Him; the wonder was noticeable in my gaze. He did not open his mouth, just lingered there; staring back at me, the supernatural green of his eyes penetrating the brown of mine. There was some kind of flame in his gaze, there was unexplained concern in his eyes which alarmed me. I noticed he hadn't blinked for more than three minutes, something that scared me to the bone. At that very moment I just wanted to run, to hide somewhere but was so immobilized by his eyes.

I ordered myself to move, to lift my feet, but couldn't. I tried again, with no positive outcome. I turned my head around, pulled my limbs and stretched my muscles. I was trying so hard to move I was gasping. I looked into his eyes again which were still unblinking and unmoving. It was like... like he was using his eyes to keep me still. It was like he was using... *magic*.

I tried to break eye contact but found myself unable to do so. In just a second my heart beat frantically. My breathing became heavy and uneven. Pure fear overwhelmed me and forced adrenaline into my veins. I tried to swallow but had no drop of saliva in my mouth. "Please, not *fear*," he whispered and moved closer. I would've instinctively pulled back but was absolutely powerless. "Fear is something you shouldn't feel..." he went on in the same low voice.

How could I not feel fear? It was out of instinct, I had no control over my body... He was something... dangerous, and kept me still with that deep set of eyes he had. I'd lost my voice and kept on staring at him with that disorientated and terrified look I certainly had. That feeling of safety I had initially felt with him was long gone. "It is hard to understand... but you have to realize, we have no luxury of time..." he whispered and for just a moment his eyes darkened, almost predatorily.

Fear transformed into horror. He detected that. "Please, do not fear **Us**... **We** mean no harm," he said, his voice softer, milder than before, as if to reassure. *Us*? *We*? Currents of electricity made me shiver. He suddenly blinked, freeing me. I dropped to the ground at once as I did not anticipate that unexpected release. I swallowed as hard as I could and prepared to scream for help – the only thing I could think of. He covered my mouth with his palm just on time. I tried to shriek, to shout but his firm hand muffled my cry. I opened my mouth and bit his flesh. He seemed completely undisturbed by that. He pulled me up, made me stand on my feet and held me tightly by the arm, so hard blood stopped reaching my fingers.

I fought for a moment and then gave up realizing it was pointless, he was much bigger and impressively strong. I was panicking; I couldn't think clearly, I couldn't make any sense out of this situation.

"Just let me show you," he said, moving his hand off my mouth. "Just let me show you..." he repeated. The green of his eyes liquefied and his gaze softened. I opened my mouth but couldn't form words. There was something in his stare, something that did not mix with that harshness of his eyes.

Honesty.

I looked at him for a moment, gave him a look of surrender. He immediately let go of my arm and allowed me to walk in front of him. I don't know what made me gather myself up, control my anxiety, but I think it was mainly because of his eyes, that honesty I distinguished.

The breeze had turned into a mighty wind carrying snowflakes – a snowstorm.

"*April Josephine Smith...*"

It was the voice! I was so surprised my breath stopped. My name, how did they know my name? "*Come...*" the voice ordered, sounding so satisfied by my presence. I obeyed and walked closer towards the glow. I was hypnotized again, had no sense of my surroundings, and was unaware of anything else. Nothing else seemed to matter to me.

The circling glow sent out an intense wave of heat. From a distance it was pleasant, but from just two feet away where I was standing, it was insufferable. I felt myself sweating and my body temperature rising. My breathing had evened out and my pulse was much calmer than before though, and all because of the voice.

"*The Chosen...*" murmured the voice in apparent pleasure. "*You are a creature of perfection. The three virtues in you are so perfectly balanced... It is so hard to believe something like you can exist...*" the voice went on, now sounding admiring. What was it admiring? Me?

Impossible.

"*Love, kindness and forgiveness. Things so simple, but yet so rare, and especially in the perfect ratio you have all three,*" continued the voice. "*Stretch your hand in front, April, allow the Powerball to be absorbed into you, for you are **our** only hope...*" instructed the voice, any trace of harshness had disappeared...

I followed the instructions and stepped closer submissively. I hesitated for just a second, feeling the warmth, the heat which now seemed life-threatening.

"*Do not fear destiny, my child...*" whispered the voice, musically, giving me some courage. Courage enough for me to push my right hand all the way down the big rotating sphere.

At first, it was just a tickle on my fingertips and then it travelled up my fingers and then up my hand. Pain, excruciating pain followed making me scream desperately. He came up behind me and covered my mouth with his palm. He tried to murmur something to me, something reassuring and soothing, but I made no sense out of it as I was so taken over by pain.

I felt it. The energy of that golden glow travelled in my veins, it moved from my hand to my entire body eventually. There was a point when every cell in me was stung by pain, the more the glow got into me, the more I screamed. My cry was impossible to muffle, impossible to stop. It was the kind of pain that you never forget, the kind of torturous pain that scars your memories forever. I tried to move my hand, to pull it away, but he stopped me, he pressed it down again, deeper into the *Powerball*. "Don't do this," he said mildly. Another series of shouts came out of my mouth.

The pain felt like burning. It was like someone had thrown me in a fire, in a wild, huge fire. Every bit of flesh on my body burned. He was there, muffling my shouts with one hand and pushing my hand deeper in the glow with the other. His body kept me from dropping to the ground. Why was he doing this to me? Why? Tears travelled out of my terrorized eyes and down my pale cheeks.

And suddenly, just as suddenly as it had begun, it stopped.

He slowly let go of me, first moving his hand from my mouth and then uncurling his fingers from my wrist, which had gone absolutely white because of his strong grip. He allowed me to fall to the ground making sure I didn't hit it hard.

I stayed there, gasping; my heart kicked my ribs, so totally terrified.

What had just happened? What was that? What am I even doing here? I started questioning myself but was unable to answer. And as the night unfolded it got even more complicated, far more complicated than I could've ever imagined.

My body had instinctively recoiled, I was facing the ground trying to make sense out of everything but was disappointed to find out that nothing made sense. Absolutely nothing.

"I'm sorry you had to live through this…" he murmured, I turned my head around abruptly, so fast it wasn't *human*. He was leaning against a massive pine tree, his eyes showing in the dark exactly like a feline's. It was something so creepy and so interesting simultaneously.

"You see, I had no other choice, I just follow instructions…" He excused himself staring at me. Instructions from whom? And instructions for what? I was incapable of stopping my heart from pounding in my chest.

I feared him now, I feared him a lot. "Why would you fear me?" he asked, sounding so surprised and made a step away from the pine tree.

"How do you know that?" I enquired, astonished.

"You're a human. Your heart beats fast, your eyes open wide and you have this light shaking. You sweat as well, you have trouble breathing and your body curls protectively… That's how I can tell," he replied emotionlessly, just stating the facts.

"I've been observing humans a while now... Intricate creatures..." he said walking towards me. It was so dark now, the only thing I was able to see was his eyes glowing as he approached. "I know you must be very confused."

Confused was a very mild term. I was more than that; I was lost – in multiple ways.

He froze. Just like that, he stopped moving.

What happened? I could've sworn his heart stopped beating for a moment and then wondered if it was normal for me to *hear* his heartbeat from this distance. I turned my head around alarmed now, but just saw darkness stretching endlessly, saw nothing but that. His eyes had opened wide and focused on something far away.

"Can you feel *that*?" he asked. His voice was full of concern and his eyes did not move from that faraway spot he was looking at fiercely. I didn't answer immediately unsure of what I was supposed to be feeling. "Stand up," he said firmly. "Stand up now!" he ordered protectively and I knew I couldn't argue. I managed to stand up, though my knees were still wobbly and unstable. "April, this will most probably freak you out. Don't try to make sense out of it," he said alarmingly.

And in that intimidating silence of the woods, in that veiling gloom he started uncurling a pair of fluorescent green wings, huge wings. So slowly, so amazingly slowly. I lost my breath at the sight. They glowed in the dark, exactly like his eyes. From that point on I was sure that something was terribly wrong, that nothing was normal that everything was just insane and crazy.

Out of this world.

"We need to leave..." he said walking towards me. I stepped back when he outstretched a hand to grab me. I was backing away instinctively, running away from a creature I didn't recognize. "Listen, we have no time for this. If you want to stay alive, you'll just give me your hand so we can get out of here. Okay?" he said and I could tell he was really agonized now, very impatient, he was almost growling at me. His breathing was heavy and his gaze concerned.

Stay alive? Is there a threat?

He just grabbed me by the wrist and tossed me closer to him. I didn't fight back, still overwhelmed by shock. He started walking mechanically in front, towards the woods dragging me with him. "Damn it..." I heard him muttering. "Not now, just not now," he said through a stiff jaw, pulling me with him in the woods.

"Where are we going?" I asked disorientated.

"Shut it," he replied abruptly.

He stopped for a moment and just listened. His eyes scanned our surroundings, I couldn't distinguish a thing; it was amazing, his senses were so sharp. He cursed, badly. "How did *They* find us? How?" he asked himself, so frustrated.

"What's wrong?" I questioned in a terrified whisper. He didn't answer my question maybe because he wasn't sure himself. I started feeling weird, as if someone was following us, I felt exposed.

"Get on my back," he demanded. I wasn't sure if he was addressing that to me. I hesitated. "Get on my back now!" This time it was a yell, a deep yell.

"How am I supposed to do that?!" I retorted raising my voice. There was this panic I sensed between us.

"Just do it!" he shouted impatiently through clenched teeth. For some reason we were both breathing unevenly, fearfully. He knew, but I didn't know what for. I just felt something, I felt being monitored.

Followed.

He kneeled down and I placed my body between his wings, I curled my legs around his waist and my arms around his neck. "What do we do now?" I wondered, discomforted by the velvet texture of his wings.

"We fly," he said and took off immediately. He was flying, his wings moved, slapping my body. I was scared like hell. He maneuvered mechanically avoiding the numerous trees surrounding us.

I was holding my breath, if I didn't remember to breathe I would've suffocated. I held tighter, I remembered I was afraid of heights. Then I heard it, something was approaching. I felt him going faster responsively – slicing the air. He was running away from it.

Suddenly, I saw fire, flaring flames ahead of us. He didn't stop, just kept on going, seeming to be unaware of the danger ahead. "We need to get out of here," he said, taken over by panic and turning to fly towards another direction. His heart along with mine created a symphony of wild beats. Adrenaline ruled his actions and kept me on standby.

He flew a distance of a kilometer in less than a minute, there was fire again and flames eating up the trees creating dark smoke traveling up the moonless sky. The smell of combusting wood made me feel dizzy. In just an instant we were surrounded by flames and smoke threatening to burn us alive. "*They* are planning to kill you while you're still human," he said over the snapping sound of smoldering logs; searching for an exit.

"Who?" I asked, horrified, clinging on to the fabric of his shirt.

"*Demons*," he said.

4. Formulas and problem solving

I felt myself turning into steel. My body reacted to the word immediately and that stiffness of surprise took over. *Demons.* The word had an echoing effect in my head. I didn't want to ask because I didn't want to know, it seemed like something so repelling. The word itself. The fear had never loosened its grip on me throughout that night though now, it wasn't fear anymore, it was an emotion so powerful I cannot possibly describe.

I couldn't help myself from hyperventilating.

There was this noise; I heard something. Barely distinguishable over the sound of crunching wood was the sound of voices. Panicked voices. He heard that as well and I felt him tighten underneath me. It was the kind of reaction you get from a disorientated, confused animal. The smoke around us was getting thicker, made breathing so incredibly hard. "What are you doing? Get us out of here," I said, not even trying to sound composed.

"Humans. They mustn't see us." He breathed sounding equally anxious.

"Well do something about it!" I pressured coughing as he kept on circling, flirting with the life-threatening flames. The voices were louder now and the sound of a siren was discernible. We were cornered, absolutely trapped. I did not actually realize how he managed to get us out of there just on time; just before the flames ate us alive, but he did. He somehow maneuvered in that suffocating smoke and got us out.

With the same astounding skill he flew just a foot above the ground and came to a stop landing on his abdomen. I quickly got off his back and imitated him; lay on my belly.

"Just keep quiet and they won't notice," he instructed in a breathless whisper.

Mayhem and destruction were all around us. Firefighting units and vehicles arrived. People battled with the ravenous flames, it was chaotic. I found it hard to believe it would be so challenging to put out a fire in such cold conditions. I immediately realized this wasn't a fire of the normal kind. Nothing was of the normal kind. We both, silently watched hiding behind curved snow. I felt a knot tying itself around my heart; it was painful watching my memories of the forest turning into ash. It was one of the few places I loved the most.

The people seemed so puzzled, lost, disorientated. There was a massive hum of yells, instructions, orders and fright. He suddenly turned his head around to face me. "It will go out only when *They* want it too…" he confessed quietly. *They*; I was right to think that this was something abnormal.

We were facing a road packed with people, firefighters, police cruisers and trucks. The sight of my mother in her nightwear made me squeak. We were too far away from each other for her to hear that weak sound I got out of my throat but He still gave me a silencing look. Her black eyes looked haunted; she seemed as if searching for someone. My dad. My breath caught.

A police officer came up to her. "It's too dangerous for you to be here, ma'am," he said with a distinctive rough, deep voice.

"You don't understand, officer. I have to find her!" she cried in obvious panic.

I realized who she was searching for. And it hurt.

"I have to find my daughter!" she insisted, attempting to walk past the cop. "I'm sorry, ma'am, but you can't," said the policeman grabbing her firmly by the arm.

My mother turned hysterical. She screamed and yelled and cried as the man dragged her away from the flames. "I need to find my baby!" she shouted desperately, her every scream came out louder than the previous one. Before I could think of anything else He grabbed my wrist. "Can you run?" he questioned nervously.

"I think…" I replied startled.

"Good," he muttered and pulled me up with one move. And in just a moment we were darting through the woods.

I wondered how I could keep up with him, running so inhumanly fast, but yet I could do it. We ran so rapidly everything around us turned into a blur. And I wasn't even putting effort in it. I gave myself no time to question, just ran making everything else's significance trivial. I followed him absolutely silent.

We stopped on the edge of a cliff where he turned around and stared at me. He looked deeper into my eyes and I couldn't help myself from looking back into his. His stare was intense, almost... hypnotizing. Gradually, my picture of the world obscured until I lost consciousness. I felt a pair of arms catching me just before I would hit the ground.

I was sweating, the pain was excruciating. I'd never experienced anything like that before, that kind of unbearable burning pain. He helped me swallow my screams; my head was propped on his lap and he cradled me softly. A shriek made it out of my throat, a loud shriek of pain.

"It's okay. You'll be okay..." he whispered melodically to me. He reassured me, holding my head gingerly in his hands and pushing strands of stringy moist hair out of my face.

He was so gentle it was hard to believe. His green eyes looked anything but hostile. I shook and trembled uncontrollably as the pain intensified. I pressed my jaws closed, clenching my teeth. My face took different grimaces of unease, and my body recoiled out of instinct. I brought my knees to my chest. He softly pushed my legs back to the ground wiping my soaked forehead.

"It's okay," he whispered again, his eyes had somehow softened, he was so empathetic. Apart from the boiling pain, I felt heat around me; the smell of combusting wood reached my nostrils. I panicked, were we in the fire? I tried to move and whenever I tried to do so, pain speared me again – viciously. He saw that, he somehow saw everything. "It's okay... Don't move..." he said comforting me again. A sound came out of my mouth. Something between a cry and a scream.

The pain hit me in waves and eased a bit for a few moments. But now, I could feel the heat build up again, it came from my fingertips up to my hands, and then traveled all around my body. It was the climax and it was torturing, I felt helpless. I screamed. He whispered to me, attempting to stop me but I made no sense of his words as I was so taken over by my suffering.

I pulled my limbs closer to me protectively and stopped shouting only when the burning had relatively lessened. I allowed my body to relax gulping huge amounts of oxygen as I prepared for the next wave to hit. It worked like that; as soon as you thought everything was over it started again in the same torturous way. So I didn't allow myself to think it had stopped, I ordered myself to prepare, to wait for that wave of ache to attack me.

He never left. He was always there, holding me. His complexion shined as the golden light of his camp fire illuminated our tiny, muddy cave. I looked into his eyes and met that soothing softness of his gaze.

I didn't look away the entire night.

Sometimes they tell you it is better not to ask, but I guess I'm the kind of person that cannot help it. How could I stop myself from wondering? Questioning? I'd always been a person of facts and I'd been afraid of the unknown ever since I remember myself. This didn't just scare me, it terrified me. Things I couldn't explain always terrified me.

He was sleeping deeply, snoring lightly. He was facing the muddy floor of the cave and his wings extended over his body exactly like a blanket. The fire he had lit to fight the night's lethal cold had gone out. I remember myself staring at him, just staring at him curiously. My irritated eyes wouldn't move away from him. *What was he*? He was an interesting creature indeed... Wings and glowing eyes and... *Magic*? Was that the word? I didn't dare to repeat it in my head.

He moved his wings over his face covering his eyes from the blond rays of the sun. His body remained paralyzed under his huge wings – he was still asleep. I don't know what made me approach so inquisitively, but there was something so amazing about his wings I couldn't ignore. After last night he didn't seem so dangerous though I still was extremely cautious.

For a moment I just stared at them, at their shape, their pale green color, the muscles controlling them. I stared at them fascinated. I extended a hand but immediately stopped myself from touching his wings giving it a second thought. But could I actually resist? I was curious by nature and it was my curiosity that won. I didn't want to wake him up, to disturb him; I touched him as gently as I could manage.

I touched velvet. It was so soft and fragile in contrast with his tough appearance. The wing was covered in invisible colorless fluff; I could feel it with my fingers. Their shape didn't look like an angel's, looked more of a butterfly's but not even that, maybe something in between. His wings were impressive in size, they had bones and joints. Muscles all over them. Arteries and veins fed them with blood carrying his pulse. A steady rhythmic pulse.

I ran my fingers over the muscles, the veins and allowed my hand to travel down just a bit lower from his shoulder bones. This was where his wings were rooted. His shirt had holes allowing his wings to pass through. They were attached to his back; they seemed like a part of his body. They were a part of his body.

Suddenly, his wings curled. Turned into tubes reducing their size with the sound of crumbling paper. I responsively pulled back in shock. "What are you doing?" he asked in a low voice forcing my breath to catch. Was he awake all this time? I didn't reply, so scared my eyes had popped open exactly like a vulnerable animal's. I swallowed. He sat up and looked at me with the same intensely colored irises only that now his eyes didn't glow.

"Good morning – by the way," he muttered and rubbed his sore eyes. There was no response from my side. "Look, it would be really helpful if I didn't have to guess your answers…" he said and turned to rest his back on the wall uncurling his wings. I couldn't move my stiff body from my spot and neither could I look away from his wings. They moved fast, sharply.

I had to say something, I knew I had to but I just couldn't make my lips move. I opened my mouth but was unable to form words.

He pulled his head back and rested it on the wall exhaling heavily. "Last night... It was really close..." he breathed as if he was re-living the night before, with the same nervousness. The identical concern.

"Everything seems complicated," I said surprising him. It seemed complicated indeed, and I was never a friend of complication. A small sarcastic smile pulled his full lips.

"Well, it certainly is what it seems..." he said and a single forced chuckle left his throat. He was avoiding my glance and stared at the corner of the low ceiling instead, afraid his eyes would betray something. "Everything about *you* is... complicated." He exhaled erasing the smile from his face.

"I'm a problem?" I asked making him turn his head and look at me through tired eyes.

"No, you're the formula solving it..." he said with a mysterious, intriguing voice.

I found myself moving closer towards him. The ceiling of the rocky cave was too low for me to stand so I crawled instead. I still kept a distance between us, he was a stranger.

"Don't expect me to give you answers..." he said turning his head away from me, overlooking outside.

"I suggest we begin with the basics..." I said cowardly, my whisper was barely audible.

"Like what, April? That *They* are trying to kill you or that you're still not ready for *The Truth*? That you're not a human anymore?" he argued, unaware of what had slipped from his lips. I looked at him and questioned myself. *Do I really want to know*?

"I'm Peter – just so you know," he added fixing his eyes on me; his gaze was harsh. For some reason my pulse had accelerated, my heart banged against my ribs. I guess it was out of response, maybe nature. Only then did I realize I had pressed my back against the moist wall of the cave – almost defensively.

I swallowed. "What are you?" I breathed staring at the floor.

"*A nothing*. A big piece of nothing..." he replied; his tone only was enough to make me look up and meet his eyes. "Nothing compared to you and I'm kind of glad about that. I guess I wouldn't have the strength to endure what you have to endure..." he went on narrowing his eyes skeptically. I wouldn't open my mouth and interrupt, it was too interesting. "You, darling... are the *Chosen One*. Though *we* just call you the Chosen..." he whispered just a bit sarcastic — slightly.

"Who are 'we'?" I asked immediately, curious and ominous.

"Big pieces of nothing like me," he said joking coldly pointing at himself with his index finger. He suddenly froze. Stared right through my eyes seeming so astonished by something. He moved, walked on four towards me uncurling his wings and flapping them behind him. I pulled my limbs closer to me defensively and my heart bounced in my chest. He moved closer and closer until his face was just two inches away from mine, he looked right into my huge pupils and I looked into his.

"I can't believe it..." he muttered in a mesmerized whisper. "Your eyes... how...?" he asked himself in obvious disbelief. "It's impossible for it to work so fast..." he said grabbing my face with his hand and examining my irises. "So fascinating..." he continued in amazement. My body was totally paralyzed the moment his skin contacted mine — I did not react, just shook like a leaf in the wind.

"A creature of perfection indeed..." he murmured and let go of my face as suddenly as he had grabbed it. "The *Three Virtues* are reflected in the three colors of your eyes," he said addressing me, moving his face away from mine. "Just like The *Prophesies* claimed..." he muttered in realization of something. "Blue, green and yellow..." he breathed, the sound of his voice was barely detectable. He was considering things, seemed thoughtful and stared at the dripping wall of the cave while his mind traveled miles and miles away.

"My eyes are brown," I argued, in apparent confusion. "And so is my hair..." I said and pulled a strand into my face.

I remember my heart stopped beating; I remember my body freezing on spot — functionless. It was like a tsunami of shock had smashed me. I was demolished, I stayed there – wrecked. Speechless, as I tried to find a rational explanation for my electric blue and fluorescent green hair. Peter stared at me with the same surprise – he hadn't noticed that either.

"It's happening... The Metamorphosis..." he muttered to himself and started moving away from me. I stared at him through horrified eyes. *Metamorphosis?*

He moved to the edge of the cave, to the entrance. "No one must witness this, I have to leave..." he said panicking almost, and flew out.

"Where are y –" I didn't manage to finish my sentence and was interrupted by pain.

I wish I could just forget about it but it was an experience so intense it is imprinted in my mind permanently. The memory is inerasable. And every time I think of it I feel myself burning again. I feel the same pain. It was nothing like the night before, nothing to be compared with. Indescribable. The brutality of the pain, of the fire sizzling my body. I couldn't give an end to the screams. My body was outstretched on the cave floor, my limbs shook and vibrated wildly as I cried – helpless. No one was there to reassure me, to hold me now that I needed it the most – desperately.

This time I was all alone.

5. Instinctively

Wings. Wings of my own. They extended over my body and I could feel their amazing weight. I couldn't move because of my exhaustion, I don't remember when the pain stopped, I just remember how much I suffered that night. I felt them coming out of me, ripping my flesh, tearing my skin though blood never ran down my sweaty body. I shouted and cried for Him but he didn't return, I felt abandoned, lost in this nonsense.

My wings were still wet, as if I was a butterfly and I'd just broken free out of my cocoon. It was morning and the winter sun entered the small cave. I dragged myself to the light exactly like a moth is drawn to a lighting lamp. I somehow stretched my wings so that the golden rays showered them. I was using muscles I hadn't used before, strong muscles. I stayed there, feeling relief after what felt like a long time. The sun had a soothing effect as it heated my sore body and for the first time I relaxed. I literally relaxed, allowing my joints to loosen and my body to drop. I remained unmoving breathing slowly, absorbing the revitalizing warmth.

What happened? What is wrong with me? What... am I? Questions. Terrifying questions I did not want to answer. I was too tired to move, I lay there lifeless. My wings felt lighter and lighter as the sun dried out their moisture. I had absolutely no idea of how to use them, to move them or flap them; they just dropped over me uselessly. They started to color, at first they were transparent, almost see through, but after a while they gradually became blue. A beautiful blue, electric blue. The outline around each wing was lime and faded out in the wing till it turned into fluorescent green.

I am like Him... Like Peter... I thought to myself in disgust and suddenly the damp cave felt so microscopic, claustrophobic. The possibility of that paralyzed my body, disordered my thoughts;

caged me physically and mentally in a moment of madness. It wasn't the answer I wanted to get; it didn't calm me nor did it relieve me, it just caused me more anxiety. I didn't know much yet, it was my first step into *Their* world of complexity, of confusion and uncertainty. And I had a lot to learn.

There were no answers to my questions, no explanation reasoning this.

I remembered his words. '*You're not human anymore.*' That phrase echoed in the cave turning me into stone. My body tightened as I realized what was certain, the only thing I could be sure about.

I weren't *Homo sapiens*.

I swallowed hard, pushing the truth down my esophagus. Was this *The Truth* he was talking about? What I was? Something inside me, just a tiny whisper warned me to expect something far worse. Something way more shaking. But could there be anything worse than *this*?

Unfortunately, the answer to that question was a positive one.

I spent the entire morning under the sun, uncurling my newborn wings and considering the possibilities. Just thinking.

Thirst.

The next thing I remember is my dry mouth, my sore throat. A thirst so severe it was like someone was ripping the inner of my neck with razors. No drop of saliva was left in my mouth – so abruptly – unnaturally. I found difficulty in breathing as the air I took in gashed my dry throat.

I acted out of instinct, an instinct which wasn't human. I dragged myself out of the cave in panic, breathing heavily through my waterless mouth, though what I searched for wasn't water – I didn't know what I wanted. I got out of the cave to find out I was on a cliff. Rocks, dirt and snow created a filthy slush. I didn't think of my actions, of the possible consequences. I was guided by a foreign instinct commanding me to move.

I was on a tiny projection, staring downwards, realizing how high up I was – over four hundred feet. If I fell from this high up there was no chance of survival. My wings were useless to me, they were big and I had no control over them. I thought the only way for me to get down was climbing; something extremely jeopardous considering all that it took was one lethal slip. But at that particular instant I didn't have the ability to consider, or think, I did things impulsively unable to bear the torturing thirst.

I buried my fingers into the dirt and stone of the steep cliff and started climbing down mechanically, growling lowly exactly like a starving animal. I wasn't human and I wasn't acting like a human anymore, I was... wild. My grip was firm and steady, my feet never slipped. As the levels of adrenaline in my body increased so did my precision. I was so unbelievably strong and that was surely an effect of *The Metamorphosis*.

What was I looking for? Why was I risking my life?

Instinctively. I risked my life because of an instinct I couldn't recognize, a foreign, inhumane instinct controlling my every move, my every feeling and my every breath. An instinct so tough that it made me lose my sense of logic. Turned me into an animal. A savage.

I was down the cliff so fast I had a hard time believing it. Just seconds before I didn't have the energy required to lift my chest to breathe and now I was digging in the snow in search of my desire. The pain of my thirst got worse by every breath; it was so intolerable the low growling sound I produced wasn't low anymore. My hands shook as I dug deeper into the snow.

I had no idea of what I was looking for. The same unidentified instinct just told me to dig, to search for something in the ground. By the time I curled my fingers around it, my growl of pain had turned into a wild shriek of impatience.

Flowers. Nectar and sugary pollen.

I pressed my lips around the center of a small wild rose, sipping the liquid out of it. I allowed the dense nectar to run down my throat slowly, soothing my unbelievable thirst. I breathed in relief licking my sticky lips and bit off a tender petal. Something was wrong with me, with my mouth I mean. I must've developed some kind of new food breaking enzymes and as soon as the petal touched my tongue it dissolved – instantly. As if my saliva was acidic.

I had to finish off at least another ten of those precious wild roses for my logic to return, for me to realize and be conscious of things. First, I felt relieved; I swallowed down the last petal of the flower I held and then, I froze.

What am I doing? I asked myself, dropping the thorny stalk on the snow in realization of what I'd actually done. What followed wasn't actually shock or bewilderment; it was milder than that, I kneeled there, skeptical – tornadoes of questions formed in my head.

I stared at my dirty hands blankly; the mud and dirt underneath my fingernails, I had held the stalk so tight the thorns had cut my skin and little wounds oozed blood. What was I supposed to do now? How was I supposed to react? My pulse raced as I searched for the explanation. The snow soaked my filthy clothes and seeped into me all the way to my bones sending currents of shiver all over my body.

Suddenly, and out of nowhere a hand grabbed me. I felt firm fingers curling around my arm.

Before I could even take in another breath I was in the sky hanging from Him; Peter. My legs hung down and I clung on his arm as we flew over the Lake. "What are you doing?!" I squeaked and looked at him through surprised eyes.

"We have to leave. *They're* searching for you," he said and continued flying with the same breathtaking speed.

"Who?" I asked panicking; my feet were cutting the surface of the water.

"Humans," he replied coldly, sighing emotionlessly.

I felt my guts twisting. Humans; my parents, the half-burnt forest, memory after memory and picture after picture flooded my mind. The same confusion pulled my eyebrows and made my heart bang restlessly. "You'll probably end up in a lab or something if *we* don't get you out of here…" he murmured quietly, more to himself. "The *Human Side* was never safe. Wars, conflicts… a world of troubles…" he muttered again, even lower. Two chuckles came out of his throat. "As if *Our Side* is in better shape…" he said ironically to himself not seeming to notice

I was clinging on his arm uncomfortably, listening to every single word he mouthed.

"Where are you taking me?" I questioned anxiously; we were now flying above the forest and I could hear distant voices.

"You need to fly," he said as if he hadn't heard my question in the first place. "I can't carry you everywhere, you have to use your wings," he said sternly.

"How am I supposed to do that?" I asked in total dread.

"You flap your wings." he said and somehow his voice softened a bit.

"How?" That was almost a scream.

"Calm down and flap your wings in and out," he said and now suddenly sounded very reassuring. I had no idea which muscles to use, how to move those immense wings of mine. They seemed dead, hung insensibly over my body. "Tighten your back, pull from there," he instructed realizing I had a problem. I swallowed and searched for the right muscles.

I felt muscles I'd never felt before; when I tightened, my wings moved instantly inwards and when I loosened, they dropped outwards.

"Good. Now move faster," he advised me as he dragged me with him over a huge patch of burnt forest. I resisted the temptation of looking down knowing that it would only scare me even more – I'd always been afraid of heights. I tried to flap my wings faster and now felt other parts of them come to life. Blood vessels pumped blood into the muscles making my wings fold and unfold so softly; the movement was continuous and wavy. "Flap them steadily." he added monitoring my progress.

And I did so. I moved and pushed my wings in fascination of this new part of my body, a low musical hum was created and I felt myself elevate. I pushed even harder, soaking myself in sweat and felt myself weigh less.

"Maintain your speed," he ordered now, loosening his grip around my arm but not completely. Big droplets of sweat ran down my forehead finding their way to my eyebrows as I desperately tried to keep my wings moving. And they were heavy.

I somehow managed it, I miraculously did. He slowly uncurled his strong fingers around my arm, one by one, until I didn't have his support at all. I gasped in surprise' and fear.

"Keep on going," he simply said, softly this time, very tenderly as if he was talking to a small child.

I liked his firm grip and I now had nothing to cling on to which made me feel incredibly vulnerable. I flew around clumsily but kept my balance. I travelled slowly staring straight ahead so overwhelmed by emotions; both positive and negative. The dominant feeling was disbelief. Everything seemed so unreal and crazy, my wings, my thirst, the voices, the pain, and the *Demons*... everything looked so false and iconic, vivid images just like in a dream. Though this dream was a real one and nothing about it was fake.

I found my lungs once again and inhaled deeply sucking everything in. My pulse was still abnormally quick as my heart was still pumping blood to my wing muscles. My eyes remained unblinking and wide open, I was stunned by what I was capable of.

"Good. Though it's kind of weird you can do this so fast..." He interrupted my thoughts and flew lower next to me. "I'm not risking it though," he said and curled his warm hand around mine. "I lead, you follow..." he said and thrust himself forward pulling me gently after him.

"Where are we going?" I asked in a hushed, breathless whisper.

"Somewhere safe. I promise you..." he said, looking at me for a brief moment and moved on, holding my hand in his even tighter. I had no idea of where we were heading, but something inside me just told me to follow him. To trust him. He was the only person – slash – creature I had trusted. I realized that I was alone except for him, which is why I allowed myself to trust him, I guess.

It was something very weird; because although I was still sort of afraid of him, I liked the fact I had someone to hold on to, I liked the fact I wasn't on my own in this mess. And most of all I liked his warm hand tightly around mine. It made me feel secure, safe and right now, I felt like deer lost on a highway.

The lights of the cars blinded me; their sound as they rushed around me was nearly as unpleasant as the ear-piercing sound of wild horns. The scent of petrol made me feel dizzy; and I was in the middle of all that chaos, not knowing what to do, upset, disorientated and frightened; unable to identify my role in this intricate situation.

Though I had a very significant one...

"This is a mess." I breathed.

"I told you again... It is what it seems..." he replied sighing slightly, his voice was gentle and his words sincere.

My senses were so powerful, stronger than ever; inhumanly and unnaturally powerful.

I heard barking dogs though my sense of sight could not find them. My sense of sound was so strong, the sound of dogs mingled with the sound of human speech. I could hear their feet, the sound of their energetic legs as they sank in the snow; the sound of their heartbeats both animal and human was discernible. And then scents came from everywhere.

The smell of pine spiraled around me, a scent so intense it almost made me faint. He had a scent as well, a sweet smell of flower nectar; the cold air even carried an odor I had never sensed before; the scent of water. I was so amazed I almost lost my balance against the cold but soft currents of wind.

"It can be very distracting; so much detail is sent to your brain, information of such great quantity you sometimes can't process it. But please even though this must be very exhilarating to you, keep on flying," he said pulling me closer to him in one smooth, single movement, stabilizing me. I remembered to breathe, and tasted a whole new world. I tasted water droplets flying around me; I tasted the pine and cypress trees, the oaks and the tempting smell of flowering plants hundreds of meters away from me, lying underground.

It was a world I'd never felt before, this was planet Earth through a different set of lenses. The real ones. Everything around me was so alive and vivid, even the leaves themselves appeared to breathe. The soil had a taste; the distant melody of a bird was so much more complex than what I'd thought as a... human. As a weak human...

It was very exhilarating indeed. Fascinating, mind-blowing. I realized how much I'd been missing, how weak, and incapable my previous senses were, how much I'd been ignoring. Life itself. I can describe the feeling with one very accurate word.

Beautiful.

He froze.

His body stiffened, turned iron hard and I knew that something was terribly wrong. His pulse accelerated instantaneously and his heart beat hard in his muscular chest. He was out of breath in milliseconds.

"What's wrong?" I asked and his sudden panic seemed to infect me as well. There was a pause for a second; his eyes stared at something faraway, wide with anxiety.

"It looks like the humans aren't alone; *They're* coming..." he whispered.

I felt my world spinning at once.

6. Chaos

"*They?*" As if I needed to ask, my voice broke.

Suddenly, Peter pushed hard forward and flew so fast everything around us turned into a speedy blur. I tightened my fingers around his hand, clinging for my life. It was all so new, all so confusing and unreal.

Just chaos.

"*They* know you're still here and *They* know you're unprotected, we need to get to *The Other Side*!" He was panicking, his voice was deep and coarse; he'd forgotten to breathe. Perspiration soaked his body; big drops of sweat ran down his forehead as a response to his anxiety, his grip around my hand was so hard I could not feel my fingers anymore.

My expression was that of blankness, the air flickered hair into my eyes blinding me completely. "Why are *They* here?" I squeaked through a tight jaw, his apprehension turned out to be dangerously contagious. He accelerated even more in reply to my question. "What do *They* want?" I enquired, trying to hold on to him, he was climbing up the sky faster than sound now.

"*You*," He mouthed breathlessly, flying perfectly vertical, flapping his massive wings hard against one another carrying my weight along with his own as my wings had curled up functionless reacting to his answer.

Me. *They* wanted me.

My heart started pounding, reacting to his astonishing answer; I felt my universe spinning, I felt I was losing touch with reality, I couldn't tell what was real and what was imaginary, everything seemed to blend together creating the feeling of nonsense. Why would *Demons* want *me*? A blood cooling shiver traveled from my head all the way down to my limbs; *Demons*, what a disturbing word...

"We're surrounded! Can't you *sense Them*?!" He was shouting, stressed out, he changed direction in a sharp motion forcing the breath out of my lungs.

"What am I supposed to sense?!" I retorted; the feeling of fear flooded my mind, took over and dominated my body.

Screams. Our charged conversation was interrupted by spearing screams.

He stopped, allowing me to see. I could see a meadow, police officers and dogs; the screams came from both animals and humans. Officer after officer fell to the ground lifeless. Crazy spasms shook their bodies and then, in just a split second they dropped to the snow breathless; dead. I stared speechless; in my entire life I'd never seen a human die, I was terrified by the thought and now I saw people dying exactly like poisoned animals.

They even killed the dogs.

"It's a display of power; *They* cannot claim the souls of animals, *They*'re just trying to frighten you…" he said out of breath and started pulling me away.

I unfolded my wings and started flapping them pushing myself towards the people. "We can't just leave them there, we need to help…" I insisted in a shaky mumble.

Peter pulled me hard towards him. "There's nothing you can do, their souls are lost… if we go… I lose my soul too…" he said, harshly and gently simultaneously.

"But…" I tried to argue.

"There is no time, April! *They* can be anything! Literally anything. The air you take in your lungs, the snow, the trees… *They* can kill everybody if *They* choose to," he shouted at me and sped up, flying recklessly, dragging me with him.

For a moment I was afraid to inhale. I was afraid to do anything.

Suddenly, and out of nowhere a tornado formed, a real one, just above the patch of burnt forest. This tornado though wasn't of the normal kind, it was black. It rotated madly, the wind created shook and bent the trees dangerously. The circling winds reached up the sky as far as the eye could see, it seemed unending.

Peter climbed higher, using every resource of energy he had left. I clung on to him; wind slapped our faces and battered our bodies. Oxygen became less and less and there was a point where the blue of the sky turned purple and I knew we were almost out of the atmosphere. And then, with one abrupt movement he started declining nose down, like a falcon. I shouted as we fell in the tornado; darkness covered us and we continued falling.

One end of the tornado closed and another opened. We fell deeper into the gloom, I closed my eyes.

I knocked to the ground and immediately lost consciousness.

7. Safe and sound

What was it chasing us? What did it want from us? What did it want from me? My life was in danger, his life was in jeopardy as well; what could I do? I didn't know why I was the hunted, why was I the *prey*; what was so valuable about me?

I'd seen a dream. I pulled up showered in sweat. Shrieks hung from my tongue. "You're alright, we're safe now…" I heard his voice; he was just a few feet away from me, extending his hands towards the flames of his fire.

The scent of moist grass reached my nostrils, there was no snow and a pleasantly warm breeze spiraled around my body. It was dark; the only light was that of the fire. Chamomile blossoms surrounded me, little daisies were scattered around. Intense aromas danced in the air and made my stomach twist with hunger; my mouth was so unbelievably dry.

Suddenly, the sound of splashing water caught my attention. I swung my head around to see that a wide river was passing by. The currents seemed strong, though the sound created was a calming swish, so tame and soft – relaxing. I stretched my wings, flapped them some times, trying to compose myself and erase that look of fear from my face.

His gaze met mine; his eyes glowed in the dark exactly like the night before, like a cat's. His expression was that of peace, he was calm. "We're safe here." His voice was soft, a tone so deep and tender it surprised me that a sound could be so amazingly crafted, with such a balance.

"Where are we?" it was a whisper, the panic was still controlling my body, I could not help myself, I could not make myself relax.

"*They* can't reach you here, you're safe," he reassured me, discerning the fear reflected in my sleepless eyes.

"*They* can't?" I asked back in a breath, afraid to feel relieved.

"Yes," he replied fixing his stare on my blank face, his glowing eyes softened.

I found my lungs and inhaled deeply, *They* couldn't reach us here, wherever we were. I forced myself to swallow; my throat was so dry I thought I was pushing down blades. I had no energy in my body, all the adrenaline was gone now and I was left to deal with exhaustion and excruciating pain whenever I moved. I curled my fingers around a daisy, pulled it from the soil and brought it up to my mouth. I sucked out all the liquid with just a single push of my cracked lips.

"You drink nectar?" he asked seeming puzzled, astonished almost.

"Yes; why?" I asked back, staring right into his shining eyes.

"Nothing, it is so interesting..." he mumbled out, his characteristics betrayed wonder.

"What?" I enquired sighing intensely without wanting to.

"You're adapting very fast...that's all," he answered flatly, appearing equally worn.

There was a long moment of silence. We were both unwilling to speak, to open our mouths because it consumed the little energy we had left.

"Look, why don't you go wash yourself?" he suddenly suggested, he sounded tired. It took me a few minutes to filter his words and then I nodded. I crawled to the river bank as I didn't have the strength required to stand up. I stared at my reflection on the water's surface, I could not recognize myself.

Sweat and mud made my complexion shine filthily; I was still wearing pajamas that now were mostly brown instead of red, my hair was messy and stringy with perspiration. But what spooked me the most were *my* glowing eyes. Three colors, blue, green and yellow shone brightly in every iris. I felt my jaw drop open in reaction but I was too sleepy to be shocked or dazed, I instead shut my lids and unbuttoned my shirt. There was one thing I could not stop and that was the frantic trembling of my wounded fingers, I was taken over by emotions I could not ignore even under my severe state of exhaustion.

I didn't care if He was staring at me; I slipped out of every piece of clothing I was wearing and submerged into the water up to my neck. My wings curled automatically and I started rubbing the filth from my skin, washed my hair and combed it with my fingers. The water was warm and soothed my sore muscles more than anything else, eased the pain better than any painkiller.

I felt my muscles and joints loosen, the soft currents of water forced me to relax. I extended my arms to the river bank and grabbed my clothes – I washed them as best as I could. I had no towel and my clothes were wet, but I slipped into them anyway unwilling to leave the soothing warmth of the water and walked up to the fire. I was two feet away from him. I hesitated.

"What? You're afraid of me now? I don't bite," he said and a tiny, nearly teasing smile drew itself upon his full lips. I sat down and pulled myself closer to him, moving my body slightly forward towards the snapping fire. I touched my side to his side reluctantly, absorbing the heat of his body. Tension pulled my sore muscles again, our touching bodies was the reason. "You know you can relax, don't you?" he said sounding slightly concerned.

"I know," I replied dryly, the images of my new face circled in my head.

"Is it normal for my eyes to glow?" I asked in a distressed whisper, turning my gaze towards him.

He stared at me right in the eyes for an instant and then answered, "Very normal."

I uncurled my wet wings. "Should they glow as well?" I questioned again, flapping my wings once as an indication to what I was referring to.

"Yes," he replied in a calming breath, detecting my anxiety.

"I sometimes think that humans are lucky…" he began talking out of the blue. "It's good they don't know how life actually is…" he said and his voice started trailing off.

"Well, how is actual life?" I asked cowardly in a murmur, curiosity made my organs tighten.

There was a long pause.

"I asked you something," I said, looking at him. His eyes did not move away from the vicious flames of the fire.

"Do you know what the fire triangle is?" he asked, surprising me, his question seemed utterly irrelevant.

"Yes," I replied; confusion pulled my eyebrows.

"Do you know what is needed for a fire?" he questioned again; his gaze was fixed on the flames and would not move away.

I thought about it for a moment. "Fuel, heat and... oxygen?" I was unsure of my answer, I'd learnt this in year nine, and I was a bit rusty.

"Correct," he said. "Think of life like that, like a burning fire," he added, in a whisper, staring at the hazel flames intensively.

"Well, what is needed for a... life triangle?" I wondered interested.

"*You* are *The Fuel* – the humans I mean, *We* are the heat and *They* are the oxygen," he explained. It took me a moment to process what he was saying.

"You mean the *Demons*?" I asked breathlessly, shocked.

"Yes," he replied.

But how could it be? He said: *They* kill, *They* can be anything; how can *They* be a part of life?

"It sounds impossible to me..." I said struggling to maintain my fragile composure.

"You can think of it like a cycle, all *Three Sides* are linked to each other and we all rely on balance," he said calmly. "You humans are the weakest link," he whispered.

"Three *Sides*?" I questioned, confused and curious.

"*Dimensions*, is what you humans call them," he clarified, turning to look at me; my eyeballs were pinned on him. "You see, *The Fuel* is running out. Nothing is in the correct ratio. Everything has lost its balance," he explained. "What happens to *The Fire* in that case, April?" he asked softly, allowing me to analyze his words.

"*The Fire* goes out," I replied in a breath, an electric current running along my body.

Life goes out.

We sat there, in an eerie silence.

Was that how fragile life was? Could it just go out exactly like a fire, as easily as it sounded? The thought electrocuted my body. "Can we stop it?" I questioned staring at him expectantly, trying to find hope to cling on to.

"Maybe..." he told me, trailing off staring at the famished flames.

"This must be shocking to you." He breathed.

I did not reply, why bother stating what is so obvious only a blind person would not be able to see. For some reason, just at that second an image of the nightmare I'd seen circled in my head forcing a shiver to travel down my limbs.

"What is it?" he asked, slightly concerned.

"A dream," I said in a dead voice.

"How is it to dream?" he enquired and his eyes glimmered with fascination.

"What do you mean?" I asked back thinking I'd misheard. "Everybody can dream in their sleep," I said; the weariness made my voice come out coarsely.

"*We* can't dream. *My* kind does not have the ability to do that," he said; his eyes were nailed on me. I didn't know how to reply, what to say. It took me a few moments to find my tongue.

"Tell me about your dream before..." he pleaded, breaking the silence. "You screamed it seemed like something so real... Like something you were experiencing." He went on; the amazement and the curiosity made his eyes shine brighter.

"I think it's a bad idea," I retorted bitterly, discomforted by his thought; I almost snapped at him.

"Why? I thought you trusted me..." he murmured.

He gave me a look.

"Trust is earned; you still have a lot of work to do to earn mine," I said as calmly as I could.

"Just tell me how it is, why you woke up gasping, soaked in sweat, just tell me how real it is. It's just so interesting." He pressured me.

I swallowed hard, uneasily. "Stop! Just stop it now!" I was panting and boiling in anger for some inexplicable reason – maybe it was the exhaustion.

He didn't say anything, just looked away seeming very surprised by my attitude. I realized I had actually shouted at him. Guilt tied itself around my chest – he hadn't done anything. "Look, I'm sorry," I mumbled out lamely. Guilt was one of the feelings I couldn't bear, I had never managed to.

"It's fine, you're just tired – I should've respected that," he said, sounding apologetic himself.

"I need to sleep..." I confessed in a weak whisper allowing my head to drop on his shoulder – I could not lift it.

"Yeah, me too," he said in agreement. His voice broke with sluggishness for the first time. My lids shut automatically and I was unable to open them again. He picked me up and it sent currents of pain all over my body even though his touch was extremely gentle. He laid my body on a soft mattress of greenery.

He brought his lips to my ear. "Trust me," he said in a breath. "I'm the only one left..." he whispered and pulled away caressing my cheek with his fingers for a brief moment.

I immediately fell asleep.

Where were we? This question remained unanswered. It seemed like this place wasn't a part of the Earth I knew. The colors were much more intense, the scents were also unnaturally strong and overwhelming. My new senses were unbelievably stimulated, so much information was sent to my brain it caused me a painful headache analyzing it. I brought my knees to my chest, covered my ears with my hands and hid my face in my lap, breathing heavily in unrest.

Even in that state, curled in a ball trying to lock the world outside of me, I sensed his approach. His sweet scent traveled in the air, the ground vibrated with his heavy, steady steps, the sound of his heartbeat echoed around me. The rays of the sun shadowed around his muscular silhouette. It was futile trying to block my senses, because although I folded myself as tightly as I could data was still sent to my brain clearly and unchanged;

only then did I realize how powerful my consciousness of the world was.

He kneeled down next to me touching his warm hand on my shaking shoulder. I was breathing through clenched teeth – his hand sent new waves of information mingled with unfamiliar emotions to my head. Emotions of pleasure. I pulled my head out of my lap.

"Must be confusing..." he said; his black hair shone under the blazing sun.

"Rather painful..." I corrected him, turning my head to face him.

"You need to learn to ignore some things..." he told me, pulling his hand off of my shoulder, something which mysteriously bothered me.

"How can you ignore a world like this?" I questioned; my eyes were filtering a ray of sunlight, passing through the canopy.

"Good question... I have problems with it sometimes," he admitted.

"What are we going to do now?" I asked sounding nervous unintentionally.

He thought about his answer for a moment, formed his answer in his head. "I don't know, but we have to move on, *Our People* have been waiting for you for centuries..." he said, standing up and offering me his hand.

"*Your People*?" I retorted puzzled, grabbing his hand eagerly. He pulled me up with one gentle move.

There was just silence from his side.

"You need to be patient; everything will clear up very soon..." he whispered, making me walk deeper into the woods with him, his firm fingers curled around my trembling hand. "Trust me..." he said skeptically.

"You're the only one left...?" I murmured completing his sentence. He just nodded approvingly and pulled us both into suffocating silence.

8. Dead or Alive

"I told you, you should fight the current; see, it's pushing you sideways!" he said loudly as I fought against a strong mass of wild wind. He insisted on teaching me how to fly properly, but I had never imagined it could be so challenging. I felt my back muscles spasming as I pushed towards the opposite direction. The wind pressed me, dragged me wherever it wanted to and I was afraid I would knock to the ground at any moment, fall into the narrow canyon. The air carried dirt and it scraped my skin like nasty sandpaper.

I moved anywhere the wind wanted me to, like a lifeless ragdoll, I had no control over my body and no matter how hard I tried I couldn't gain any.

"Oh, C'mon! You're stronger than that!" he yelled trying to sound persuasive, he was standing on one edge of the canyon monitoring my disappointing progress. I tightened my jaws, gritted my teeth and pushed even more; I felt blood washing through my veins immediately, running in my tireless wings, feeding my aching muscles.

I started fighting back.

My body was about to give up, the mental and physical exertion had worn me down; I was using the remains of my energy to thrust myself upwards, to make myself ascend vertically up the glimmering sky in a desperate attempt to escape from that single current that had tortured me for hours now. The feeling of freedom filled my chest with the air I could finally breathe in.

The slapping of the vicious wind gave way to the silky touch of a warm breeze draping itself around my sweat-soaked body. The weight of the pressing air which had tyrannized me demanding the oxygen out of my lungs was replaced by an amazing lightness; I had the freedom to breathe again, to inhale and exhale in remarkable comfort. The grimace of unease had pulled and stretched my characteristics in an unnatural way, in that of suffering almost. Now, while I breathed in, wildly sucking in as much air as I could store in my lungs, the hard lines on my face eased out forming a mask of genuine relief.

I did not stop flying and I wasn't planning to. The sense of freedom was addictive; exactly like a drug, it was narcotic. A tiny smile of victory drew itself upon my cracked lips, although I knew I was anything but a victor. The vast unending sky pleaded me to fly higher, to ascend even more, it was a feeling I had never experienced before, it felt like I couldn't help myself, like I had no way to stop, like the appeal of the clear sky was an irresistible one. It felt like I was succumbing to a temptation.

"Don't go too far!" I heard someone shouting at me, exclaiming an apparent warning. I was anything but alarmed by his excessive concern; I didn't bother answering just flew even faster, slitting the air, enjoying the freedom I had never felt before in my entire life as a powerless human. I didn't know what exactly was so desirable about the sky and I realized it was another unfamiliar instinct because of *The Metamorphosis*. The urge was running in my veins, in my blood, the desire filled my tissues, made me lose control from the inside out, moving my body without my brain's approval.

I behaved exactly like when I was searching for luscious flowers, in the same obsessive way when my throat was burning with thirst; – like an animal. I was driven by an unidentified instinct, an instinct I could not control – a completely untamable yearning. But what did I want?

"Hey! April! Stop!" He was following me, the yell was closer to me now; he was flying as well. I accelerated as though he was hunting me – in fear of captivity. I needed to go higher, I had to go higher, I had to reach a point. My shaking fingers curled into stiff fists, cold sweat ran down my skin and my eyes would not look away from the endlessness of the atmosphere. What I was doing was insane from every point of view; there was no logic in my actions, none at all.

Then, I felt it.

A feeling in my body; satisfaction overwhelmed me. My heart beat frantically inside my chest the first moment and then it just stopped for a single unending second knocking the air out of me in a gasp. A gasp of pleasure, of *victory*. The next thing I remember was me ducking down, recoiling my wings, falling vertically exactly like a falcon with no interference of fright whatsoever. Actually, I was content, amazed, utterly mesmerized...

I closed my eyes and allowed that powerful feeling to control me wholly. I could not breathe – the strong slapping of the wind on my face would not allow it, my heart thudded hard against my ribs, I was sucking in the moment. The appreciation was drawn upon my face and pulled my lips into a winning smile. This was a real victory. I had satisfied my desire.

Adrenaline.

The temptation wasn't the sky itself, but the experience it provided. A unique experience of adrenaline; a total rush. I longed to feel the rush of adrenaline making my pulse frenzied, making me feel free.

Alive.

He was close by, his heart beat faster than mine – stressfully.

I declined in unbelievable speed, so fast the air around me hissed as I passed; gravity pulled me down and I realized that I would shortly have to start reducing speed.

I didn't know how.

My eyes fluttered open, that very thought pushed me back into reality. I had no idea of how to stop myself. The danger of death sent currents shivering all the way down to my limbs freezing them into place. Panic took over and an alarm sang in me. My pupils were black and wide with shock, immobilizing my wings which I now wanted to use more than anything. Horror dragged me in a state of inability.

I had to scream, but I could not find my tongue, I was unable to form words. The breath was knocked out of my pressured lungs. My arms and legs hung lifelessly and I lost my balance against the brutal wind. I fell into the narrow canyon and realized my rescue was impossible as I came closer and closer to the ground. Closer and closer to my *death*; I realized I was condemned.

I suddenly screamed; I found my vocal cords.

I was staring at the ground wide-eyed, it seemed like I'd frozen up, like my joints did not exist. I was doomed and no matter how badly I wanted it I couldn't move my wings an inch. I shut my eyes and shut my mouth preparing to face the pain only seconds away.

I never hit the ground.

A pair of solid arms grabbed me, held me against a chest of steel. A *human* instinct told me to hide my horrified face into the vastness of his chest. His heart pounded wildly and I could hear it amazingly clearly. His breaths were sharp and deep, his lungs demanded oxygen he was unable to provide them with, betraying the extensive exhaustion, the amazing race he'd done to catch me. The movement of his chest pushed me against the security of his arms wrapped around my shuddering body. Our heartbeats created a panicked symphony; our bodies were under a thick layer of icy sweat making our clothing glue on us.

His scent was a familiar one; one that I would recognize miles away even though I'd just met him three days ago. Peter.

He leaned towards my ear, but did not touch it with his lips. "Gotcha…" He breathed barely audibly and I responsively hided deeper into the safety and the warmth of his still body.

"WHAT WERE YOU THINKING?!" He was furious, just so totally furious. His amazing calmness was replaced by uncontrollable anger. "Are you suicidal or something?" he wondered. There was concern in his voice. "I can't afford losing you! Do you understand? *We* can't afford losing you!" he was shouting taken over by rage; walking up and down in front of me. The darkness of the forest made him look intimidating, close to spiteful. "What were you thinking?" he asked again, his look was desperate.

"Nothing. I wasn't thinking at all..." I lamely murmured. The guilt I felt was pulling a string tighter around my neck every time I looked at his exasperation; at his amazing worry as if he was responsible for me. Like if I died the blame was on him.

"What do you mean?" he asked edgily, stepping closer towards me. His eyes shone brightly with resentment.

"I mean I was flying and I didn't know why..." I mumbled out staring at the mud underneath my feet, the sound of it was as stupid as I had imagined it would be. I felt his skeptical eyes eyeing me curiously. "How can I explain this...?" I muttered in unease, it felt as though I was choking, the imaginary wire around my neck was pulling even tighter, so tight a wound had formed.

"It was..." My voice was even lower this time, almost undetectable. His peering eyes glared when he completed my sentence. "... instinctive." He breathed in perceptible astonishment. He looked up at me searching for my approval – just a slight nod. "But of course! Your claim on *The Dimensional Universe*..." he muttered to himself stunned by his discovery, his eyes now glimmered not because of anger but because of fascination.

"I thought it was just for the rush..." I said cowardly, spooked by how long his eyes had remained unblinking.

"That is what it would seem to you... But no..." he whispered, and his amazed eyes met mine. "You wanted to make sure that you *claim* the sky, that you own it for sure, that the Demons haven't taken it..." he said putting his hand on my shoulder and tightening his fingers around it.

"And I'd do that by killing myself?" I asked unconvinced, looking deeper into his shining gaze.

"Everything claimed by Demons feels *Dead*, you can sense it. Everything that belongs to life feels *Alive*," he murmured. His lips were only inches away from my ear, like he was confessing something to be kept a secret. A gasp came out of my tight throat automatically.

"Did –?" He didn't manage to form his question.

"Yes," I whispered breathlessly, astounded. I'd indeed felt that, felt *alive*.

It was a feeling I'd never felt before, it was something unfamiliar, totally new. And it gave me so much pleasure and fulfillment. An emotion making my heart beat powerfully, but this was just a different kind of heartbeat.

"I hadn't realized you could be so strong. It's impossible..." he murmured, more to himself than to me. "Unbelievable..." he whispered turning to look at me with smiling eyes replacing that irritation that had terrified me seconds ago.

"I didn't do anything..." I said, putting my hand on top of his which was still resting on my shoulder and shoved it off of me softly.

"I'm thirsty..." I added trying to swallow, but my mouth was completely dry. I turned around and searched the green ground for any sign of blossoming plants and was disappointed to find none. I couldn't smell anything but the water of the little canal only a few meters away, running between the two sides of the canyon. I walked towards the water and kneeled down scooping water with my still frozen hands. The water slid down my esophagus but did not soothe my stinging pain whatsoever. My thirst only got stronger.

"Water isn't what you need..." he said walking towards me.

"I know, there's always hope though..." I muttered standing up, feeling the burning of my throat more than ever. He was right behind me and I knocked into him, his firm hand secured around my upper arm preventing my fall.

He leaned down towards my ear and I could feel his warm and moist breath hitting my shoulder. "Don't do that again," he whispered gently, so very gently.

"I didn't do it on purpose." I breathed, his touch sent waves of unfamiliar feelings of liking all over my body, the closeness between us made me tense, a tension I mysteriously enjoyed experiencing.

"I might not always be there to save you," he said. His lips touched my ear as he mouthed the words and I couldn't tell if it was by mistake or intended. I was still, unsure of how I was supposed to react to the soft touch of his mouth, unsure of whether I should accept it or not.

"I trust you," I said and he pulled away letting go of my arm at once. We were still very close to each other, close enough for me to feel the warmth flowing between our bodies.

"Do you?" he questioned stepping away, that shine of intelligence made his eyes look a lot more attractive.

"Yes," I replied lost in his gaze for just a single second and then stared away into the woods awkwardly avoiding his examining look.

"Progress," he commented moving away from me, the warmth between us was replaced by unwanted coolness.

He turned his back on me and started walking away, allowing the shadows of the lightless forest to consume him.

"Where are you going?" I asked moving away from the river bank.

He turned around and a set of glowing eyes stared at me identical to a lithe cat. "Somewhere safe," he answered.

"I've heard that before, safety seems like it is non-existent in *your* world…" I said eyeing him carefully, waiting for a reaction or a reply.

Two cold forced chuckles came out of his throat. "It might actually be that way…" he said slightly sarcastic, blackly humoristic.

"Let's see if you can a keep a promise…" I said.

"Trust me, *that promise no one can keep*," he murmured eerily, absolutely serious, glancing at me briefly in the eyes and then turning around pacing deeper into the woods forcing me to start following him closely behind.

9. Fire

I craved for explanations, for answers to my endless questions; though I didn't dare to ask, afraid of the untold answer, afraid it wouldn't be something I would want to hear. Afraid of how irrational the reply would be because I knew that human logic wasn't a part of this unknown *Side*.

I was going through some facts. What I had was poor, the information I had up to now was disappointingly little. I just had *Sides, Dimensional Universes, the Chosen One*, and of course, sinister *Demons*. I couldn't place the information in a satisfying answer; I couldn't make sense out of it.

We had found a valley to feast. The acidic pain in our throats was insufferable. Sucking the nectar out of the flowers seemed like drinking ambrosia; it was so soothing, it softened the pain to nonexistence. "You like that, don't you?" he murmured, watching me suck out the liquid from a water lily I'd found just by the river bank.

"You bet..." I said, smiling, licking my lips clear.

I turned down towards the ground and pulled out a flower I could not identify. It was red mingled with white almost like mixing pink on a palette, it looked beautiful and juicy but I didn't know if it was edible. "Hey, do you know what this is?" I muttered standing up, staring at the flower I had in hand.

There was just a creepy silence. "Pete?" I asked reluctantly, turning around, hating the quiet.

There was nobody.

A forceful wave of panic washed through me knocking the breath out of me. He had disappeared in just a single moment. I'd lost his scent; I couldn't hear his steady heartbeat anymore and I realized he was somewhere I could not reach him. "Peter?" I shrieked in agony letting the blossom fall out of my trembling hands. If this was meant to be a joke it was a bad one. Cold blood was running in my veins and perspiration wet my body once again. Anxiety made my knees wobble when I walked towards the murk of the woods.

I started running into the trees like a lost animal. "Peter?!" I shouted. Fear made me move stiffly. I tried to find his scent between countless different ones, but I did not manage and the dizziness that followed made me almost knock to the ground unconscious. I was disorientated, lost without *Him*. I unwillingly ran into the intimidating gloom of the forest unable to determine the direction he had followed.

What ifs were questions I hated, but while I was running they just formed in my mind involuntarily, making up different scenarios to reason his sudden disappearance. Why would he leave me? Why would he run away now? What if he wasn't running...? What if he was the... *chased*?

What if he was running away from *Them*?

My heart pounded so hard the sound of its thudding echoed around me. *Demons*, he might be running away from *Demons*. The gasp of terror was automatic; the thought itself made my eyes glare with fear and my reluctant pace transformed into a ferocious sprint. I couldn't scream his name without being electrocuted by pain and only then did I realize how much I depended on him. Just how much I cared.

What if he was *Lost*?

"Pete, you can't be serious man!" I heard a voice saying. It belonged to a stranger, and it wasn't Peter's. I immediately slowed down and walked silently towards the sound.

"I'm very serious. *She's* not ready!" It was him! The relief was displayed on my face replacing the worry which had twisted my characteristics. The gasp I was holding in my throat turned into a heavy exhale – I'd found him, alive.

"Who are you to judge?! Pete, *She* was born for this!" The male voice was deep and sounded annoyed, furious almost. I moved closer into a huge dense bush, curiosity now was the dominant feeling.

"*She's* just... *too human*! *The Spirits* will crush her like a bug!" Peter's voice got louder; his tone was close to protective. I moved as noiselessly as I could, incapable of resisting the temptation of listening in on them. There was a tiny hole in the bush allowing a weak ray of sunlight to enter.

My heartbeat was uneven because of excitement; couldn't they sense me? "I know you, Pete... You're trying to protect her, aren't you?!" The anger and sarcasm in the stranger's voice cocktailed.

"Don't be ridiculous, Logan; no one can protect her from her fate," he denied. He spoke so raw it surprised me enough for me to place my eye in the little hole and examine them both.

The stranger was big, well built. He had beautiful cinnamon skin and bright fluorescent yellow eyes, a pair of wings in the same coloration rested curled on his back. I don't know what, maybe the way he spoke made me hate him, fear him in a way. "Look, it's natural for you to want to protect her, she's got the *Three Virtues*, it makes her precious, makes you want to guard her…" the stranger said, trying to sound understanding unsuccessfully.

"It has nothing to do with *The Virtues*; she's just too weak…" Peter tightened his jaws trying to maintain his composure; I could hear him gritting his teeth. What were they talking about? Virtues? Who were they talking about?

Me?

"The *Life Commission* is waiting for you to bring her to *Us* three days now, Pete; *The Metamorphosis* should be over by now…" You could see that the stranger named Logan was boiling in exasperation; anger made sweat run down his neck soaking his T-shirt.

"I'm sure the *Commissioners* can wait…" Peter replied stubbornly. His hands to his sides were fixed tightly into fists.

There was a cold laugh from the stranger's side; discernible black sarcasm. "Wait? For what? You have to be joking." He chuckled icily. "I don't think you have realized how crucial this is, the *Sides* have no balance between them, Pete, we're gonna die without *Her* and you tell me *We* can wait? Two weeks before *The Autumn Full Moon*? That's absurd." The sarcasm evaporated quickly and suffocating seriousness condensed. Concern was reflected in both pairs of eyes, they both seemed desperate for a moment.

"*Vie* wants to see her. She wants to see the *Chosen*. You can't go against a *Life Commissioner*, Pete..." he added, in a poor attempt to sound persuasive.

The Chosen, this whole thing was about me.

"She can't use *magic* yet. She can't cast spells..." Peter murmured disappointed, like there was something terribly wrong with me.

"That's not a problem, she'll learn how to use her powers or she's just going to *die*," the stranger said sourly, spitting out the truth, being absolutely cold.

"I can't show her how, Logan, *We* have no magic. I don't know... I mean she's weak and... vulnerable... She seems so human. But then, I realize she's so powerful it scares me, she made sure she *claimed* the sky today!" he said with reasonable admiration and caution at the same time. There was clearly distinguishable confusion in his eyes and his voice.

"If she *claimed* the sky, I don't think she's that weak, she seems rather strong to me," the stranger said uncurling his wings with one, crumbling sound. "If you're not bringing her, I'm getting her myself," he said aggressively, losing his patience. "I'm not getting in a fight with *Mort* again, do you understand?" He was being loud, threatening.

"Where is she?" he asked moving past Peter who's hand was immediately on Logan's shoulder preventing him from walking away. I instinctively recoiled, hiding deeper into the safety of the bush now knowing that this man wanted to find me.

To take me.

"What? Let me get to her," the stranger said eyeing Peter.

"That's not going to happen." Peter breathed slowly, like a sour growl.

"You're not okay, buddy, she's going to die and you're attached to her? She's doomed, condemned to save *Us*, she'll die anyway. Face it," he said impassively, like he didn't care much about it. He shoved Peter's hand off his shoulder with a sharp move and made a step forward, knocking into Peter's blocking body.

"Stop being ridiculous," Logan barked at him.

Pete did not move an inch.

"I don't want to hurt you, buddy, get out of my way." The threat came through a tight jaw. You could see the flame of rage widening their pupils, and you could smell the sweat soaking their bodies. Peter raised his hand and pushed him away with one abrupt move, knocking him to the ground.

He grabbed him from the collar of his shirt ominously. "What, don't, you, understand?" he breathed, emphasizing each word. Logan looked scared for a moment, Pete was bigger than him and then, his fist hit Peter's face out of nowhere, smashing his lips, making them chap and ooze blood.

The argument between them turned into a bloody fight.

Punches flew around smashing faces and bruising bodies. You could hear their mechanical breathing; you could smell the blood dripping out of their mouths as they tumbled on the ground kicking each other violently in the abdomen. I was so startled by their fight I fell out of my hiding spot, tripped out of my bush. They didn't seem to notice me at all, too busy slapping their faces.

"Hey!" I yelled walking towards them hesitantly, keeping a decent distance between them and me. They didn't seem to hear, or sense my presence at all.

"Stop!" I screamed, louder this time, staring at them, in disgust of the blood spilling out of their wounds, creating little channels reaching the tip of my shoe. Gasps coming out of both arguers betrayed the pain their barbarity caused, though the infuriation mirrored in their enlarged pupils was not a single bit less than just a moment before.

They just ignored me.

Suddenly, I felt this tsunami of anger demolish every piece of logic in my head. I was not able to think or comprehend in one endless instant. I remember a veil of heat draping itself around me immediately and I felt myself sizzle and boil exactly like the night of *The Metamorphosis*, though this seemed different. This time, I did not feel pain, none at all. I was outraged, furious, and totally wild. My body temperature rose dramatically, to a point where I thought I was about to melt, to liquefy. I quivered from head to toe; my eyes were wide and unblinking.

Then, I felt this power, this energy moving from my burning chest down to my outstretched arm, leaving my body through my trembling fingers. A glow. A blinding, white glow.

The light grew into a large fire ball and hit a tree right ahead of me slicing its trunk in its path with a sharp, slitting sound. There was a grouped pant from all of us as the log fell directly in front of Pete, making them both freeze on spot, with obvious dread in their gaze.

I stared at them wordlessly, feeling the rage still shaking my body, feeding the burning fire inside of me.

What had I just done?

10. Secrets and powers

"CUT IT OUT! RIGHT NOW!" I yelled overwhelmed by fury. I couldn't control myself; I'd exploded exactly like a deadly bomb. They just stared at me utterly speechless; their eyes were wide with astonishment and something else, something like terror. I didn't know why I was so outraged, so angry, it just came out from inside of me like a huge fire burning my interior. The flames consumed me.

Peter tried to stand up showing his palms at me, as if I were holding a gun or something at him.

"Don't you dare come near me!" I barked aggressively, making a step backward in synchronization with his step forward, like a dance.

He didn't seem to be alarmed by my panicked order; he moved closer eyeing me tenderly. "April, you need to calm down..." he murmured at me gently, acknowledging the fact I had no control over my actions.

"Don't you tell me to calm down!" I shouted back, moving away from him, stepping backwards, tripping almost.

"Listen to me, you do not know how to use your powers properly, you need to collect yourself..." he said calmly, looking at me through a swollen eye socket. Blood was traveling down his chin from his ripped lips.

"I need to collect myself?!" I asked with thick sarcasm.

"Sit down, April. Now." He was louder this time, slightly sterner and just three feet away from me; I felt cornered.

"No." This time, it was just a pathetic whimper, the distance between us became less and less by the second. I hit a tree exactly behind me and I had nowhere to go.

"Yes," he said, detecting the weakness in my voice. He was just two inches away from me when I allowed my stiff knees to bend and slid down on the ground, pulling my legs tightly to my chest.

As soon as I hit the ground the fire had gone out as mysteriously as it had lighted.

My head was a total jungle, a paining mess. I tried to analyze, to clear up, to make sense of, but I couldn't place the pieces of the puzzle in the right spot, it caused me so much frustration I dropped my head into my lap and sobbed. For the first time in my life I felt fear, real, breathtaking fear of the unknown; and it hit me with sheer force. I swallowed down two irrevocable truths. One, I didn't know where I was. Two, I didn't know what I was. Everything else was being debated; my mind was working so hard it felt like a hammer was crushing my skull.

I never thought my life could ever get so complicated. I was never a fan of complexity, simple things were my favorite ones. And now complication surrounded me in this world, everything about this *Side* was intricate and demanded paining thorough analysis. I was tired of it.

I wanted to be human once again so badly.

How on earth had I got myself into this trouble? Why was I standing in the eye of this hurricane? I wanted to run, to flee but I had nowhere to go, nowhere to run to. I felt trapped; the feeling forced my lungs to swell searching for air.

Peter placed his bloody hand on my shoulder sending electric currents all over my quivering body. "Crying isn't a good idea..." he breathed plainly.

I looked up, my eyes stung with fresh tears wanting to slip out of my eyelids. "Why?" I questioned through a tough voice, deep because of crying.

"You've learnt nothing yet, imagine if you knew *The Truth*..." he told me pulling his hand away. "That'd be disastrous..." he muttered more to himself, looking away from me, towards Logan's direction.

He was on his knees facing the ground, spitting ounces of blood holding his abdomen. For some inexplicable reason I felt an urge to aid him, despite the fact he'd sounded so amazingly hostile before, he was suffering and I couldn't bear looking at him in that state. Peter realized I was staring at the stranger intensely, my watery eyes gazed him tenderly, empathetically.

"He'll be fine. He deserved that." His tone surprised me, the bitterness in his voice was something I wasn't used to.

"No he didn't," I argued powerlessly and crawled towards the stranger cautiously on all fours.

He was choking on blood, coughing his guts out. I slowly placed my hand on his back making him flinch away protectively; but once he recognized me he moved closer peering at me brightly with his curious yellow eyes. He looked like a little child for a moment, so innocent and full of interest. He tried to smile but did not manage it as it caused him excruciating pain; his teeth were red instead of white.

"Stand up," I whispered at him. He coughed again and did what I'd told him. "Go wash yourself," I advised him, pointing at the little river cutting through the two sides of the canyon.

He nodded.

I made sure he was gurgling with the water before I turned and sprinted back into the gloom of the forest. I had to run away from this insanity, even for just a few minutes.

My heart was about to burst out of my chest, the sweat stuck on my body, I ran faster than sound and everything around me turned into a blur. The confusion, the shock, the fear, everything created a *deadly* cocktail that almost made me turn hysterical. I felt I was going crazy, I needed something to snap me back to reality, I needed to figure out what was the product of my imagination and what was real; the two seemed to blend together so well I couldn't tell which was which.

I felt icy under the heavy layer of sweat veiling my body, my pupils had widened like an alerted animal's, like I was being hunted down by someone, like I was running away from the predator threatening to kill me. My sharp, profound breathing was so loud I knew it was a matter of time I'd be discovered. Every sound my sensitive ears perceived made me jump on spot, every scent sent waves of stress down my limbs.

Flying wasn't an option; *He* had the advantage of experience. Peter was weaker on the ground; it would buy me some time, right now I just knew I had to get away from him, I had to create as much distance between us as possible. The familiar shot of adrenaline made me bolt, dart through the trees with unbelievable precision. My pulse became frantic, making the pressure I was under apparent, betraying my panic.

C'mon, C'mon, C'mon! I silently ordered myself, *you need to go home, you have to go home!* I was screaming in my head, the humidity made my hair stick to my skull dripping sweat. *You have to leave, you have to run!* This was spoken out loud, in just a breathless mumble while I sprinted. I was talking to myself; I might as well have been on the verge of madness, the tropical characteristics of these woods made me feel dizzy.

Run to where? How would I ever escape? I knew I'd lost the game before I'd even started playing it, I acknowledged it was futile.

In spite of the knowledge of my certain failure though, I did not stop running. I knew that if I dared to halt I'd lose my mind for sure; running gave me a false sense of freedom I desperately needed at that particular moment. I wanted to feel free, to feed my ferocious run with the confusion and frustration burdening my chest.

I wanted to know. I wanted to know everything, to get the answers I wanted. Why wasn't He telling me? Why wasn't Peter explaining things to me? I don't know exactly why tears slid out of my eyelids and traveled down my colorless cheeks, but I felt so scared, it felt as though there was no possible place where I could be *safe and sound*.

Safe and sound, it echoed so beautifully in my head...

There was one thing that frightened me to the bone, something Peter and the stranger had mentioned so emotionlessly, so not disturbed by that truth while I flinched away from the sound of it in terror. *Death*. My death. And something about my fate. Maybe Peter was trying to keep me in the dark because the answers to my questions weren't things I wanted to hear; just as I'd imagined. But even though I knew that the facts would be unsettling I hoped I was wrong. But hope itself is never enough...

"Stop, April." Every working part of my body shut down. *The voice*, the voice I'd heard the very first night. It was speaking to me again, though this time I was conscious of my surroundings, I was not hypnotized. The sound of the melodic speech made me freeze on spot, made me turn as still as a marble statue. *"You cannot escape, I'm afraid..."* the male voice went on, this time the voice seemed to be just one. My face was blank from any emotion other than shock, my eyes popped open as I searched for the origin of this eerie speech, I turned my head to the canopy of trees, dropped my gaze to the forest floor but sensed no human presence. I realized the birds had stopped whistling their musical songs, something extremely alarming.

There was just a creepy silence.

"You were Chosen for this world..." the unidentified voice continued incredibly calmly, breathing slowly and lowly, unaffected by my increasing stress; I was now almost sure I was hallucinating. *"You cannot run away from who you are... You can only face..."* the voice trailed off on the last sentence, like it wanted to hide something, like it didn't want to reveal something accidentally to me.

"Face what?" I yelled out the question, my voice came out hoarse with anguish, my eyes were not looking at something in particular, it was like I was talking to the air.

"Your Enemy." There was no musicality in the answer, it was dryly said, completely raw and I realized there was no lie or implication. The reply did not need any analysis; it was just the one clear truth I'd got ever since I entered this enigmatic multi-dimensional world. I asked the most predictable question.

"Who's my enemy?" I demanded and my voice broke on the last word; I could not make my gaze focus on anything specific. Stringy strands of hair fell into my eyes and I continued shuddering unstoppably. I hadn't realized I had a foe to face, I didn't know I had a battle to fight; the current of electricity shook my body instantly; electrocuted me.

There was a brief moment's pause.

"Yourself," the voice finally replied darkly, making me wince in response. A veil of cold draped itself around me preventing me from moving. What did this mean? The puzzlement was immediately visible upon my face.

"What do you mean?" I retorted in a surprised gasp. There was no answer, just the same peculiar silence, it was as if the voice had disappeared, I'd lost contact with it. The dissatisfaction hit me like a strong slap.

"Oh great, don't tell me anything either!" It was pure frustration, I was addressing the voice, I talked to nobody and nobody could hear me apart from myself. "Who cares if I die?!" My attempt to sound sarcastic was pathetic, it sounded more like a cry, my voice broke. "Nobody." It came out as a powerless murmur. I knew I was talking to myself – a sign of deliriousness – but I had to say something or otherwise I would choke on my own tongue.

I dropped to my knees, my face turned as white as a sheet of paper, my gaze was absolutely vacant. I felt sick. Sick of *everything*. My head felt as though it was about to explode. I heard Him approaching, moving slowly, I wouldn't run anymore, I'd consumed all my adrenaline and I now felt the tiredness seep into me, immobilizing me, draining the life out of me.

His heartbeat sounded like singing to my ears once again, his unique, distinctive scent traveled around. From his pounding pulse I could tell he'd been running, obviously following me. He sat next to me quietly, being careful not to touch me. He sat there, surrounded by silence. "I've been terrible, haven't I?" he suddenly asked, smashing the stillness of the forest, the noiseless peace.

"What do you mean?" I wondered in a feeble whisper, not moving my eyes from that faraway spot I was staring at lifelessly.

"I mean, I should have told you earlier…" he mumbled out nearly ashamed of himself. I felt him stiffen next to me awkwardly.

"What should you have told me earlier?" I asked in a dead tone, a weary one.

"*Everything*," he replied immediately. The same shame was distinguishable in his words.

"I was wrong to think we had luxury of time… *It's coming…*" His words flashed with concern, with noticeable panic.

"What's coming?" I enquired, interest twisted my stomach. I sensed the agony flowing in his body radiating off to me, I turned around deeply infected by his contagious stress; I knew it was something bad, I knew it all along. For a moment, we just stared into each other's nervous eyes.

"*The End.*" He said breathlessly, darkly, ominously; something like terror was discernible in his look.

My eyes flared and for the first time since I'd been here I had the opportunity to ask questions.

11. Explanations and definitions

"*The End*?" I asked quietly. My eyes shone with identical fear.

"The collapse of *The Balance*. The death of our Dimensional Universe," he said, gazing at the ground, his words were stung by pain.

"Like... the entire Universe?" I questioned in disbelief, my fear gradually grew into horror.

"When we say 'Universe', we just mean the universe of one world," he said, turning his eyes on me. "Earth is three-dimensional, the *Sides* are connected to one another, if there is no *Balance* in one side of our world's Universe the entire *World* collapses..." he said, just a bit over a whisper. "A chained reaction, something like a domino..." he murmured reluctantly, his heart was thudding in his solid chest.

"Which *Side* is out of *Balance*?" I enquired at once, my eyes were glimmering with interest; the alarm was distinguishable in my tone.

He hesitated; I could listen to the saliva sliding down his esophagus as he swallowed in unease. "The *Human Side*..." he finally spat out, knowing he couldn't escape from my expectant gaze. The surprise immediately broadened my eyes, questions swam in my head. "*Souls are lost. Claimed*," he muttered, the disgust made him flinch unconsciously.

"Claimed by *whom*?" My voice's volume was rising, for some reason anxiety seeped into me, making my heart beat abnormally fast.

There was another pause, like he couldn't form the word with his lips without wincing. "*Demons*." He breathed, his eyes returned to focus on me, the iciness flowing between us froze us on spot. Me, because of astonishment, him, because of revulsion.

"They'll do everything for an *untouched* soul. A *human* soul," he continued whispering, afraid somebody would hear. "You see, once we die, I mean, when Humans die, the body is worthless, it's the soul *They're* craving for." The despair traced his words. "A *Clean* soul is all they want, but *untouched* souls are so hard to find among the dead, the Spirits are unsatisfied," he mumbled stiffly. He chuckled, "You'd think I've lost my mind, wouldn't you?" but I could discern no actual humor in his words.

I was lost; I had no idea as to what he was referring to.

He saw that.

"I'm confusing you, aren't I?" The humor dissolved giving way to the same miserable murmuring. I nodded, my brows had pulled together reflexively making my puzzlement obvious.

"Human logic does not apply here; to you it'll seem just like insanity," he warned me.

"I'm aware of that," I replied calmly, almost encouragingly.

Another torturous pause followed.

"Demons have been around since... forever," he began suddenly, surprising me. "At first they weren't called that way, we named them *Soul Claimers*," he said. I turned my entire body around to face him; curiosity was shining in my eyes. "Just like I said before, once a human dies the body is worth nothing, but the soul inside is the reason of this unbalance." He went on; I was still holding my breath.

"*Soul Claimers* claimed the souls of the dead, exactly how *They* were supposed to do, in order for the balance to be kept," he told me. "We don't know why this has changed, why these *Soul Claimers* turned into *Demons*. The problems with the *Balance* cannot be solved until the *Spirits* lose power. *They're* just too strong to confront..." The dread in his tone was so heavy I felt it pulling me down as well.

"You see, every dead soul needs to be consumed by *Demons*, it just has to be claimed, it's a rule, the way it has to be, you cannot leave a soul within a dead body." He went on, staring somewhere faraway; avoiding my eyes which were pinned on him. "We hadn't realized the *Demons* had preferences..." The acidity in his words stung, the hatred radiated off of him. He stopped speaking, fighting to remain composed.

"What kind of... preferences?" I asked, afraid he wouldn't open his mouth and explain, afraid he'd pull me in the dark again, blindfold me, now that I'd seen light.

"They say souls have 'tastes'. What *we* call 'Untouched' souls, are clean souls, with a few or no *faults*. 'Consumed' souls now, are souls with a lot of *flaws* and *faults*. They say Untouched souls taste sweet while Consumed souls are bitter. No matter what kind of soul *They* have *They* need to claim it though, it's a rule for the maintenance of the Balance, whether *They* like it or not," he said. Growing anger made his eyes glare.

"That's when the *Soul Claimers* turned into *Demons*... When *They* found out *They* had the ability to kill, to suck a soul out of a living body, to claim a soul that was not supposed to be claimed and leave souls within the dead because *They* simply didn't have a taste for them." The indignation made his face pull and stretch, his body reacted releasing sweat making his forehead shine.

There was another pause, this time I broke the silence.

"I don't understand... Who can guarantee that a living soul is... 'Untouched'?" I questioned grudgingly, allowing this new bit of information to register.

"Good question... It seems like *They* don't care, *They* don't care about what kind of soul *They're* dealing with; *They* just want it to be still alive," he said bitterly, not looking at me directly, avoiding my skeptical gaze.

"*They* truly have transformed, maybe into a different kind, who knows? *They* turned into something sinister, a dark creation..." he murmured, the same nauseous grimace was drawn upon his face, a grimace of repugnance. I pursed my lips lost in thought; this was my chance for answers.

"These... *Demons*... Can *They* hurt us now?" I asked unwillingly. I winced at the thought of my soul being taken, sucked out of me, the image of my lifeless body flashed in my head.

"Oh, of course, anytime *They* want if I'm not with you. But nobody can actually hurt you, you're the *Chosen*," he said matter-of-factly, his voice turned serious when he mouthed the word "Chosen".

"What do you —" I didn't manage to finish my sentence.

He opened his mouth again explaining, a cool breeze made the trees' branches bend and shriek creating a sound I found rather bone-chilling. "This... *unbalance* started centuries ago, prophets had said it would happen, we expected it," he began; turning to look at me with his bright eyes, the fury which had turned him iron hard was now loosening its grip on him. "The Prophesies said someone would save *Life*, would defeat the *Spirits*. Somebody with the *Three Virtues*," he continued a bit louder than a breath. The Three Virtues... I'd heard that before.

"These *Three Virtues*... are reflected in your eye colors," he said staring into my eyes deliberately. "Blue for love, green for kindness, yellow for forgiveness. All three equally powerful in you. You are not too forgiving, or too loving or even too kind, everything inside you is balanced out..." he said admiringly, my eyes consciously did not move away from his...

"'A creature of perfection' just like they said..." The admiration was still there, even stronger than before, it made me look away modestly. "This balance you have within you makes you a powerful soul. The strongest one that has ever existed."

I turned my eyes on him again; what was he saying?

I blocked the world out of me processing this information, analyzing it, allowing it to settle and register in my mind, the answers came faster than what I'd thought, and they were complicated... My eyes now stared right ahead of me utterly unblinking, making the connection...

"The *Life Commission* is a different story..." he went on interrupting my inner conversations, my painful thinking. "They're something like, 'Balance controllers', our *Life Commissioners*..." he murmured, observing my amazing concentration, my narrow eyes on his face. "They're immortal souls, they never die. Vie, Mort, Passion, Desire and Love. The *Life Commission* used to control everything, when the Spirits were... cooperative." His facial characteristics twisted at the thought of the Demons again.

"Why are *They* chasing us? I mean, *They* were when you... found me..." The question slipped out of my lips automatically, without me going through it.

"Oh, April…" he trailed off, lingering. "They weren't chasing *Us*… they wanted *You*." He breathed gently this time, the expression he wore on his face was that of tenderness. The jump of my heart in my chest was immediate; the shock washed the color from my face.

"You were still human, and you are a danger to *Them*. The Spirits thought they could get you out of *the game* while you were still a human being, powerless and vulnerable. Your aura is still the same though, the *Metamorphosis* hasn't changed anything, even as a human your mental balance and inner balance was incomprehensibly strong, absolutely *perfect*…" I felt his observing eyes scrutinizing me once again, with identical softness.

I looked up, my eyebrows pulled together making my confusion visible. "*They're* afraid of you," he said meeting my thoughtful eyes, skepticism spread across my face. I went through the facts again, adding this new piece of the puzzle into the mixture. I had to remember to breathe, I found myself holding my breath as I tried, worked hard, putting the events into the right place, examining the facts, allowing everything to seep into my long term memory. I wanted every explanation and definition to register, I wanted to memorize everything.

Things started clearing up, even though the explanations seemed so crazy, and so impossible they did make sense. Just like he had said, human logic was not a part of this world, and I was totally aware of that.

Something though seemed so not right. The Prophesies said someone would save life and that person needed to have the three *Virtues* just like me…

The *Chosen*.

The gasp that followed pressed all the air out of my lungs in a moment of terrifying astonishment. *I* had to defeat the Spirits; *I* was supposed to fight the Demons.

I froze.

12. Fear

My head started spinning; I didn't want to believe it. I turned to look at Him through terrified eyes, it wasn't surprise, it was horror, it hit me hard, the truth hit me so hard I thought I was going to faint, literally pass out. "I knew you'd figure it out... you're smart..." he murmured realizing what I'd realized. "That's why I didn't tell you earlier, your reaction was what I feared, but as I said we have no time to waste, *The End* is too close..." he whispered, *loathing* made his eyes widen, he spoke hesitantly. "Too close for me to care about reactions..." he muttered, more to himself.

I felt my guts twisting, my stomach gurgling and I was about to vomit. In just a breath, I felt this stiffness spreading inside of me, cold sweat ran down the back of my neck dripping from my hair. Shock hit me relentlessly, and every wave made my heart beat even faster, until I was unable to breathe.

A mess; everything about it looked so complicated and so confusing. Demons and dead souls and I, had to fight *Them*; it was just insane. I couldn't help myself from thinking like a human, I still felt like one. This conversation was supposed to calm me down, to make me understand, but instead it unsettled me even more than before, mystified me so much. I was breathing in spasms, I felt like my body was been electrocuted.

I stood up, I don't know how, but I stood up.

I instinctively wanted to run, to escape just like before, my head was still a wild jungle, the facts tortured me. I couldn't stop myself from thinking things over and over again, trying to find something, somewhere where I'd made a mistake, I wanted to believe this was a misunderstanding, a miscalculation of my tired brain, but found nothing. My heart raced when I realized I had nothing solid to hold onto to prove myself wrong – nothing tangible, I couldn't find where I'd made a mistake because there wasn't one.

This was the raw truth.

I wanted to run, to react to this truth just like I'd done before, I wanted to leave, to wear myself with the exertion, to tire my body so that I wouldn't think about anything else other than my aching muscles. But I had absolutely no resource of energy to run futilely into the forest, so I walked instead, allowing the gloom to cover me again, my fingers were tightly fixed into shaking fists.

"Don't run away again. It's getting dark, you're gonna get lost…" he said and I felt him following me, his heavy footsteps behind me.

"That's what I'm hoping for…" I breathed so quietly, I doubted he heard that.

"Don't be stupid! Come back," he said, planting his feet, standing there completely unmoving.

"Leave me alone." It came out like a pathetic growl; I didn't turn to look at him, the sudden stress that had overwhelmed me made my voice sound coarse and deep. He mysteriously and thankfully stopped following me and just stared at me as I faded into the murk of the woods, allowing the darkness to consume me, to veil me.

I couldn't find peace, I couldn't stop thinking about the same things over and over again, my walk was anything but relaxed, my legs were so strained they felt wooden, my heart throbbed unimaginably violently as though I was actually sprinting.

It was like a thick strap was pulling me around my torso, pressing my chest. The deeper I got into the woods the tighter the strap pulled around me, pushing the remaining oxygen out of my lungs, making me feel as if I were suffocating. I was actually suffocating, drowning when the stress quickly transformed into panic.

My walk changed into a spastic jog, sweat soaked my quivering body. Mysteriously, I couldn't make myself cry, I was too shocked to do so. It was like someone had slapped me in the face, first you feel the burning pain where the hand smacked you, then, you feel anger boiling inside you and then, you cry. Lastly.

Naturally, I wanted to hide. Out of impulse. I scanned around for anything that could provide me with shelter. It was getting dark, dusk was creeping in, swallowing the last rays of sunlight –

I doubted I could sleep tonight. I was never a friend of the dark, not being able to see made me feel vulnerable when I was still human. Now, this seemed to have changed, I wasn't bothered as much, I nearly didn't care. Now that my senses were so powerful, I didn't mind losing one of them, it meant less processing and analyzing, it gave my brain a bit of a break.

I kept on going, planning to tire myself to breaking point, which was what I did whenever I felt frustrated, I exhausted myself. I still couldn't manage to block every thought; I was incapable of stopping myself from going through the same facts manically.

Stupid, did you have to wake up that night? Did you? I was questioning myself, I was talking to me, I screamed in my head.

There's nowhere to go now, idiot! You're doomed! I was mad, I was sure I was. My eyes watered.

I hate you! I hated myself; I told myself I hated it. I reacted to that and the first tear slid down my colorless cheek. More followed as I ran as best as I could, tripping every few strides.

It felt as though a hammer was hitting me persistently, opening a hole in my skull, I felt the pain of it. My heart tied into a knot banging so hard it moved my entire ribcage. I put my head into my hands as I ran and ran, tangling my legs repeatedly, biting my lower lip muffling my cry, trying to stop myself from fearing.

I didn't realize when, but shortly after I'd climbed up a hill the ominous darkness of another night covered the world, so suddenly it caught me by surprise. It was inexplicably quiet, usually at night everything springs into life, but now, everything seemed lifeless, dead almost. Not a single sound, or a scent, or even a taste... nothing at all. Just the creepy stillness of the semi-tropical forest; I felt blindfolded.

My powerful survival instincts ordered me to look for somewhere to settle, to hide. I walked up to a meadow, a tiny treeless patch, barely twenty feet across. I hadn't realized I'd been hiking up a mountain, I was glad I could get out of the suppressing humidity of the forest, I was glad I could breathe dry air again. Just above my head, several kilometers away, was the mountain's naked summit. And behind it, the moon was rising up the starlit sky, it was just a fine, very fine slice of it but still, it showered everything in beautiful moonlight.

I spotted an opening in the mountain's wall where the moonlight shone like a flashlight. Probably not even a mile's distance from where I stood, I saw it clearly. I was off, limping up the dangerously steep mountainside. It was so vertical I had to grip with my hands to prevent myself from falling into the nothingness of the cliff that formed. I was worn out, I was barely conscious, one lethal slip was all it took...

I was afraid to use my wings and I was certainly not skillful enough to fly up vertically with so many trees around waiting for me to get caught in them. I instead gritted my teeth and pushed myself as hard as I could, I thought climbing was a good distraction, unfortunately though, not good enough...

It was higher than what I'd thought, but I reached it, the entrance of the little cave I'd spotted an hour or so ago. I was dripping sweat – literally. I pulled myself into it not bothering to check if something threatening lay within, I'd rather die at that particular moment, after going through the facts so thoroughly every little flame of hope I wanted to keep burning had gone out.

I recoiled, pulled my limbs so tightly around me – defensively – and covered myself with my wings. I turned into a tight, tiny ball blocking everything out of me, locking the world outside but could do nothing about the battle I had to fight in my head, I couldn't push anything out after I'd worked so hard to memorize everything...

I cried soundlessly, it wasn't even a sob, I just breathed in gasps every now and then, squeezed in my awkward position in that claustrophobically small opening.

Just like the stranger had said I was *'condemned'*. I realized that more than anything else. I had no choices, nowhere to run to and just like the voice had said I could *'only face my enemy'*. Though my enemy appeared to be something I'd never imagined existed in the first place. I didn't know how I was even supposed to fight, how I would be able to confront *Them*. Under other circumstances I would have lied to myself, I would have found another explanation, something calming, something *logical*.

Logic, what an irony. I was still thinking like a human.

I shook my head pushing that possibility out of my pool of ideas. I shook not because of the cold but because of all the anxiety that had overwhelmed me. *Think, you idiot, think*! I was yelling at myself. *You got into this mess, you can get out of it*! I was trying to convince myself there was another solution, how stupid I was...

C'mon! Think! I was going crazy, something I knew was very likely to happen from the very beginning.

"I can't!" I argued with myself out loud, and then shut up again shaking spastically. Moving kept me occupied while sitting just tortured me; it gave me the opportunity to think without wanting to, it just happened automatically. I wanted to scream, to let out that fear strangling me, but just couldn't find the strength to do so.

I shook and whined until I quitted.

Hours certainly passed before I found peace again, when my body stopped reacting to the shock, when I stopped arguing with myself. When I could *breathe*. I was alone; the stillness around me remained untouched; it was peaceful. The truth had sunk in for good, I wasn't fighting back, I wasn't trying to find ridiculous excuses. I faced it. I was still folded in a tiny ball – I loosened up a bit, still hugging my knees though.

The same exhaustion I'd felt before was just too much to bear, I allowed it to finally pull me under, I let my heavy head fall back and I lost consciousness.

He'd found me, he somehow found me up there, tightly inside the little hole. The sun wasn't up the sky yet, but the sky wasn't black anymore, it was early dawn. I hadn't managed to sleep a lot and was awakened by his scent. He kneeled just three feet away from me eyeing my uncomfortable position.

"Come out," he said gently, offering me his warm palm. I didn't take it, I instead crawled out on all fours, my joints cracked. I didn't stand up; I stayed there, sprawled weakly on the ground. He looked at me for another endless moment. "It was kind of sudden I guess..." he muttered, not actually looking at me, and I stared into emptiness absentmindedly.

He outstretched his hand and gently traced my cheek with his fingers, my eyes flared and I winced away. "How do you feel?" he asked, staring at the ground.

My stomach roared so loudly he certainly heard it. "Hungry." I breathed a bit more lively this time, still startled by his touch, looking at him curiously.

"I'm sorry about... yesterday," he mumbled out. "I should have been a bit... milder..." he said and his eyes met mine, the innocence or perhaps the regret I could detect in his voice made me feel uncomfortable.

"No. At least now I know the truth. I asked, remember?" I felt something sharp piercing my heart – guilt. But why would I ever feel guilt? It didn't make any sense... Why was I feeling so agitated? Just by looking at his face, the real but unneeded regret, the apology ready to be spoken...

"Don't hate me..." he pleaded, almost begged me with his liquid lime eyes.

"I don't hate you," I said at once. How could I hate him? He was the one who truly took care of me, I relied on him... How could I possibly hate him?

"Then what's wrong? You just pulled away from me..." He seemed puzzled for the very first time; I'd never seen his eyebrows pull together before.

He meant when he had touched my cheek, the caress. I stiffened wordlessly.

"Can you handle it?" he questioned, real concern was distinguishable.

"Handle what? Which of all?" I retorted rhetorically, not really expecting an answer.

"*All of it*, can you handle it?" he asked again, his gaze did not move away from mine.

It took me a moment to find the right words. "Do I have a choice? I mean... you know..." My words were stung by pain without me wanting to.

"You don't have a choice…" he replied sincerely, reaching out to me, touching his hot fingers on my cold cheek, this time I didn't move away, I absorbed the heat of his hand. I liked it, not just the heat, I liked his touch…

"Then…" My voice trailed off, my thoughts scattered because of his gentle caress from my cheekbone down to my chin. He pulled his hand away and I could concentrate again, I could form the sentence.

"I guess somebody has to handle it," I whispered so that the roughness of my voice wouldn't be audible, I didn't want him to realize just how dry my throat was. "You know what they say…" I mumbled, looking away from his examining eyes, staring at the very first ray of sunlight traveling up the clear sky deep in the horizon, above the summit of the mountains. "One needs to be sacrificed for the other Ones…" It sounded too melodramatic, but right at that moment I felt that way. I barely kept my sobs deep inside my throat, I fought against them, veiled my real feelings.

"Don't say that, you're not a sacrifice, *everything's going to be okay…*" he lied. The last part of the sentence certainly was a lie, he wasn't a good liar, and I saw that, he was trying to reassure me unsuccessfully.

"You know better than anyone that that *is the truth…*" I argued. My voice was edgy; it almost broke when I mouthed the last word.

There was a second's pause.

"*I don't like it…*" he said.

He stood up, pulling me with him by the hand.

13. Screams, Shrieks and Whispers

Why did I even believe this? All of *this*? Was this even true? It seemed so false, maybe it was just a dream and it would end when I woke up... but I never woke up. It frightened me; this reality was so intimidating. The insecurity and confusion I felt were overwhelming sometimes.

This time I wasn't climbing again, he'd tossed me over his back and just flew between the trees with breathtaking skill, like a weightless leaf. He was descending with ease, almost swayed with the wind; I just stared through stunned eyes, the air swished as we passed. The sun journeyed up the sky, pulling everything back into life.

The forest started breathing again the first moment there was just the gentle swishing of the wind as we flew and the next, bizarre birds started singing their melodies, some tender and smooth other melodies sounded rough and deep, but together they created a natural orchestra, it was just so beautiful, to be able to discern every single sound, every note of their synchronized song.

Then, there were scents. Countless scents, the odors of the birds themselves, the smell of water somewhere far away, Peter's body's sweet fragrance, the scent of grass, the delicious aroma of flowers – my stomach growled instantly.

I could hear heartbeats, not just mine and Peter's, a heartbeat of an animal, then I heard clawing, and then I heard a bitter hiss, the sound of snapping bones reached my ears. Then I smelled blood and realized that whatever it was, it was certainly a carnivore. Though curiosity swelled up inside me, I did not ask Peter, I didn't want to know.

The forest was predictably humid, I thought I was breathing in water, the vapor particles condensed when they reached my lungs and suddenly I felt as if I was about to suffocate. Sweat ran from my forehead, it dripped off my fingers and on Peter's already soaked body underneath me. Suddenly, the pleasant heat of his skin became insufferable, close to painful. My breathing turned spastic and mechanic.

When we reached the forest's floor, we landed.

"I think... I'm gonna die if we don't get out of here..." he murmured sharply, out of breath, pulling me with him. There was almost no sunlight, the enormously tall trees created an impenetrable canopy. The contrast was so great; up high it was shining and bright and down where we stood, it was dark and dull, almost like dusk. It just was a bit brighter than twilight.

I was still wearing my long sleeved, thick cotton pajamas; I thought of pulling my top off but then remembered I wore nothing underneath but my bra. It was intolerable. I now craved not only for nectar but for water as well; these were two different types of thirsts. The burning deep in my esophagus could only be put out with pollen; the dryness of my tongue was a thirst demanding water. I was able to tell now, to differentiate the two different needs of my body.

Peter suddenly stopped running and turned to face me, his complexion was red. I only now noticed there was a little purple bruise on his cheekbone just millimeters away from his eye. The eye socket had swollen up a bit. "Oh, good god..." he said, staring at my arms. "How on earth can you stand it?" he added placing his hands on my motionless arms, gripping tightly on my sleeves. With one abrupt move and a shredding sound, he pulled the sleeves off my shirt effortlessly. Little rivers of sweat ran down my arms to my fingers.

The relief was immediate.

We were off again running out of the semitropical forest. Why were we running, anyway? Was it the unbearable humidity or was it something else? Something *He* wasn't telling me about? Again, I didn't ask, I was too scared to. I just ran as fast as I could keeping my mouth shut.

Everything around us turned into a blur; we were going so fast again, faster than sound, covering great distances in a relatively small amount of time. Gradually, light crept into the darkness of the woods and I realized we'd reached the edge of the forest. We slowed down; relief was drawn upon our faces as we walked out of the asphyxiating humidity and breathed in dry air again. The air felt so good in our lungs, it dried the dampness of our bodies as well, cooling us down.

We sat down, under the sun.

There was the same strange flower I'd picked up when Peter had suddenly disappeared from next to me, this time I had the opportunity to look at it closely. It was red and white, and even though the two colors mingled beautifully on every velvety petal they never created pink. The two colors stayed as they were, unchanged. The smell was also appealing, sweet. I turned towards Peter who was sitting next to me, still gasping. The twisting and gurgling of my empty stomach had abruptly become excruciating.

He immediately stared at me through the kindness of his green eyes, cutting my breath for a moment. "Is this edible?" I questioned, curling my shaking fingers around the stalk. His gaze fell on the plant I was about to yank out of the ground.

"Oh, that's precious," he mouthed quickly, eyeing my impatient fingers.

"What is it?" I retorted, reading his admiring expression.

"It's called a *Scream*," he said.

"It's a what?!" I asked laughing, forgetting about my painful hunger for just a second.

"A *Scream*," he repeated smiling at me.

"How come?" I wondered curiously, examining his bright eyes.

"There's this story about the name..." he went on. "You see, when the wind blows, flowers bend and sway but what is commonly ignored is their *sound*..." he continued, a beautiful musicality hinted his voice. "It depends on the petal's shape and size, not all flowers can create music... those that can always have white mixed with another color. *Whispers* for example are black and white," he said.

"We named the flowers because of their different sounds. *Whispers* have very thin and long petals, that's why their sound is a very soft and muffled one almost like a whisper. Because *Screams* have wider petals their sound is sharper and louder, almost like a scream..." he said. My eyes stared at the flower in a different way now, not in a ravenous one...

There was a moment of stillness, of absolute silence.

"You know, I once tried to test the theory, but it didn't work..." he admitted. "There was a cool breeze and I listened hard, but there was nothing, not even a whisper..." he said, with a bit of disappointment. "Oh, I forgot... It's edible, tastes quite good actually..." he added in a monologue.

I didn't need to be told twice...

I unplugged the plant from the ground and pushed the whole of it in my mouth. The juice coming out if it was just so addictively sweet, irresistible.

Scream, shriek, whisper... whatever it was, it was just so good...

"I need to take you to the *Life Commission*..." he said when I'd finished feeding. I licked my lips in unease. "I can't delay it anymore... The full moon is just too close..." he muttered, seeming to be trying to convince himself about that. A lump formed in my neck instantly, not allowing me to swallow.

"What... What will they do to *me*?" I asked him, the tightness of my jaw did not allow me to speak above a whisper.

"The Life Commissioners? Nothing..." he reassured me unconvincingly, it was nearly a pathetic attempt to it. I wasn't an idiot. I'm not an idiot. He felt my gaze on him; he deliberately looked away avoiding my suspicious eyes. "They're probably going to kill me... They've been waiting for millennia and I am sitting here protecting you from something that is inevitable..." He spoke to a tree, still not looking at me directly but with the corner of his eye. "I'll have to excuse myself, tell them why I kept *you* to myself..." he went on, turning his head towards me, concurrently.

We glanced at each other for a few heartbeats. "What do you mean?" I questioned, I was lost – again.

"You're *aura* is something I never came across before... it's just... so... clean." He breathed, amazement made his eyes glimmer intelligently.

"Is that something... wrong?" I retorted still feeling confused.

"No..." he muttered, somehow leaning closer towards me... "It's incredible..." He breathed in my ear, I hadn't noticed how close he was it caused me anxiety. My pulse slammed the instant his lips touched my ear, I moved away at once. What was he doing? Silence of awkwardness followed.

"This Life Commission... Where is it?" I finally wondered.

"*The City of Miracles...*" he replied.

"How far is it from here?" I enquired swelling with interest.

"About a day's flying, not much..." he murmured thoughtfully.

"Why is the city called like that?" I demanded, looking at his skeptical features briefly.

"Because miracles happen inside the city's walls..." he answered.

"What kinds of... miracles?" I questioned again, looking at him directly, the sparkle of curiosity made my eyes wide with anticipation.

"April, I'm sure you won't be impressed... You're still sort of too... human..." he whispered. "It's actually about life we're talking about. *Life* is a miracle itself..." he said, eyeing me softly, as though he was talking to a little kid, someone incapable of seeing the obvious. "If you were less... human, you would've been able to see, to realize. Humans are the only creatures tending to... forget life's value..." He went on stiffly, like he had just mouthed an insult.

"Oh." It was the only sound that came out of my pursed lips. "Are you taking me there today? To the Life Commission?" I enquired in a breath; I closed my eyes and leaned a bit back supporting my weight on my arms, absorbing the sun, exactly like a plant.

"No. Tomorrow," he told me. With the corner of my eye, I saw him imitating me; there was one distinguishable difference between us though. I was acting to be casual and he was actually casual. Next to him, my attempt to appear relaxed looked so ridiculous, I'd never been a great actress.

"You're gonna be *okay*, I promise you..." A lie, he wasn't a good liar; I heard the hesitation in his voice.

"You know I don't believe that," I said flatly, not looking at him, still having my eyes shut.

He didn't respond just stayed wordlessly by my side, under the blazing sun.

14. Beautiful souls

"Um... Okay, an alien? Am I getting any close?" We were walking; a smile pulled the corners of his lips. He laughed.

"No, April, I'm no alien..." He chortled, the light of the setting sun made his black hair glisten. "*What* are you? Why won't you tell me?" I whined, my voice pleading.

"Because I don't have to. You'll figure it out..." he replied and squeezed my hand in his. How long had he been holding it, in the first place? I pulled away abruptly when I became aware of that.

"You okay?" he questioned, feeling the wave of tightness washing through me. Why had I allowed him to touch me? Why had I found my fingers between his? It had happened completely unconsciously... "Yeah, I'm... fine." I forced myself to murmur, my jaw was still tight. I pushed a strand of hair behind my ear with my fingers pretending nothing had happened – pretending I was totally and utterly comfortable. Was I "fine"? I wasn't even aware of my actions now. What was *wrong* with me?

I stuck close enough for me to feel the heat of his body without touching him. I'd fixed my hands into fists, so I wouldn't find my palm in his again; it was almost like... like I was fighting a desire...

Dusk draped everything in a beautiful twilight. His eyes along with mine glowed again, just like they did every night. He'd sensed my caution, the hardness of my body, and now kept a distance between us as well. I could not feel the heat of his body anymore, there was a huge gap allowing cold air to pass through. I didn't like that.

We walked in silence; the sound of our breath was the only thing disturbing the peace around us. I didn't like it. The silence consumed us. "Um... Peter... it's getting dark, shouldn't we camp somewhere?" I tried to ask, my voice was still thick though.

"Right," he said, allowing his eyes to scan our surroundings, to search for something that we could use as a night refuge.

His gaze traveled around us several times, until his eyes locked on something far away. "Can you see that opening? Up on that hill?" he asked pointing at the spot with his index finger, moving closer towards me, shifting his weight.

I searched, initially disorientated but then finally found a miniature cave on the mountain directly ahead of us. "Yes," I said. There was no light left around us; we were covered by complete and unfriendly darkness.

The night had veiled the world once again.

"Wanna walk, or fly? You choose..." he told me, looking at me.

Fly? In this blindfolding murk? The idea frightened me, it just seemed so reckless. He sensed that, my instant panic, he acknowledged I lacked experience.

"Don't freak out. I thought you would've preferred a walk from a flight..." he said, joking lightly.

Relief demolished every little piece of worry left in my system in just a single heartbeat. Despite the glow of our eyes, we did not see much better in the dark. He had explained that to me, neither he, nor I, was nocturnal. It didn't bother me much; I still had very powerful senses, the night relieved me a bit from the constant headache I felt during the day. Apart from the relief though, my relatively poor eyesight made me feel extremely vulnerable as well, because I knew exactly how much I was ignoring and I knew there were a lot more things out there than what I could perceive.

It made me feel sort of... *human*. Which for some inexplicable reason, I didn't like; I didn't like feeling weak again after I'd met so much power. Even if it was just during the night hours. I felt a vulnerability I hated, truly detested...

I knew I would hate the walk. The darkness seemed very threatening, and, I instinctively moved closer to him.

The forest looked so hostile and ominous in the dark. There were smells I couldn't link to a memory and terrifying, cracking and snapping sounds coming from all directions, squeezing their way into my tired mind, hitting me relentlessly in massive waves of information. I reflexively wanted to recoil; I wanted to fix myself in a tight ball again, although I knew it wouldn't make much of a difference.

I intuitively stopped and started bending my body down to the ground flinching with pain, clenching my teeth, holding my head in both hands. It was like bombs were exploding within my skull cracking it in the middle. If I opened my mouth and tried to complain I would burst into tears; it was just insufferable. Peter grabbed my arm and pulled me up preventing me from hitting the ground forcefully. He dragged me with him as we walked. "Try and ignore everything, block your senses..." he whispered to me.

A low whimper of pain came out of me. A complaint.

It was real torture, the hike up to the little cave. How could I follow his advice? How could I ignore everything? How could I possibly block my senses? I clung on to him as he pulled me along with him. The heat and dampness of the forest had not changed, it was still awfully suffocating. When we reached the treeless meadow, a cold breeze hit our soaked bodies, freezing us. He pulled me into the cave with him, this time though, he carried me.

And then, a fascinating color made my eyes flutter open.

He put me on the ground, allowing me to examine my surroundings. In the far end of the tiny cave, a spring of crystalline water swished calmly. It was glowing, the entire cavern shone because of the water... It was not a single bit as dark as I'd imagined, gentle turquoise rays of light beamed out of the spring showering the petite hole we were in with the most spectacular light I'd ever seen in my life.

It looked almost... *magical.*

The gasp of admiration that came out of my lips echoed lightly against the walls of the cave. "Pretty, isn't it?" he said, sitting down as well. I was still sprawled on the ground, unable to move, not because of my physical and mental exhaustion but because of astonishment and amazement. Awe. I was mesmerized.

I pulled up clumsily and rested my back on the wall. I allowed my wings to drop over my shoulders and wrap around me exactly like a blanket.

He was in front of me, staring at me. The illumination of his green eyes was different this time; because of the blue light the color of his irises seemed to liquefy, to melt. "What is this?" I asked in a worn breath, my eyes – half open. "A *Mirror*," he said and crawled to the edge of the spring – the ceiling was too low for him to stand.

"*It reflects your soul*," he explained looking at the water's surface, staring at his own reflection. Curiosity was my motivation. I moved my ragged body, aching with pain. Curiosity was a strong feeling I could not ignore even when I was a human. I crawled beside him, lying on my abdomen imitating him and stared at my complexion. The light was almost blinding.

I looked at my reflection. I was frightened at the sight of my eyes and my hair. The fatigue was visible in my features and the dirt and sweat made my forehead shine. But still, even though I looked so dramatically different, the expression on my face was still April's, it still looked exactly like it had when I was human.

I turned my gaze on his reflection.

It seemed like he had... aged. Not much, although the change was clearly visible. The smooth skin of his face was folded in light wrinkles, it had lost its gloss and shine of youth, his midnight black hair had fair gray in it. It surprised me so greatly I turned to eye him, to make sure I had the same person next to me. Confusion seeped into me at once. I looked from him, back to his reflection, and vice versa, the bewilderment twisted my characteristics.

"April, it's reflecting my soul, my *real* face..." he explained in a dark whisper. The shame in his voice was intense, his eyes suddenly darkened with mortification.

What?

I felt him swallow, swallow hard.

"What's *wrong* with your soul?" I asked in a murmur, eyeing him gently.

"A lot of *mistakes*, April... Just a lot of *mistakes*..." He breathed, he stared at the ground humiliated.

There was a cold moment of stillness and absolute silence. Neither of us dared to open our mouths.

"Peter..." I began, shattering the quiet.

"Yes?"

"We all make mistakes..." I whispered to him, for some reason I felt an urge to comfort him, to make him hold his head up high again. It was like my heart had tied into a knot.

"Yes, but not *my mistakes*..." he said lowly, so shameful again, avoiding my eyes.

I'm not sure what happened next, it was like I was next to a little child experiencing guilt for the very first time. It just made that maternal instinct inside me flare. I raised my hand and caressed his cheek, caringly. From the cheekbone down to his chin. I wouldn't have done that under other circumstances, but this, for some inexplicable reason, was so different.

Very different, it was a sentiment from deep inside my chest, which, I couldn't label.

"Just look at you..." he mumbled, pointing at my reflection with his eyes, envying me. "Clean... just so... *balanced*," he said as I turned my head to look back down at my soul.

"What a *beautiful* soul..." he whispered, with respect for me.

No one had ever called me beautiful before...

"I'm not beautiful, I make mistakes myself," I argued.

There was bitter laughter from his side. "Like what, April?"

"I lie, and I curse and I make fun of people. They're all considered mistakes, aren't they...?" I said.

His laugh was louder this time; it was still edgy though, not a single bit genuine, there was too much anxiety in it. "Yes, but that's not what I mean..." he muttered, turning to look at me momentarily. "You're *balanced*... It has to do with the *Three Virtues, you're perfect because of your imperfections*, because even though you make mistakes you have no real *evil* inside you," he explained with his eyes fixed on me.

"And do *you* have?"

Ominous silence.

"No, but I was close once…" he said.

I was already biting my tongue until I tasted blood. What had I just spat out? Something stupid. Obviously. A slip of my tongue. I'd just hurt his feelings, I'd actually insulted him. My nature ordered me to apologize.

"Sorry, I didn't mean to –"

He cut me mid-sentence. "See! I told you, you never do anything to hurt people, never," he mouthed. There was this sharp and piercing edge of pain in his words once again, and this time it pierced me as well.

Suddenly, as I stared into the bottomless little pond, I saw something moving in it. Figures, women swimming up towards me.

Silver, there was no other color.

A captivating melody with no actual words reached my ears.

The two silver female figures sprang out of the water and grabbed me by my shirt's collar, pulling me down with them, mumbling some kind of anthem or song – a beautiful one.

I screamed.

Then, I saw they had no legs, except only a fish's tail.

I screamed even louder.

15. Reflected

Mermaids... At least that's what I thought they were. They were silver, their eyes, hair, skin, were all colored in shining silver. They sang, an enchanting melody, an exquisite song. They're voices were perfectly synchronized; it was a soft and silky sound, with no gaps in it. It was beautiful, truly beautiful.

Their wet hands grabbed me and pulled me down towards them, their fingers traced my hair, my face, with an admiration beyond belief. I shouted and fought against their unexpectedly strong grip. My entire torso was under water, these fragile-looking creatures were very powerful. Peter placed his hands around my waist and dragged me out of the spring. I was choking on water, I looked up at him through terrified eyes; I was still trying to free my arms from their hands.

"*Reflectionists*... don't let them pull you down!" The panic in his tone alarmed me even more, made my already crazy pulse speed up.

I managed to pull away, to crawl to the cave's entrance, shivering in pure horror. The *Reflectionists'* arms reached out to me cravingly, their eyes pleaded me to move towards them. They splashed water everywhere, fighting to get a hold of me. Their hypnotizing song stopped abruptly and instead of that, there were just moans and whimpers of disappointment, maybe even pain.

It was an unpleasant, screeching sound.

I could see it, their urge to reach *me*, their urge to reach my *soul*.

Peter placed his body in front of mine protectively – shielding me. "Just don't look at them. Don't talk to them and they'll leave, they *always* do..." He breathed through clenched teeth. I stared at them over Peter's shoulder, I was shaking.

Always?

"What do they want?" I breathed, coughing water out of my lungs.

There was another startling pause and I felt his joints tighten. "*Me*," he finally murmured. My blood was running icy, freezing me on spot. Why would they ever want him? I did not understand. "They want my *soul*..." he continued bitterly, shame was now replaced by hatred.

"*Reflectionists* were *Soul Readers*. Now they're just a part of the *Spirits* and the *Demons*. *Sly, satanic* creatures..." he said in a whisper sensing my petrifying anxiety, the same revulsion came out of him. "*Whenever I come here, they just come out of the Mirror. I'll never be free again, they're my punishment, April...*" he said and the same mortification condensed.

"Why? What have you done?" I questioned still panicked. Why should he be punished? It made no sense...

The *Reflectionists* were screaming, they screamed so sharply it was like I was being stabbed in the ears. They yearned for *Him*; they wanted him so badly... I could feel the heaviness of the atmosphere, the incredible discomfort my question caused him.

"*Murder*," he replied in just a humiliated breath.

"The Life Commission punished me in this way..." he said and the pain dripped out of him. "When I die, I'll turn into one of them... a *Demon*..." he whispered sourly, disgusted at himself.

I froze in shock; I felt the blood solidify in my vessels.

Should I be afraid now? Should I feel the identical repugnance he felt? The same disgust? I didn't know how to react, what I was supposed to do now. I was completely blank – my expression – vacant.

I had to remember to breathe.

"Then why did *They* attack me?" I breathed still unsure of how I was supposed to react, I couldn't comprehend – I was too overwhelmed to. "Because *They* cannot *touch* me if you are with me. They have no real power over me if I'm with you..." he said in a nervous breath.

I felt like a knife had been pushed into my flesh instantly. Pain and concern hit me like an enormous tsunami, two feelings I shouldn't feel for a possible killer...

"*What do They do to you?*" I demanded, as protective as a lioness with her cub. I impulsively wanted to guard him. He swallowed and spoke sourly and painfully.

"They *Mark* me..."

What?

The *Reflectionists*, at some point, gave up. They stopped screaming and whimpering and dived back down, to the unfathomable depths of the *Mirror*. Even though, they'd practically left, I knew they were underneath us, lurking, waiting for the right time to attack, to *Mark Him*. I'd noticed that their silver eyes shone differently – darkly and cannily.

I was so scared that, even though I was thirsty I did not move towards the water in front of me. The cave felt haunted, it freaked me out...

My confusion was like a balloon being blown and I wondered when the balloon would actually pop, when *I* would explode. I was panting a long time after the Reflectionists had backed away, the shock was hard to shake off, but when I finally did relax I could not move an inch from my spot – terrified.

Peter did not move either; he placed his body in front of mine in my defense, alert. Only then did I notice his shirt was torn on one side. There was a wound swelling with dark red blood at the top of his arm, just a bit below his shoulder. He noticed I was staring at him with great concern. "It's nothing... I just hit a rock when I was pulling you out..." he reassured me unconvincingly. The wound now seemed deeper, like a patch of his skin had been scraped away. It pained me just looking at it.

"Let me have a look..." I whispered, standing on my knees, moving closer towards him. He remained still and allowed me to fumble around the wound, to examine it. His jaw was tight and his body unutterably tense, it pained him a great deal. When I pressed my finger on his injury just a little harder, he flinched away in discomfort. "I think I should clean it... it could get infected..." I murmured moving my hand away from his shoulder.

"I, I could... um... use your shirt," I suggested cowardly, moving my fingers to the buttons of his top. He pulled away sharply as if I was about to hurt him and shoved my hand away from his chest. His eyes shone with something like fear, he puffed so incredibly startled.

"What's wrong? Does it hurt that much?" I asked worriedly, turning my gaze from his wide eyes back to his wound and vice versa.

"No. I'm, gonna be... *fine*," he spat out in an anxious, cautious breath.

I noticed his long fingers had curled around the fabric of his shirt self-protectively. "Let me take care of it... You won't feel a thing, I promise..." I insisted, too blind with concern to sense the genuine fear reflected in his enlarged pupils. I extended my arm towards him again and he pulled away, banging on the cave's wall.

"I can't let you do that..." he muttered through clenched teeth. "I cannot let you see *me*, not my *real* self..." he said and his deep voice broke weakly.

"What do you mean?" I asked moving closer, forcing him to press his body harder against the rigid rock. He could've pushed me away if he wanted to, he was strong enough to crush me like a powerless insect if he wished to, but he didn't.

"*You won't like the sight...*" he breathed bitterly, moving his hand off his shirt. He surrendered. Perhaps he was as exhausted as I was, perhaps he was tired of hiding whatever he was hiding.

I pulled him away from the wall, gently. I placed my fingers on his chest and started unbuttoning his shirt; under my hand his heart thudded hardly. Once his top had split into two, I could see *It*. What he was talking about.

I didn't know what they were, tattoos maybe. Just black lines spiraling and twisting over his muscular chest; I tried hard not to look surprised. I slowly slid his arms out of the sleeves and he did not fight back at all, just knelt there quietly. I then realized that the lines were all over the skin of his torso, covered his wide chest and strong back.

I tried to look at these mysterious marks the least I could and cautiously crawled to the little pond to soak the fabric I now had in hand. Afraid the Reflectionists would spring out; I wetted the shirt as fast as I could and started wiping his wound gingerly. I noticed that the black *scars* completely covered his left chest – his heart. He was quiet; he did not even flinch when I pressed his injury, too ashamed of himself...

"*Marks of Hell*, that's what they are..." he suddenly whispered mortified. "I'm *stigmatized*, just a *killer*," he spat out disgusted at himself. "I shouldn't complain, should I? I *do* deserve this." It seemed he was talking to himself rather than to me. Thinking out loud he added, "It'll never leave me, April; my sins will *infect* my soul forever..."

I did not know what to tell him, how to help him lift his burdened chest. I instead wiped his wound a little more, thinking of my reply, trying to form answers in my head.

For some reason, I could not feel fear, I could not make myself feel fear and that was the only thing frightening me. I felt this way maybe because I could see the sincere regret and guilt he felt – these two feelings torturing him.

At some point, I was done cleaning his wound. His eyes were pinned on me, making me look up to meet his worried gaze. "What do you *see*, April?" he questioned, and I, instead of answering, crawled into his arms, cold to the bone because of my soaked clothes. For a moment, I felt his body tighten with surprise. I pressed my face on his bare chest, over his heart, and replied to his question in a worn whisper.

"What I see, is *genuine* and *honest* – *true*."

He hesitated, processing my declaration; and then, slid an arm around me, holding tight on me. I felt like I'd achieved what I really wanted – to comfort him. It gave me so much satisfaction, to see the pain of his guilt ease, to listen to his heart slow down, to feel his body relax. I curled my wings around us, to protect us both from the deadly cold of the night.

I fell asleep and so did he. I did not feel fear, the exact opposite – I actually felt safer than ever. Right there, in the arms of a *murderer*...

16. Fundamental

I woke up first, but was too afraid to move away from him, too scared of the *Reflectionists*. So, instead I stayed next to him. He snored lightly and his expression was that of peace. I *listened* to his heart beating steadily and calmly, something I liked. He looked vulnerable, powerless, and almost fragile when he slept. He looked like an innocent little child, even though I knew that his soul held darker secrets...

I did not fear him, not a single bit, I was just *curious*. Who had he killed? Why had he killed him? What was his motivation? How had he killed him? Was it even a man? Was it a woman? I still could not picture him in that way, but the *Marks* spiraling around his muscular torso reminded me of the truth. The skin over his heart was covered in lines, in these enigmatic deep scars.

The Life Commission punished me in this way... he had said. This... Life Commission seemed like something threatening now, like something menacing and torturous. We had planned to go to this Commission; they needed to see me for some reason. I was the *Chosen*, although at that time I didn't know what that meant exactly, I did not know I was fundamental.

There was another thing I could not understand, another thing I could not explain. This innate desire I felt to protect him. It was ridiculous, I barely knew this guy and yet, I wanted to guard him as if he was my child. It made no sense, like most things in *this* world...

"We're late!" he breathed, sitting up. He seemed startled.

"What's wrong?" I questioned. I still held his bloody shirt in my hand. He grabbed it and moved towards the water to wash it. He put it on wet.

"The Commissioners need to see you; we've already *wasted* a day..." he murmured, moving towards the entrance of the little cavern. "Come," he said and I followed obediently.

We both stepped out of the hole and were instantly showered with powerful daylight. "We'll have to fly, it's quite a distance..." he told me and my expression turned into one of unwillingness at once. "Calm down, you're designed to fly, *accept your nature*..." he told me, smiling encouragingly, offering me his hand which I eagerly grabbed.

Before I could hesitate we were flying.

It wasn't as bad as I thought it would be. But, I wasn't perfect and I lost my balance now and then, but he did not let me fall. I did not hate the flight but I did not love it either, it was tolerable.

We didn't feel like talking and we were very quiet. Maybe what had happened yesterday with the *Reflectionists* and his soul were still making him feel uncomfortable – mortified. I should be scared but I wasn't. Maybe I was stupid and reckless but, did it really matter? What were the chances of me returning back to *reality*? The reality of the human world? And even if I found a way to escape would it be the same as before? *Normal*?

I was a fool to think there was a chance of fleeing, but I couldn't help myself from thinking that way. From thinking of ways to run away, to return back home.

It was mysterious though, one part of me wanted to leave and another part of me ordered me to stay. Perhaps, it was the urgency of the situation, how much I was needed and right at that moment I started acknowledging it. I was too important to *them*, and if I turned my back on *them* everything would be destroyed. I didn't know in what way and I didn't know why I believed this scenario of *Universal Balance*, but I did. And apparently if their *Side* went down the *Human Side* went down as well which meant only one thing.

The death of my parents.

I felt like it was my responsibility, my duty to do whatever in my power to protect anyone I could – it was almost instinctive and it made no sense. It was so confusing. It was like a weight on my chest and *it grew greater and greater day by day...*

A *burden...*

It was dark and we had stopped to feast. The distance to the Life Commission was long. Longer than what I'd expected. We would move on, we had to move on and *He* constantly murmured that we'd *wasted* another day. A thin layer of fog had obscured the world and an icy breeze blew against our bodies – I'd curled my wings around me responsively.

From that point on, I was scared. Scared because of my lack of knowledge, scared because I relied on someone I did not know, scared because everything seemed abnormal. I was terrified of this reality, of the *souls*, the *Demons*, the *Sides*, but there was also another thing I hadn't forgotten and it haunted me.

The glow.

The fire ball that had flown out of my hand when I'd got agitated the other day. And I felt it again. The suffocating heat coming from deep inside my chest, spreading along my veins, I burned, and I burned so much it hurt. I breathed harder, violently; in an instant I felt my knees buckle and I fell.

I screamed.

I was paralyzed, in just a breathless moment I was unable to move myself and I shrieked sharply – painfully. The heat now melted me, burned my tissues and sent currents of excruciating pain everywhere. Hot needles punctured every single bit of me, stinging me, electrocuting my flesh and I shouted even more. Wild spasms controlled my functionless body and suddenly the only sensation was that of pain. Pain I had never experienced before.

He was towering me in just a breath and he seemed as shocked as I was.

Another shout burst out of me; the panic was so obvious in the green of his eyes – he did not know how to react, how to stop the violent shudder and spearing pain I felt.

With shaking hands he grabbed my face and lowered his, just inches away from mine. In just a moment his lips had attacked mine and he kissed me ravenously, hungrily but with noticeable agitation. I wanted to pull away, to shake him off – my eyes had fluttered open in disgust. Suddenly, that heat melting me traveled all the way down to my fingertips and left my body in a powerful, blinding glow slicing the distance.

The shaking stopped and he dropped my head spontaneously. We were both breathing in gasps, out of breath – speechless.

"What. Was. That?" I whispered between my breathing. His lime eyes stared at me vacantly for a moment, he was still standing on top of me.

"A *Powerball… Magic.*" He spat out, panting; and my expression was as vacant as his…

We were running in the darkness of the night, our speed surpassed that of sound. Peter was in panic and dragged me along with him. He didn't seem of thinking to fly, running demanded less processing and less effort and he appeared to be too overwhelmed to risk flying. His heart along with mine created a chaotic beat.

"What's wrong? Why are we running?" I breathed as we darted through the pine trees. At this point the forest seemed to transform from semi-tropical to deciduous.

"I don't know! *I don't know what to do with you!*" he squeaked, distressed, pulling me with him. "*You're too strong! I don't know how to handle you!*" he murmured in panic, sheer fear.

"The Commission! I need to take you to the Commission!" he whispered in shock and unspeakable stress. The fog was thick and heavy, the smell of the moist soil was dominant, the moonlight beamed through the dense canopy. "You've got just twelve days, just twelve days until *The End…*" he breathed, I could smell the perspiration soaking his body, his hand was cold in my mine.

Panic. Panic. Panic.

His panic was contagious and I was soon infected. Adrenaline dissolved into my blood and flowed into my arteries – alerting me. Something was wrong and in spite of the fact I didn't know what exactly, I felt it. Something was wrong with *me* – certainly. And there was also something terribly wrong with that glow that had flown out of my fingers.

Everything was *wrong*.

Surprisingly, I now anticipated to go to the Life Commission, I felt there was a chance of reassurance and safety once I was with the Life Commissioners, but when I went through the facts a second time, I realized how far away from home I was, how far away from safety I was and I knew, in that instant, that I could not be reassured, and it terrified me.

From the night when I'd heard *The Voices* I felt constantly exposed, in danger, like I could not hide. And I was constantly on the run, escaping from all sorts of things: Demons, Humans, Reflectionists. It seemed like everyone wanted to eliminate me, it felt like everyone felt threatened by me and all this time I didn't know why.

And now I knew.

He had said *Magic, Powerballs...* Peter seemed like he was scared of me, of the strengths I didn't know I possessed; powers I'd just began to explore. I felt unwanted, I was afraid of what I was capable of and somehow in all that panic and bewilderment, Peter's kiss lingered on my lips and the more I thought of it, of the way his mouth had attacked mine the more my heart pounded.

And this was a different kind of pound. A pound I liked...

A pound I perhaps *loved*...

PART 2
"Confronting the ugly truth"

17. What?

Confusion.
A feeling I was now familiar with. We ran and ran into the darkness of the night. I didn't know what had caused Peter's panic and I didn't want to know – I was tired. Sick and tired of knowing.
And I was tired of running; I didn't want to run anymore. I didn't want to be afraid but in all that panic, feeling fear was inevitable. I feared myself; something was wrong with me.
Everything about me was *wrong*.
"Stop." I breathed, squeezing his sweaty hand. He definitely had heard me but chose to ignore me. "Stop!" I said; louder this time. He turned his head. His beautiful eyes reflected horror; his pupils were enlarged exactly like a hunted animal's. "Stop," I whispered as calmly as I could, pulling him towards me.
He surrendered. He came closer.
His heart beat crazily, in an unsteady way and he breathed in gasps.
"Walk with me..." I told him; equally exhausted, dragging him by the hand.
"But – the – Commission?" he questioned, looking at me through wide eyes, drops of sweat slid down his forehead colliding with his eyebrows.
"We'll get there..." I said; knowing that if I gave him a negative answer, he'd be twice as panicked. My reply seemed to calm him a bit, but not enough. The adrenaline that had once made our muscles incredibly strong was now diffusing leaving us in insufferable pain. A cramp made me whimper, my entire body burned.
He picked me up; in just one move. His hands shook, they betrayed his physical exertion. He tried so hard to move me around.

"Let me down," I murmured. "You can't do this." I breathed; trying to pull my aching body away from this. He did not let me down. He pressed me harder against his soaked chest.

"Just stay still," he ordered weakly. I did not argue with him; I couldn't resist his offer of carrying my wrecked body.

Stillness; absolute, intimidating silence.

Gradually, my lids felt heavy and my eyes closed without me wanting them to. It took all the energy I had left to keep my eye muscles stretched, to prevent myself from falling asleep. I counted Peter's heartbeats; I pressed my ear on his chest and listened. I synchronized my breathing with his pulse.

Beat. Inhale. Beat. Exhale.

He was silent; anguish still flowed in his system, he handled me particularly gingerly, as though he was holding a newborn and I stayed still, breathing in coordination with his heart. I quivered; my entire body trembled – my muscles were spasming violently and I couldn't stop it.

Pain.

I was scared, very scared. And who wouldn't be scared? Despite that though, I did not cry. I guess the moment was so charged I couldn't even make myself cry. I closed my eyes but knew I wasn't allowed to fall asleep no matter how worn out I felt – I had to stay awake.

But everything blurred eventually and I was too weak to stick to my promise...

Light. Blinding light.

Am I dead? I hear the words coming out of my grandfather's mouth. "APRIL RUN!" Panic; the haunting feeling I can never run away from. My grandfather? But he's in a coma...

I sprint towards the voice, his eyes; their pale, grayish green is staring at me. A smile pulls the corners of my lips, I open my arms in a welcoming embrace but then, I hesitate. Suddenly, the unique color of his eyes darkens, his face loses its warmth and his features sharpen – he is reshaped as if he is made out of dough.

He transforms into an unrecognizable, threatening creature. His eyes are black, just a cold black, shining predatorily – a Demon.
I scream.

"Do you think she is alright?" an elderly woman asks –, I can tell from the tone of her voice.

"I think she is… Humans sleep like this, don't they?" a man asks reluctantly, unsure of his speculation.

"She seems fine to me…" another female voice declares. This woman is a younger one though.

"We need a bed for her…" Peter says tightly, sliding his arm around my waist.

"You won't touch her again! What don't you understand?" someone shouts at him sternly, aggressively almost. He immediately pulls his arm away letting my back hit the tile floor. A grouped gasp comes out of everyone. How many are they? Six? Seven?

"You idiot! You could have damaged her wings!" the elderly woman whispers agitated.

I can feel their warm breath over me; I can hear their accelerating heartbeats. It's not fear nor is it anxiety; this is more like excitement…

I move, I open my eyes and stare at them.

I could've sworn their hearts stopped beating for a moment; their eyes wouldn't let go of me, they eyed me with amazing curiosity. No one talks and no one breathes; the room is silent.

I sit up and everyone pulls back; everyone but Peter.

He outstretches his hand and I try to grab it but I don't manage it; someone has shoved his hand out of the way in a noisy slap before I can curl my fingers around his warm palm. I look up at a man dressed in black, he is blond and his pale blue eyes meet my questioning gaze, he still has Peter's wrist clasped in his hand. I move my eyes from his to Peter's wrist – this makes him feel uneasy.

He releases Pete's hand; avoiding my forceful, accusing look.

I stand up on my own; even though every single move is painful, I don't want anyone's help, not even Peter's. I flick my wings and flap them open producing a sharp sound; this makes everyone move away – it gives me space.

I try to swallow, but my mouth is completely dry – I'm thirsty. I examine my surroundings, I'm in a building, in a big, high ceilinged room and I smell pollen, it tempts me but I do not move towards the appealing scent. I notice that the walls are exclusively made out of gold; the floor is made out of glimmering marble, black and white, I feel like a pawn in a chess game.

Maybe I am part of a game after all...

I twist my head to view the five strangers staring at me wide eyed, in total inquisitiveness.

Should I say something, or should I not? I silently question myself, moving my eyes from person to person, examining and analyzing even the slightest detail. Finally, my eyes lock on to Peter, the only one I could recognize, I look at him puzzled, completely disoriented.

Were these five creatures what I thought they were?

"No one can harm you here, April, relax..." Peter told me, making a single step towards me. He did not manage to reach me; a hand pushed him back. The same fair-haired man was in the way, I stepped forward trying to disguise my reluctance. The man lowered his gaze to the floor but did not pull his hand off of Peter's chest.

The man's heart thudded hard. "Could you please let him go?" I asked tranquilly, eyeing the stunned man; he looked up at the sound of my voice.

"Is that what you *desire*?" he questioned, narrowing his eyes, so very pleased for some reason. I stared at him for a moment. What did he mean?

"Yes," I said vacantly, examining his expressive, expectant blue eyes.

He obeyed. He moved out of the way. I turned my gaze to stare at an old woman, her hair was short and gray, and her eyes studied me with amazing concentration. Next to her stood a much younger woman, her skin was a beautiful cinnamon color and her eyes were a golden yellow; she looked like a feline. Several steps behind the beautiful catlike woman stood another one. Her hair – a fiery red and her eyes – a mysterious gray.

I feel someone's breath on my shoulder; I twist my whole body around in one, abrupt, fast movement. The glimmering dark eyes of a man immobilize me. Everything about him seems so hostile and looming – I move away disorientated – I want to leave.

Peter's body is in my way.

"How extraordinary… So *powerful*…" the ominous man exclaimed in obvious astonishment.

"*Just feel her aura, it's Her*…" the blue eyed man said lost in thought.

Every single pair of eyes gazed at *Me*.

"We should take her to the arena; we have no time to waste…" the old woman whispered.

"What arena?" I enquired, suddenly alarmed – my heart raced. There was a moment of silence; they looked at me again, unable to believe I could actually speak, unable to believe I actually *existed*.

"You'll fight off a beast…" the red-haired woman mumbled out grudgingly.

I panicked.

"But what if I die?" I asked. I knew they weren't joking about it; nothing in this world was meant to be a joke.

They laughed their heads off. They started pacing away, into the corners of the room that could not be reached by sunlight. Their feet tapped on the solid marble floor.

Tap. Tap. Tap.

"Honey, you can't die…" a voice began.

"*You're immortal*…" a voice finished.

I lost my breath.

What?

18. Lifeless

"*Immortal*? I'm immortal?" I questioned in a forbidden whisper; Peter was dragging me out of the huge, high-ceilinged room and into a dark hallway lit only by candles scattered on the walls.

"Yes," he replied lowly.

I remained quiet for a moment, digesting the fact. "So, I can't die..." I mumbled, more to myself, having difficulty believing it.

"Yes," he said again, confirming it.

"Why?" I asked. It seemed unfair to everybody else, why did I have the right to live *forever*? *Forever*... it was such a long word...

"Your soul is... Um, your soul is too powerful to die..." he said, unsure of the way he presented it.

I did not understand.

"Are you immortal too?" I asked, looking at him. We were pacing down an endless staircase.

He chuckled coldly, sarcastically perhaps. "No, and I don't deserve that..." he muttered stiffly, avoiding my expectant and curious gaze.

"Why do I deserve it?" I enquired.

"Because you're not a killer, April, because whatever you do you never do it to hurt anybody. You're soul is *perfect*..." he said, still thoughtful.

"But you're not trying to hurt anybody either..." I retorted.

"Now, now that I am paying for it..." he murmured, meeting my eyes.

I hadn't realized the stairs were over; we were walking on solid ground, the floor was dressed in luxurious red carpeting.

He stopped moving and pulled me with him inside a room – the first room he came across.

"Aren't we supposed to be going to some sort of arena?" I wondered. I looked around; the room was absolutely empty, there was only a tiny little square window allowing some light to enter.

He did not reply; he acted as if I hadn't asked at all. "*Powerballs...* do you know how to form them?" he demanded, suddenly nervous.

I thought about my answer for a second. "You mean the *glows*?" I murmured.

"Yes. Do you know how to control them, to make them on demand?" he pressured, anxiety was discernible in his voice.

"I don't know... I don't make them... I don't –"

"You have to use magic in there, in the arena, or you're going to lose..."

"What happens if I lose?"

"You mustn't lose."

"But what if I do?"

Silence.

"Listen, you have to kill that... *thing*; do you understand? No matter what," he said; there were traces of panic in his words.

"What *thing*?" I asked, distressed.

"What *Mort* will create for you, you've got to kill it," he said and his heart raced again, creating a chaotic symphony along with mine.

"The heart, that's what you must go for... '*The spot of the soul*'," he said, placing his hand on my chest gently, feeling my heartbeat.

"I – I can't kill..." I argued, terrified, my voice barely passed a breath.

"You must," he insisted.

"But I can't..." I repeated.

"You will."

I could not even breathe. Who were these "people" and why did they make me kill, commit murder? I wanted to run, to escape but there was nowhere to go, I felt trapped.

"Stand in front of that wall, under the window..." Peter instructed; it was so dark in that room, our eyes glowed as if it was night.

I listened to him and moved under the window obediently, having my hands fixed into shaking fists to my sides. My fists were so tight my fingernails cut through the skin of my sweaty palms. I stood there for a moment, absorbing reality.

"The heart," he whispered and pushed me on the wall forcefully. But instead of hitting the wall as I'd anticipated, I passed through.

I fell on to my face and managed to prevent any damage by landing on my elbows with a loud thud. The astonishment was obvious on my features. Did I just pass through a wall? Adrenaline was already flowing in my circulatory system – I was alert. There was one word echoing in my mind – danger. Fear seeped into me and infected every part of my brain, making me instinctively want to flee.

My breathing turned heavy – burdened.

Where am I?

A hiss makes me turn my head in search of its owner. Fear transforms into horror as I uncurl my wings slowly, trying not to agitate *It*. I do not dare to look at *It* and I know it's very close. I make myself roll up to my knees, knowing that I'm in an extremely vulnerable position. I hear the flap of wings, big, powerful wings; the sound makes goosebumps travel up my spine, immobilizing me.

Run, I tell myself. *Leave*, I think. But again, I'm cornered, trapped. Horror swells up into terror and it stings me. My hands are trembling, I'm lost, completely disorientated and most importantly I'm by myself, all alone.

I feel *It*; it's on top of me, I freeze.

A single drop of thick, warm, dark, blood lands on my hand and slides down my index finger – my heart beats frantically. I stand up reluctantly; my enlarged pupils cannot move away from that single drop of stinking blood, I turn around slowly, trying to find the courage to confront *It*. I have to. I *must*. I try to swallow but my mouth is painfully dry.

It moves – rapidly, like lightning. It's fast. Faster than *me*.

I can smell *It*. I hear *It*. I can taste *It*, but I cannot see *It*. I clench my teeth and squeeze my hands into fists once again.

I turn around.

Nothing.

Surprisingly, there is nothing to see. I hold my breath as I examine the arena. It is massive, colossal, a perfect circle. I look up, there is no ceiling and a flame of hope for a possible escape warms my soul immediately. I roll up to my knees and flap my wings. *Where is It now? I can't sense It.* That little flame of hope grew into a raging fire as I stared at the open sky. I pushed myself up, flew as fast as I could but then knocked onto the invisible, electrical field I couldn't pass through. I hit the ground hard, and the same coldness and desperation was restored inside of me.

I heard a hiss again, I could listen to *Its* heartbeat, this time *It* was much closer. *It* was breathing over my shoulder, *Its* breath smelled like rotten flesh and blood. I was on my knees, shaking, analyzing possibilities, speculating, calculating. My brain now worked very differently compared to a human's, much more efficiently, inconceivably fast. My pupils widened, adrenaline reached every part of my system alerting me, sharpening my senses to an unimaginable point, I didn't even think could be possible.

If I couldn't run, there was only one alternative – to confront *It*.

Even though so much had changed I still thought like a human, I didn't feel powerful, nor did I feel immortal; I didn't believe it at the time – I genuinely thought I was going to die. I felt I were the prey, the hunted.

I could feel *Its* eyes fixed on me, analyzing me, probably detecting my weaknesses. I was breathing unevenly, Peter had said I should use *Powerballs*, but I didn't know how to create them, I felt vulnerable, so frail compared to *It*. I had to do something or *It* would attack me first.

I tried to stand up and *It* caught me by the leg, sinking *Its* teeth into my flesh.

I could not feel the pain; I was so overwhelmed by adrenaline I did not feel a thing. *It* was huge, enormous and I started fighting with *It*, twisting my leg away from *It*, trying to fly in the opposite direction. *Its* jaws wouldn't open, but I pulled away anyway and a chunk of my leg was ripped off. I screamed, not because it hurt but because I was terrified. Fresh blood started streaming out of the wound forming a puddle around me.

I couldn't stand up; my entire calf muscle had been torn off; I lay on the ground helpless staring at *It* in disgust. Twelve snake heads were attached to a birdlike body. The whole creature was bigger than a bus. I had to think fast. I couldn't walk but I could still fly, only then did I remember that I had wings. But I couldn't use them, I was laying on them – I had to turn over. Although I was fast, faster than sound, *Its* speed surpassed mine. I had to think deviously if there was a chance of me winning.

I wasn't allowed to lose, even though I didn't know why exactly.

I needed something more than deviousness though, I needed... I needed... *Magic*. But how could I create it, how could I control and use it? I was at a dead end. In the meanwhile, the snakes hissed at me and started snapping their jaws at me trying to bite my wings; their fangs dripped deep yellow venom. A drop of acidic venom landed on my palm and burnt me, opening a wound.

The beast moved forward and I dragged myself backward. The snake heads were only inches away from my face and continued to hiss at me threateningly.

A noise made the monster turn around giving me that nanosecond I so desperately needed to fly. I darted up, trying to comprehend, to think, to come up with something.

Heat. Anxiety makes me feel like I'm on fire, as if I'm burning. I feel it in my chest.

I zoom in at every detail of the creature's body trying to find a weakness, but it seems to be flawless, so perfect in every aspect. *Its* perfection terrifies me to the bone. I start feeling dizzy and I'm not sure if it's because of blood loss or the toxic venom that has been injected into my system. I know I don't have much time – I might faint.

'*The heart.*' Peter's words echo in my terrified mind. '*The spot of the soul.*' I try to listen in search of the heart, but I can't; *It* has grabbed me with *Its* sharp claws in less than a breath, and *It* is deliberately banging my body on the ground, smashing me over and over again with unbelievable force and hatred. I cannot help myself, I scream and shriek as my skull cracks, and my bones snap. For the first time pain stings me, and it stings me viciously.

Magic, you need to use, magic! I think, fearing my end. *Come on! Create some!* I'm yelling in my head. *Magic, Magic, Magic...*

And then, I felt it. Heat traveling from my chest to my fingers. Everything happened in a matter of seconds. I was underneath the creature's body; I was facing *Its* abdomen, *Its* claws wouldn't let me move and *It* was pressing me down, harder against the ground. *Its* heart was directly above me. My eyes locked on my target. Another wave of pure adrenaline hit me, washing the pain away once again and I pulled my arms free, I outstretched my hand and the Powerball flew through the creature's chest, burning it.

The beast shrieked in pain, and it lost balance, giving me the opportunity to free the rest of my wrecked body. I pushed my arm in the hole I'd opened in search of the organ I so desperately wanted to pull out. The snakes tried to reach me and bite me off. How could I deal with that? I just thought of them being locked in a cage, of them being unable to reach me.

And just by thinking about it, Magic happened...

Somehow, I'd created a little "bubble" around me, an electrical field they couldn't pass through. Shocked and falling apart I pushed my entire arm deeper into the wound. Black blood and mucus flowed out of the creature and *It* cried in pain, but I couldn't feel empathy for *It*, I was a monster myself, my instinct of survival was stronger than my ability to feel and think. I just wanted one thing.

To kill.

I was covered in feathers, in slimy blood and overwhelmed by adrenaline; I was determined to not let go of *It*. The hole was too small for me to reach deeper so I placed my hands on either side of the perfectly circular cut and tore the skin, widened the opening with a physical strength I'd forgotten I possessed. The creature was desperate but I still couldn't find myself lost in that chaotic moment. A bitter emotion flooded my soul – loathing. I hated *It* with every part of me.

I pushed my arm inside the creature once again. I felt tissues, flesh and blood, even though the fact was hard to believe, this thing was alive – it breathed. *It had a soul.* I couldn't find the heart, it was so close but I couldn't take hold of it. Then, I decided to push myself inside the opening. I took a breath, closed my eyes and crawled into the wound up to my waist. I fumbled, searching for the particular organ. As panicked and overpowered by my wild instincts, I tried to stay as focused as I could.

I got my hands on something, but it wasn't beating – I assumed it was a lung and let it go. Time and adrenaline were running out and pain started attacking me again. I reached even deeper and I was sure I was just an inch away from the heart; the beating echoed around me, it was pounding hard.

I grabbed it, held it in my trembling hands.

It beat inside my palm, so real, so... *alive.* I thought about what I was about to do for a second. I was about to kill a soul and I had no other choice.

With the pain stinging every part of my body I tightened my fingers around the creature's heart and pulled it out. The beast gave a cry and fell on the ground dead.

Lifeless.

19. Ethics and Conscience

I was in shock, shaking, as the heart still beat in my hand. I had just taken a soul, killed it. Reality hit me hard as my ability to think and feel returned to me. A salty tear slid down my cheek. As a person, I always thought of life as something sacred, I wouldn't even kill a fly, because of my theory that everything had a reason of existence. And now, I'd gone against that deep principle of mine and I wasn't at all proud.

I stood there quivering. A thick layer of black blood covered me. I stopped producing adrenaline and pain attacked me savagely. I fell down screaming and bleeding. Breathing became harder and I was losing consciousness.

I heard Peter's voice, felt his arms wrap around me. I whimpered in pain even though he touched me so gently.

"Shhh, it's okay…" he whispered as he picked me up.

I felt something; a feeling I hadn't felt in a while now – safety. I allowed my eyes to close, trusting him fully.

The fact I had magic inside me hadn't registered until that moment, the moment I started fixing myself. I remember water, someone washing me, cleaning my body from the mucus, the blood and the feathers. I then remember the soft touch of clean fabric. I feel hands, lots of hands handling me gingerly and placing me on a hard mattress. Though, there is one thing I cannot recall.

Pain.

I wasn't actually unconscious; I was in a lethargic state, and in that state I started recreating myself. I felt magic flowing in my system, pulling my snapped bones together until they fell in place and it was that magic that acted as a painkiller. The bleeding stopped and new tissue grew from where my calf muscle had been ripped off. Magic even dealt with the burning venom.

I was putting myself back together; I had the ability to repair myself.

Though magic could fix my body perfectly yet it couldn't deal with my panicked soul. I saw dreams, visions of me killing people, ripping their hearts out and that's when I began to fear my own strengths. My powers. That's when I realized I was capable of killing.

It caused me revulsion.

Maybe I was defending myself and maybe killing an animal wasn't the same as killing a human, but I felt guilt. A lot of guilt, I felt like I was the true monster. And the responsibility of that creature's death burdened me. I pitied it, it was forced in that arena with me and it was sentenced to death because I was obliged to execute it, though the reason still remained a question.

Time ticked by incredibly slowly. And I tortured myself with remorse, thinking about what I'd done over and over again. I wanted to wake up but I couldn't, my brain was alert, it was awake but I had no control over my body. I panicked but I could do nothing about it, I couldn't open my eyes nor could I scream. I was trapped in my own body.

Maybe magic was responsible for that too.

I was fighting to gain control, but I couldn't and at some point I just gave up knowing that what I was trying to do was futile. I couldn't run away from the responsibility so I let it torture me, *punish me*.

I screamed; I couldn't take it anymore. I woke up soaked in sweat. He was sitting next to me, looking at me. I stood up and held my head in both hands, shivering. Tears streamed out of my eyes and I gritted my teeth. "I didn't want that!" I mumbled out, "You know I didn't!" I said in a husky voice.

He stood up, moved towards me and attempted to touch me. I pulled away, moved to the center of the room rocking my body back and forth, overwhelmed by panic.

"April, you need to calm down..." he said slowly and quietly, staring right through my wide eyes.

"How can I calm down? I just killed it, ripped it apart!" I squeaked. "You did well; you were supposed to kill it," he whispered stepping closer.

"How's that right, Peter? Since when is killing the right thing to do?" I retorted, allowing my regret to take control.

"*Our* story involves a lot of loss and death and you are a part of it now," he told me.

"What if I refuse to take part in your story?" I argued gazing at him accusingly.

"We all die."

It was enough to shut my mouth.

There was a moment of silence, though, his words still echoed in the room.

Then, he came close, *really* close, his face just inches away from mine. "That's how I felt when I killed for the first time. But after a while, I didn't feel much, I got used to it. There was no guilt, I had no conscience. I was a real monster..." He breathed ashamed, looking at me right in the eyes. For some reason my heart galloped, as if I was anticipating something.

"What changed you? When did you start having a conscience?" I enquired in a whisper. My throat was tight.

"I don't know. When I lost everything perhaps... But my conscience is not a single bit clean..." he muttered, meeting my gaze, trying to crook a smile unsuccessfully. "You shouldn't think about it, April. You didn't do wrong..." he murmured and tried to step away but my next words stopped him.

"I'm scared," I said quickly, panicky.

"I can see that," he replied.

"I was expecting something a bit more comforting..." I murmured and for some reason a tiny smile pulled my lips.

"I can't comfort you, April. I just say truths, not what you want to hear. I'm... too straightforward," he confessed and it was that honesty and harshness that made him even more appealing.

He turned around and I grabbed him by his lower arm. "But how can I deal with *this*?" I begged through watery eyes, truly desperate.

He stared at me for a moment, weighed my desperation. "Just don't think too much, thinking is painful…" he finally declared.

It wasn't an answer good enough.

I let go of him, released him, but he wouldn't move away – he didn't want to. Instead, he slid his arm around my waist and pulled me closer, pressed me against his muscular body, he then placed his hand on the side of my face and leaned down to kiss me. My heart was about to jolt out of my chest in expectancy of what I knew was going to follow. A kiss, gentle and soft, so intoxicating.

Truly comforting, *sensational*.

I clung on to him, drunk. Every thought drained out of my mind, I could think of nothing else and that was soothing.

Very soothing.

"Where are we going?" I asked; the taste of his lips still lingered in my mouth. "The Life Commission," he replied.

My throat was burning and my stomach was completely empty. "How long have I been out?" I asked thirstily.

"About two days. The sun will rise in an hour from now…" he told me and pulled me with him in a passage; a narrow, dark hallway.

I smelled dust and burnt vanilla candle, the red carpet underneath us absorbed the sound of our feet. It was warm and even though I'd been out for quite a while I felt sleepy – still tired. My head felt heavy.

I outstretched my arm and allowed my fingers to stroke the golden wall as we passed by; I felt every detail of the complex carving on it, I examined it curiously with my glowing eyes. He didn't pay much attention to what I was doing; he just made sure I arrived in front of the Commission room just on time. Before sunrise.

He stood in front of the massive doors for a moment. "I'm not going in, I can't," he whispered, afraid someone would hear him.

"Why not?" I asked.

"The Life Commissioners have a very interesting ability. . ." he went on, avoiding my gaze.

"Which is?"

"They can *read your Aura*," he said.

My eyebrows pulled together making my confusion apparent.

"I know; it's hard to understand. But it's like they can... know what you've done," he said quickly, in a hushed voice.

"And why are you hiding?" It was more than obvious.

He swallowed with unease, as though he was cornered. "I... I kissed you," he breathed, as if he'd just committed a crime.

"So?" I still hadn't made the connection.

"It's not right. I'm not supposed to," he said, matter-of-factly.

"You know, I've noticed some things about you. You hide a lot," I stated.

"Correct," he agreed.

"Don't you get tired of that?" I questioned, looking at him carefully.

"Sometimes..." he admitted, walking away. I knew I couldn't change his mind; he was stubborn and adamant.

I placed my hands on the door handles but I did not managed to push or pull, they opened at my touch. Parted with the grace of a blooming flower.

The Commissioners sat on their thrones directly in front of me. Their eyes – unblinking, the sound of their breathing – inaudible; they could be compared to statues. They were at the far end of the colossal room, staring at me like a famished predator. They frightened me so much I started sweating.

I tightened my jaws and stepped into the room allowing the door to close with the same smoothness as it had opened. The room was covered in twilight; I noticed the curtains were pulled back from the huge windows and I didn't understand why. I was about to make another step but then I hesitated.

My eyes locked onto the *ominous* Commissioner – *Mort*, and a bitter feeling of repugnance stopped me. He smiled with my reaction; a cold, sarcastic smile. I felt my guts twist and it wasn't because of my hunger. He moved in his seat, sat more comfortably perhaps.

"Approach," he ordered me, with his clear, thundering voice, eyeing me with his cold, black eyes.

20. The Life Commission

I moved, approached them grudgingly.

"Come closer, don't be afraid..." the old, gray-haired woman told me, outstretching her hand to me, as if she was encouraging a toddler walking for the very first time. I hesitated, but her pressuring gaze made me move. I unwillingly outstretched my hand too, but she pulled away as if she'd just been electrocuted.

"Oh, good God! Did you feel that as well!? So powerful, I don't even have to touch her to *read* her!" she exclaimed in amazement.

I pulled away too, scared, for just a moment she appeared to be mad.

"You're scaring her, *Vie*..." The blond, blue-eyed man murmured.

How did he know I felt fear? It surprised me.

"Oh, excuse me! My name is Vie; I'm a Life Commissioner..." the old woman mumbled out awkwardly, smiling a bit.

"I'm aware of that," I reassured her, and again at the sound of my voice, everything stopped, their eyes pinned on me.

"And you are...?" I asked after a long pause, addressing the blond man.

"*Desire*," he replied quickly, surprised I'd talked to him.

"I'm *Passion*," the beautiful, catlike woman purred.

My eyes turned to gaze at the red-haired woman and her shadowy gray eyes stared back at me with the same intensity. She didn't talk though, she was focused on me – she was *reading* me.

"That's *Love*," the voice of the commissioner I was avoiding looking at replied – *Mort*. My eyes narrowed automatically. "I'm –" He didn't manage to finish his sentence.

"*I know who you are.*" I breathed, while repulsion swelled up in my empty stomach and suddenly I'd lost my appetite.

Mort smiled. Coldly.

"Do you know why you're here, Chosen?" Desire asked me.

"Yes. Demons," I answered.

"Do you know what a Demon is, April?" he questioned me.

"No," I admitted, I had no idea, I couldn't define it.

"You see, April; we believe life has a flow, a balanced, *perfect* cycle. A Demon is anything that tries to go against the laws of life. That is why it is something, so malicious and evil. Something that has to be destroyed," he said.

My brows pulled together in concentration.

"The problem with Demons is that they're too powerful. And only you are strong enough to capture the *Core*," he went on.

"The *Core*?"

"Their leader," he explained.

"And how can you capture the Core?" I asked curiously, full of interest, absorbed in the conversation because I was finally getting what I wanted – Answers. I don't know what happened at that moment, but I instinctively felt a responsibility to do everything in my power to capture that thing. I just changed my way of thinking and I still don't know how.

"You need something that is hard to find. A special medallion. The *Locket of Hell*," he breathed, enough for me to hear.

"Where can I find it?"

"Nobody knows..." he said absentmindedly.

"What do you mean 'Nobody knows'? If it were so important to you, you would know!" I barked.

They stared at me, surprised by my attitude.

I bit my tongue till it bled. "I apologize," I said taking a deep breath, trying to compose myself. What actually bothered me was that so much was being jeopardized and they seemed to simply not mind, it really made me furious.

"It's good you care so much, April, and with just *Eight Days* ahead, I believe it is very natural for you to be... nervous," Vie told me, trying to sound understanding.

"Eight Days?"

Nobody answered. Just creepy silence.

I wanted to walk out, to leave but something inside me told me that by doing so I'd be considered as disrespectful.

"You may leave, April, if that's what you *desire*..." Desire told me. My breath caught; it felt like all of them were reading my thoughts.

"*No, not thoughts, your Aura,*" Vie corrected me. A lump formed in my throat.

"B – But, how can you be so... accurate?" I was stunned and shocked at the same time.

They all just smiled, accepting my comment as a compliment. "Must be quite a transition, April... You didn't have these *things* with the humans, did you?" said Passion. Her way of speaking was quite unique, it always sounded as though she was purring – even her way of talking reminded of a feline.

"No," I muttered, realizing how much I'd taken for granted in the Human world; how everything made so much more sense and a sweet wave of nostalgia hit me hard.

A sunray reached my eyes. The sun was rising, emerging from the distant mountains. My head turned. "You may go now, April..." Mort told me.

"Yes, we cannot afford wasting time... It's just too close..." Vie murmured.

"What's close?" But, anyway, I didn't need to be told, I knew exactly what was close.

The End.

I was in the arena – again.

"Do we have to do this here?" I demanded through a stiff jaw.

"As a matter of fact, yes. Here," Peter told me, eyeing my reaction.

"You know, stop amusing yourself or else I'll crack your head open," I threatened, annoyed.

"You're too soft to do that," he whispered, so sure of himself, being playful.

"I wouldn't be so confident if I were you..." I argued, in a joking tone.

"Then prove me wrong, use your magic..." he suggested.

He was supposedly going to help me use my magic properly; show me how to control it.

"So here's a question I've had for a while now. If you don't know spells and if you don't cast spells, how do you use it?" he enquired.

"I just think about it," I mumbled out reluctantly.

"Think about what?" he asked again.

"About what I want to happen and it just happens. At least that's what I did with that... *thing*," I explained in discomfort.

He froze.

"*You mean you control magic just by thought?*" he questioned, speechless and his pupils widened predatorily. I swallowed in unease, I couldn't understand whether his eyes accused me of something or admired me instead.

"Yes," I spat out after a few heartbeats.

He was petrified once again.

What had I done wrong, what was my great mistake? He grabbed me by my arm and dragged me through the wall of the arena and into a tiny little room that was black, with no windows and no doors.

"That can't be possible..." he muttered, more to himself in a state of shock.

"What can't be possible?" I asked confused.

"Only *dark magic* works like this; not our kind..." he whispered, his glowing eyes seemed terrified.

"What's *dark magic*?"

"The kind of magic the *Core* uses, it's no good," he breathed. "He controls it with his mind, that's why he's considered *undefeatable*," he added after a second, sensing my puzzlement. "If you... use magic in that way... I don't know if it's a good thing," he said through a tight throat.

"Why?"

"If your magic works like this, it's dangerous, if you hurt someone, no one can stop you..." he explained, and I could smell the perspiration soaking his body once again.

"But I won't hurt anybody! What makes you think I could do that?!" I retorted surprised and a little offended.

"*Power, power is dangerous, April*, that's what can make you kill," he said in a whisper, staring at me. "And you are exceptionally powerful, no one knows if you're going to take advantage of that, power is addictive you want more and more..." His voice trailed off.

"Okay. Shut up!" I snapped. "I know myself!"

"You think you know yourself, truth is you don't," he muttered calmly.

"And what do *you* know about me?" I felt insulted.

"Not much. But I do know your soul is *perfect*; that though, doesn't mean it can't change," he admitted.

"Look, I don't think your conscience is clean enough so you can judge me; I'm not the murderer..." I breathed sourly, my chest burned with rage.

His heart raced responsively at my accusation and I bit my tongue realizing what I'd just spat out. A heavy feeling burdened my chest once more – guilt.

"I'm – I'm sorry... I didn't mean to –" I mumbled out apologetically.

"No you're right, April! I'm a killer, I'm *Marked*, you remember? But I'm just trying to help you, so you don't make the same mistakes; I think you should appreciate that," he said bitterly and my heart tied into a knot.

"I have a problem with trusting others..." I felt like a total moron, an idiot; my voice was shaky.

"How does trust have anything to do with this?" he asked confused.

"In order for you to help me, I've got to trust you and I don't know if I can do that..." I explained hesitantly.

"Because of my past?" he suggested.

"No. It has nothing to do with that. I'm just scared of this whole story, of the Spirits and the Demons. I feel... alone," I confessed sincerely and a shiver traveled down my spine.

"Loneliness is just a choice," he told me.

"I don't choose that," I said in a breath.

"Good." He approved my decision and a little smile pulled the edges of his mouth.

Trust is a big word. A word I feared. But trusting Peter came so naturally, I didn't even have to try. Maybe because I knew he was one of the few that cared about me – genuinely cared about me. Perhaps, it wasn't just his concern about me that made me trust him. His kiss was so true; at least it felt that way, as though he actually *loved* me. But I couldn't be sure of that either; love is a big word too.

21. Just a thought is enough...

"I still want to see you do that," he said and there were traces of excitement in his features.

"What?" I asked Peter.

"Use your magic; I want to see you do that," he explained.

"What do you want me to do?" I looked around; the arena was completely empty.

"How about that mosaic in the center?" a voice suggested – *Desire*. I turned around and he was just an inch away from me. How was it possible for me not sense his presence, to smell him or hear him? I was surprised.

"You could try and bring that butterfly to life," he told me indifferently, calmly, eyeing me with his expectant blue eyes.

I moved my gaze to the center of the arena and I noticed there was indeed a mosaic, I zoomed in and realized the tiny stones composed the image of a butterfly. "I can try," I declared after a moment's thought, feeling pressured.

I inhaled and exhaled slowly – heavily.

For just a second I wasn't sure what I was supposed to do but I focused, thought about the butterfly flying out of the stones. And in just a breath the rock appeared to liquefy – to melt. But I was so surprised I lost my concentration and the rock condensed once again.

"Focus, Chosen, focus."

The voices! I could hear them instructing me, ordering me. My breath caught. "Is everything alright?" Desire asked, looking at me carefully, *reading* me probably.

"Yes," I replied in a hushed voice afraid I might be mad. I blinked a few times and locked my gaze on the lifeless object I was supposed to bring to life.

I *imagined*. The blue wings of the animal emerging from the picture, flapping. Pulling the rest of its body out of the liquefied rock. And just by thinking about what I wanted; it happened.

My body was stiff and my hands were fixed into tight, sweaty fists to my sides.

It was like the stone had turned into mud, a dense liquid. And I saw the blue wings I'd imagined slicing through that mud, moving in and out, lifting the rest of the body out of the rock but they were wet and couldn't manage it. So I thought of them being dry and in just a moment there wasn't a single trace of moisture on them.

The butterfly pulled its body out of the liquid rock with ease and grace. It was much larger than what I thought, slightly bigger than a car. It looked at me with its bulging, shiny black eyes and then flew away, up, until it was out of sight.

I couldn't believe it myself, it was hard to accept that just a thought was enough...

A creepy silence followed; I turned around to look at them, I couldn't tell whether it was shock or admiration – maybe a mixture of both.

"Yes. She's the right *One*..." Desire told Peter in the same calm and unsurprised tone, as though he was expecting what had just happened. The Life Commissioner then walked away, slowly – the commissioners didn't have wings.

Peter waited until he was out of sight. "What did you just do?!" He jogged towards me, he sounded as confused as I was.

"I don't know..." I murmured, lost in thought, my eyes stared at something far away – blankly.

Powerful.

Yes, that was the right word. I wasn't the weak girl I used to be – I was powerful and I liked that. I liked it so much it made me change my way of thinking...

I wasn't the hunted.

I. Was. The. *Hunter.*

"What happened to your parents?" I asked him. We were under a tree.

"I killed them," he said shamefully.

"May I ask why?" I whispered, trying to disguise my shock.

"No," he refused coldly. He exhaled heavily. "Why do you even ask me these things? Nobody cares, I'm *Marked* for life; it's irreversible..." He breathed through a coarse throat.

"Do *you* want that to change?" I questioned eyeing his mortified eyes – detecting his discomfort.

"No one cares about what *I* think..." he whispered, and somehow he appeared to be pained.

"I care," I said.

"It's none of your business..." he mouthed, slightly aggressive, maybe trying to hide that wound I was sure he had somewhere on his body.

"I know. But I thought... that if I could trust you... you could do the same thing. I thought it was something mutual..." I reasoned myself. He looked at me for a moment and chuckled crookedly.

"So the tables have turned..." he said and I smiled. "Sorry, April, that's not going to happen today, I can't..." he said apologetically, avoiding my eyes.

Long silence.

"Last night, I was thinking about what you can do with your Powers..." he declared, changing the subject of conversation. "If you're actually using your mind to control your magic then there's nothing that's impossible for you..." he said. "Though I have to say it's quite dangerous considering you can go against the *Natural Balance* of things..." he added.

"I won't do that," I argued.

"Maybe not on purpose..." he corrected me.

"You can influence seasons, space and time," he continued. "You don't even need a Side Shifter to move from dimension to dimension..." he went on.

I processed what he was saying, for a long moment. "You mean I can leave?!" It was hard not to sound surprised; it was hard not to *hope*.

"Yes. But you'll choose the right thing to do. The Commission trusts you – no one is keeping you here, April, no one other than yourself..." he explained; demolishing any kind of hope I had managed to create within that nanosecond.

I always did the right thing – regardless. It was a matter of ethics. Of clear conscience.

"I hate myself for that," I mumbled, though it sounded more like a painful whimper.

"It's what makes you so different," he told me. "It's what makes you powerful," he whispered after a second.

It would be so much easier if I just simply did not care, but I did and that was the problem. I cared too much, so much I said "no" to an opportunity to flee, to reunite with my own family.

My family – the thought made my heart tie into a tight knot.

I crawled next to him and pressed my back against the trunk of the eternal oak we were underneath. "Close your eyes and think about them..." he breathed in my ear, it wasn't advice, it was an order.

I listened; I shut my eyes and kept them closed tightly. Then, all I had to do was to think, to tell myself how badly I desired to see them – over and over again, until everything else drained out of my brain.

I tried to stop myself from thinking about them; it creates too much pain. I can't. Gradually, the image of a snow-covered meadow replaces the faces of my beloved ones. Suddenly, I have no control of the thoughts in my mind. I shiver – it's cold.

An icy wind spirals around my body; snowflakes are dancing their way down the gray sky. They touch me, fall on my rigid shoulders and melt, soaking my short sleeved T-shirt. It's so cold I wrap my wings around my torso in desperate search of warmth. I need to find warmth, heat, or else my limbs are going to go numb.

The dense forest is dressed in white and creates a fence around the clearing. A question I've been struggling to form is finally complete.

Where am I?

And then, I see a tiny channel of frozen water dividing the meadow into two. The river is not even a meter wide. I've been here before. I can hear the sound of swishing waves. I've heard that sound before; it all seems so utterly familiar. I follow it, the echo of the moving water. I un-wrap my wings from around my body and use them to jump on a tree.

I move from tree to tree, as silently as I can. I know I'm close – I can smell it. I'm moving fast and agilely; like a feline, a predator.

I reach the edge, the land has ended and a colossal, powerful mass of water is running fiercely. In just a fraction of a second my eyes widen as I have finally recognized my surroundings. The shock is so strong I almost lose my balance and fall into the wild waters.

It's Lake Michigan, St. George, Wisconsin.

Home.

How did I get here? Is this true? Is this actually happening? All sorts of questions create a chaotic storm in my mind. I start to hyperventilate; I do not feel happy with this. This means I'm in the Human Side, this means I'm in danger. I'm not a human, I am a freak with wings and colorful eyes – I hadn't realized that up to that moment. An ancient instinct tells me to hide as the sound of a conversation reaches my ear drums.

I stick to the tree's trunk. I can hear barking dogs – police dogs. I look down with the corner of my eye and I try to even out my breathing. *Cops? Why are the police here?* I question myself, not understanding the reason for their presence. "Is it possible for *the girl* to be here?" a man asks someone and you can tell by the tone of his voice that he is very skeptical, doubtful.

"Sir, can I be honest with you? It's been nine days; I don't think we're going to find *her*," a police officer whispers, a whisper I wouldn't have heard without my supernatural hearing. "And even if we do, I don't think *she* could've made it in this kind of cold…" the man continues.

"I can't accept that! You're telling me you're going to stop searching for my daughter!?"

It's my dad. My heart stops beating for a moment. I cannot make myself look away, it's him; his eyes are sleepless, he looks pale – so *sick*. But there's something that is just radiating off of him – desperation. And I had never seen my father more desperate in my life. It stunned me.

"That is not what I meant, sir..." the officer apologized. "I'm just saying that you should be prepared and aware of the fact that we might just find a body..." The policeman breathed with a significant amount of sorrow.

Who's body? Mine?

And then, it all suddenly made sense.

I looked down again and saw something I thought I'd never see in my life. A single tear slid down my dad's cheek and forced me to swallow a whimper.

Somehow my leg slips off the tree's branch and a dog barks. I manage to slide on the tree again but I know I made a noise and that the canine underneath my tree caught my scent – and it's still barking.

I only have a second... I think of myself being invisible, transparent, see through. I don't know if I can manage to disappear so quickly but I don't have another choice, or enough time to think of an alternative. I close my eyes and stay as still as I can.

My heart is about to jolt out of my chest.

I hold on to the tree with all of my strength and just think of one thing – me being invisible. My fingers lock around the trunk like claws. The dog is still barking and I know that someone must be looking in my direction. I take a deep but silent breath and let my eyelids open. I can see them, I can see them so clearly but their searching eyes scan the canopy, the branches, the trunk, but cannot see me.

The German Shepherd won't stop barking, but the animal is also obviously confused as it can still smell me but lost sight of me.

After a minute or so, they all walk away, dragging the dog with them. A heavy exhale that I'd been trying to hold inside my lungs finds release. All of the adrenaline in my blood dissolves and I suddenly feel exhausted.

I close my eyes again; I know how I'm going to leave – the same way I came here – by thinking. So I think, realizing just how powerful a thought can be. Accepting the power of my mind. Respecting it.

I imagine being in the arena once again, being next to Pete, being safe. I don't even have to try so much, it comes naturally. And there I am, in the enormous arena of the Life Commission building, next to Peter, full of thought.

"How did you do this?" I breathe, not wanting to believe what just happened, afraid of the fact that I'd done this, all by myself.

"I didn't do anything; it's all you…" he whispers in my ear and touches my cheek with his lips.

22. Cassandra

In my entire life I had never met so much power. And it was so addictive. Peter was right. Even my "perfect soul" had trouble with being perfect – staying like that. Just thinking about the potential, the possibilities, and the open doors – I started thinking in a different way.

Power was trying to corrupt me.

Fortunately – for my own sake – there was another part of me that warned me. A little whisper in my mind telling me: *"Don't mess with the balance of things; you don't have the right to."* And I really fought to maintain that balance, to stop myself from asking for more, and it was harder than what I thought. Because, once that little temptation finds its way inside your brain, you have to fight it off forever.

I was in my room in the Life Commission building. I was in my bed, accepting the caress of my white, satin bed sheets, allowing the soft fabric to slip around my tired body. It almost had a soothing effect. The image of my father crying kept returning and I couldn't help it. Only then did I realize how much pain and grief I had caused. My family, the entire police department of my hometown was searching for me.

But they wouldn't find me; ever.

Then, I thought of how life works. They would get over it, overcome it because life works like that, it *always* moves forward.

"Can you listen to me?!" a voice, a female voice called out. I jumped out of my bed, out of breath. I looked around, searching for the owner of that eerie whisper. *"Do not be fooled, Chosen..."* the voice went on, she sounded nervous. *"Sometimes he who we believe is our greatest friend can be our greatest foe..."* The tone of the voice was calm, but at the same time warning.

"Who are you?" I asked out loud, walking to the center of my room, my eyes wide open – scanning my surroundings. I was soaked in fear already. *"Someone trying to save you from yourself..."* the voice answered, surprising me.

"Conscience?" I questioned.

"Yes, think of me as something like that..." she said, sounding satisfied with my speculation.

I waited; she was gone.

"Hello?" I shouted out, but got no reply. In just a heartbeat someone has gotten a grip of my arm and is dragging me out of my room in blinding speed. I think it's a man; he is so fast I don't have time to react or even fight back.

We're in a room, it's pitch black.

"You can communicate with the *Spirit of Cassandra*?" the man questioned me ominously, he sounded panicked.

"What do you mean?" I was still gasping.

"Answer my blasted question!" he yelled at me with impatience.

"I don't know what you're talking about!" I argued, confused, staring at nothing but darkness.

"Okay, I'll make this simpler for you to understand... Did you hear *a voice* or did you not?" He tried really hard not to sound intimidating.

"Yes, yes I did," I whispered hesitantly after a moment's thought.

Silence. It was like shock had forced the breath out of the man.

"Don't you listen to what she says, she's lying; The Spirit of Cassandra is a Demon... She's – she's trying to deceive you, play with you!" He was right in front of me, holding me by the shoulders, he was shaking – terrified.

"That is a lie!" A thundering female voice screams out in my head – she sounds desperate. I look around reacting to her shout; it was as though she was next to me, whispering things in my ear. *"Do not be fooled! Friends and foes, foes and friends, they have no great difference between them..."* she declares, in a more subtle way.

"She's talking to you right now!" the man breathes out in utter dread.

"Who are you?" I ask him, he's so scared he's squeezing my shoulders to non-existence. He removes one hand from my right arm and snaps his fingers once – flambeaus scattered on the walls illuminated the colossal Life Commission room automatically.

I look at his face and I freeze. My hate for him is so great I feel my guts twist at the sight of his threatening features.

Mort.

I pull away, his touch is cold. His black eyes reflect something I had never seen before – horror. "*Listen, Chosen, please listen to Me...*" Cassandra whispers hopelessly. I can barely hear her, her voice is fading away.

"What is she saying to you?!" Mort demands. "Don't you dare lie to me... I can feel her presence..." he spits out, trying to hide his panic even though his heartbeat is betraying him. A salty droplet of sweat slides down his forehead and collides with his eyebrow.

"*Shush...*" she tells me, in a rather calm and confident manner. I listen to *Her*; there is something about her that is so believable and honest. Am I agreeing with a Demon? "*No, I'm no Demon...*" she answers immediately in a mumble, and again it is that same sincerity that makes me trust this Spirit.

"Answer me!" Mort is screaming, his eyes have almost watered as if he is about to cry – true, pure fear.

I decide to lie. "She's gone! She's not talking to me anymore..." I state as convincingly as I can.

"What did she tell you?!" he questions in anticipation.

"*Lie...*" she encourages me.

I've got to think fast.

"She just called out my name, she didn't tell me anything..." I said with all the boldness I could master – What if he *read* my Aura and realized I was lying? He was a Commissioner, he could do that...

"Really?" he enquired in a breath, he appeared to believe me, his eyes shone with hope, but he was afraid to allow himself to calm down.

"Yes," I replied, sure of myself – he was obviously too panicked to care about my Aura, or my quickened heartbeat, or even the fine layer of sweat soaking my body.

He exhaled heavily, as if he was Atlas, carrying the weight of the entire world. He was truly relieved.

"I was scared for a moment, my darling..." he began with his sketchy voice, wiping his wet temples with the sleeve of his shirt. "Demons are trying to hurt you, take advantage of you. I promise to do anything in my power to... protect you from these kinds of dangers; this is just unacceptable, it won't ever occur again."

I was full of suspicion; was he lying too? It seemed so...

"*Hello?*" I think, call out in my head. Is *She* still there?

No reply.

"So, April... Hum, I thought of testing you..." Mort suddenly said moving to the center of the room, where a carved, golden, round table sat. "Come closer, there is something I want you to see..." he told me and I followed him. He placed his hands on the table and so did I, imitating him. "Tell me what you see, April..." he said staring at me expectantly. I allowed my fingers to brush the surface of the table, feeling every bump and shape on the precious metal.

I saw trees, flowers, a mountain, the starry sky, animals I couldn't recognize – the carvings represented a forest. "Can you see the Oaks? Bring them to life," he ordered me.

"Desire asked me to do the same thing with the stone mosaic in the arena; I don't think I have to do this again..." I argued cautiously.

"I know, but I won't believe it until I witness it," he retorted and the determination was apparent in his eyes.

I realized he wasn't joking.

This time I didn't have to struggle or even think that much. It just happened the moment I thought of it – mechanically. Huge Oaks grew out of the gold reaching up to the high ceiling of the Life Commission room. Mort appeared to be totally speechless. I was just surprised by how easy it had become.

"Extraordinary..." he breathed, staring at my creation, examining it. "*Useful, powerful...*" he continued slowly. "*Deadly,*" he whispered in amazement. "*The power of thought,*" he said to himself as though I wasn't even in the same room with him, he looked like he was hypnotized, like he had just discovered *absolute authority.*

"Reverse it," he finally said, turning his eyes on me again. "Reverse the spell," he repeated, his voice thundered and echoed. I nodded but wasn't quite sure whether a spell could be reversed in the same way it had been cast in the first place, but I didn't have time to argue or even ask for help, his pressuring and impatient gaze made me feel nervous.

So, I reversed the spell the same way I'd cast it, with my thoughts.

"Tell me what you see, April?" Mort had his hands on the table. I just had this terrible gut feeling from the very beginning; I'm lost, confused for a moment. "Can you see the Oaks? Bring them to life," he ordered me. I pull away from the table in total puzzlement. What does he mean?

"I just brought these Oaks to life, just like you said; now you want me to do this again?" I wondered mystified.

"April, what are you talking about? You haven't done anything yet..." he disagreed, seeming equally confused.

"No, I have done something, I turned the trees in the carvings into real ones and then you told me to reverse the spell; and I did. How can you not remember?" I insisted, not realizing the great mistake I'd made.

"Listen, this isn't a very successful joke," he said sounding quite angry; his eyes shimmered with growing fury.

"I'm not joking, I really did cast the spell and then I reversed it, just like you said! I swear!" We stared at each other awkwardly for a moment.

I was going through things, facts and moments, something was wrong but I didn't know what precisely. And then, I remembered what Peter had once told me in the arena. "Did you know you can influence seasons, space and *time*?"

Time. I had traveled in *time*!

I didn't even think at that moment, I just ran out of the Commission room in total panic. *Find Him! Just find Him!* I thought to myself over and over again. There was only one person I could think of; *Peter*. I was disorientated; I didn't know which direction to follow, the Life Commission building was huge, I could be running forever.

I was afraid of myself and afraid of what I'd done. In just a few seconds a heavy feeling of guilt started squeezing me around the chest. I stopped in a little corner, panting, my pupils had widened like a hunted animal's. I looked around; I'm in the same hallway and it just seems endless. Countless doors lie next to each other; there are no windows and once I realize that, the passage suddenly appears to be so airless; my body is asking for more oxygen as I start to respire much quicker but the air around me is insufficient, so my breathing becomes deep and loud.

You messed this up! You messed up for good! I think to myself.

I'm harsh on myself, it's like I'm abusing myself mentally. It's almost like I'm trying to punish myself; I am fully aware of the magnitude of my mistake. I went against the Natural Balance and knowing that this wasn't my intention didn't fix things.

Think, don't be an idiot! I order myself, realizing that sitting in a corner and sobbing wouldn't make things right. I try to pull myself back together and walk down a staircase – even though I have wings, I don't want to fly, I feel better when I walk, it makes me feel... human, *sane*.

I'm barefoot and I find out that I'm in my sleeping shorts and a very thin night top – suddenly I feel naked, exposed. But I do know there is no time to waste, I still need to find Peter. I pace down the stairs as fast as I can – my entire body is shaking.

I can smell him! A smell of sweat and gardenia blossoms. A fragrance I found particularly pleasant. My eyes stretch, and I follow his scent like a dog.

I end up in another hallway, and I can hear him – his beating heart, the inaudible sound of his blinking eyelids; the sound of his clothes as they swish on his body. He's close. I stop walking and I start running, in a few seconds I can hear his voice; he's talking to someone. I gallop, sprint with all of my strength and find myself standing in front of him in less than what appeared to be an eternal second.

"What happened to you?" he says, staring at me, questioning me with his eyes.

"You've. Got. To. Help. Me. I. messed. Up. Mort. Wanted. Me. To. Cast. A. spell. for. Him. I did. But I. Reversed it. And. We. Went. Back in time." I stopped between words to breathe.

"I know. We all felt it; Vie is dealing with him as we speak. Relax," he told me indifferently. I stood there for a moment, trying to understand, swallow the fact and calm down. "Come, Vie wants you to join them…" he added after a long moment, offering me his hand which I eagerly grabbed just like a little toddler, relieved because I'd finally found comfort, relieved because I finally felt safe.

This time we flew, Pete wasn't so used to walking, he preferred flying and he was much better at it than I was.

We enter the Commission room in less than a second – that's how fast we are, even though we are flying effortlessly.

"What are you searching for, Mort?" Passion asked the suddenly frightened Life Commissioner.

"Nothing," he murmured timidly.

"Don't you lie! There is something you desire; but I cannot tell what exactly…" Desire declared skeptically.

"I was just curious!" Mort said grudgingly, obviously feeling trapped, cornered.

"Really? So curious you went against the natural flow of things…?" said Love, in a rather sarcastic tone, having trouble believing the words Mort had just gotten out of his mouth.

"I apologize… I was impulsive, that's all…" he reasoned himself, staring at the other members of the committee exactly like a terrified pup. They appeared merciless.

"Oh calm down, Mort, you're not getting the *Ultimate Punishment*…" Vie said after a moment.

I turn towards Peter who is standing next to me and whisper in his ear, "*Ultimate Punishment?*"

"Death, April…" he replies in a breath knowing that our private conversation is not at all private…

23. Dreams and Visions

I used to be a very impulsive kind of person, but lately, I had been spending a lot of my time just thinking. Doing absolutely nothing else – I would lock myself in my room and daydream, comprehend, speculate and imagine. I would try to analyze everything that had been happening to me, trying to fit it in human logic; I still thought like a human, I hadn't realized those days were over.

But even just thinking seemed like something risky and jeopardous now. I couldn't find peace. I couldn't sleep and even if I did sleep dark nightmares would haunt my nights – and it was the same dream every night. Images of massive destruction, dead bodies, and people screaming their hearts out, hopelessness surrounded me in this imaginary world my mind would create night after night. And I, would be standing in the eye of this hurricane, this sinister tornado and I would hear myself whisper to me: '*Your thought...*' I would spit it out so wickedly and accusingly it made my hair stand on edge. And then, at the apogee of my vision, where I grabbed a child and strangled it, I would wake up drenched in sweat, panting uncontrollably; and for some mysterious reason I would always find Peter next to me.

He would calm me down, make me sleep again; I found his presence rather comforting, he was the only tangible friend I had left. Friend; I wasn't very fond of the particular word. Since that time we kissed he was being careful and quite distant – it looked like he was bothered by something or someone. It was more than apparent that he was trying to restrain himself; he was pulling back – a fact which I hated.

"Kiss me..." I told him. I had woken up for the third time that night; he was sitting on a stool next to my bed.

"Why should I do that?" he retorted, in a diplomatic voice. I was caught off guard because I wasn't expecting him to argue with *me*. What should I tell him? Then, I thought of the virtues of honesty and sincerity. I would tell him the truth.

"I think I love you," I said staring out of the window; I couldn't find the courage to tell him that looking at him because that would make me feel vulnerable and I always hated vulnerability even though at this point I couldn't avoid it. I could feel his glowing green eyes narrow with skepticism.

"I'll kiss you only when you are sure," he replied, clearly and powerfully, so prestigiously my head turned towards him unconsciously and I examined his wakeful eyes. His complexion was pale; he looked ill.

"If you don't care about me and talk to me with such contempt, why do you spend every night with me?" I questioned, and my inquiry seemed to unsettle him.

"What I feel and believe has no value and no importance. I'm a *Marked* criminal…" he answered, fixing his right hand in a shaking fist as though he was trying to bear some kind of torture.

His heartbeat accelerated. I could hear his heart throb against his ribs. And he knew that, because he could hear it too.

He stood up abruptly, spastically almost, and paced to the center of the room restlessly. Then walked back towards me and sat on the edge of my mattress. He closed his eyes, having difficulty ignoring the heavy load clearly squashing him to the ground.

He exploded.

"I think I love you too," he whispered in my ear and ran out of the door in less than a nanosecond, dripping with guilt and soaking me in satisfaction instead, because I had finally made him say it.

PETER

I hated myself. I hated myself because I had allowed myself to kill and although I thought I had an excuse, reasoning my actions it wasn't enough for me to get away with it. I have to admit, it was a terrible mistake I'd made but I did have my reasons…

Vie was the only commissioner that had shown me mercy; she believed me. Believed I had murdered my parents thinking they were possessed by Demons, when we were under attack two years ago. She gave me the option of living the rest of my life Marked and work for the Life Commission or get the Ultimate Punishment instead. I chose the first option of course, but never thought it would be so hard to live stigmatized and marginalized by everyone else. Sometimes, I wish they would've killed me and got it over with.

And when I started accepting the fact that I would never have a proper life she came. "The Chosen." I wasn't quite sure about what she would be like, I thought of her as something flawless and perfect and really, everyone thought she'd be the representation of the ideal.

But she was human. Something so puny and deficient, so flawed and lost. We actually had a saying about humans. "If it's bad, then it sure is human."

And it was very true, very wise. There is no other species in the dimensional world that would hurt its own kind deliberately. Humans were and are as low as you can get, we thought of them as dumb, unbalanced masochistic creatures, and they were worth no respect.

But she was different. She was the most imperfectly perfect creature; she loved, she detested, argued, agreed, joked... She used a part of her most us had forgotten even existed – sense, logic. She made me realize that perfect is not balanced or healthy, what is normal and healthy is to think before you act, to think of every aspect of your actions and every possible outcome – positive or negative; something I never did up to that moment. And only then are you the true master of yourself, only then are you balanced.

Maybe she just gave me hope that perhaps one day I would be forgiven by the Commission and my Marks would disappear. I was so used to misery I had forgotten how it is to step into the sunlight, to be happy even for just a brief moment. Happiness is very important for any creature's survival, without it you have no reason to live, you are never satisfied.

I guess that was why I was so scared of the other side of the coin, because there was another aspect of The End, something that could be translated into her end too. That sensible, bold, honest girl could transform *from our only hope to our doom. I couldn't imagine her in that way but, the possibilities of her betraying Us were greater than the possibilities of her supporting Us and that would be the end of everything.*

But most importantly, I would lose the only thing that ever made sense in my life and if that happened I wouldn't have the strength to overcome it. Because, once you meet the light you can never be blindfolded again and if you are, you cannot survive.

I had new orders; I had to take April to the Prophet. The Prophets used to be seven, the Spirits killed the six and only one survived thanks to the Life Commission. They supposedly had prophesized April's existence thousands of years ago. The well-known prophesy of The Chosen, or the so called prophesy of Hope.

"Come, you need to meet someone," *I told her as she walked out of her room, I had been waiting for her.*

"Who?" *she questioned, and her eyebrows pulled together skeptically.*

"I'll tell you on our way, we need to hurry..." *I said, grabbing her hand, pulling her down the hallway with me; there were no formalities between us, it felt like we'd known each other for years now, it was hard to believe we had met just ten days ago.*

She didn't argue, she followed me out of the Commission building, over the wall and into the tropical forest. It was so humid it was like we breathed in water and our clothes stuck on our bodies. She was rather small and fragile-looking, but in that average female body a greater power was found – the power of the mind. It was so much stronger and precious, but dangerous at the same time. Her power, just like any power was a double edged sword.

"How far away from here is this place?" *she wondered, sweating even though we weren't running, we moved slowly, almost human-like.*

"Just be patient, we're almost there," *I answered – we had been walking for more than three hours; she liked moving slowly, she once said it was easier for her to take things in that way. If she traveled fast her senses would work so quickly, it made her panic, if she traveled unhurriedly she claimed she could analyze every little piece of detail in peace.*

"There's one thing I can't understand..." I began, breaking the silence, "why don't you use your wings?" I questioned her; it was true, she almost never used them in spite of the fact flying was easier and faster.

"I don't know... I guess I don't like them..." she admitted, looking at me briefly, shamefully.

"Why?" I asked, surprised by her reply.

"Because they remind me of what I'm supposed to do," she said reluctantly, staring at something undefined, far away.

"Truly, it's no great honor..." I stated rather sarcastically, smiling crookedly. She laughed; just as I intended. She didn't have a choice really, she was either going to cry or laugh. And I didn't want her to cry.

Suddenly, sunlight found its way through the dense canopy and blinded us as our eyes had adjusted to the forest's twilight. She let go of my hand and followed the light, as though she was hypnotized by it – this was a different kind of light. She moved quickly, started jogging and I jogged after her. Then, she started running and I ran after her; she finally stopped, exactly where the forest ended and a clearing stretched in front of us.

She stared at it; the grass-covered meadow, and she wouldn't move.

"What's wrong?" I asked, alarmed by her stiff posture and her wide eyes.

"Someone is here," she declared in a careful whisper.

I looked around – I hadn't realized we had reached the location. "I know," I mouthed, trying to calm her down. For some reason lately, she was being careful and hesitant about anything and everything, maybe due to what happened in the Life Commission building with Mort.

She eyed me for a long second, trying to find reassurance in my eyes. "There's someone you need to meet before the Full Moon..." I told her in an encouraging voice, walking out of the safety of the woods and dragging her with me by the hand. She followed me grudgingly, without confidence because she still had trouble trusting me, a fact which I didn't like. But talking realistically, who could trust someone like me...

Perhaps she had trouble trusting anyone – that fact was my comfort...

She didn't make a sound, she never liked being the vulnerable one, she thought she should know and do everything, she burdened herself as if the real task she had wasn't a burden enough. And if things didn't go her way, she would get frustrated, shout and talk to herself with such harshness and severity — herself was her greatest judge.

The meadow's light was strange, and I imagined how strange it must've appeared to her, to someone new to our World. The Real World. The fresh grass cracked and snapped under our bare feet, the soil was moist and the smell of mud was overwhelming; for some reason however, there was no trace of humidity in the air — it was absolutely dry.

Movement.

Something moved behind a tree; we were standing in the middle of this perfectly circular field, and something had moved right in front of us, between the trees — it was so abrupt and unexpected my heart skipped a beat and so did hers. We stood still, wouldn't even move our chests to breathe in or breathe out properly. She let go of my hand stood in front of me protectively, another thing which I was bothered by; it hurt my male ego though I knew she was the powerful one — always. It just felt out of place, a girl significantly smaller than me, shielding me? — I sometimes still forget this wasn't about size or physique...

"What was that?" she questioned me in a reluctant breath.

"I don't know," I replied, almost inaudibly. Her hands slowly tightened into fists and she started sweating — in just a few seconds. I didn't know what to expect, in spite of the fact I'd been spending most of my time in the forest away from everyone and everything; this was unknown territory.

Footsteps. The sound of heavy walking reached our ears — it was loud and clear.

A man stepped out of the shadows and allowed the eerie light of the meadow to shower him. He was old, very old; his skin was folded with deep wrinkles, his white hair rested down on his shoulders and his blue eyes surprisingly, looked so young...

The Prophet, the Visioner...

I put my hand on April's shoulder, reassuring her — there was no danger, just an old Visioner, probably thousands of years old, probably older than the members of the Life Commission itself... He gazed at us with tenderness and warmth, he appeared to be so harmless and weak.

"Come closer..." he mouthed with his coarse, weathered voice, outstretching his hand towards April. She stared at him for a moment, and then looked over her shoulder and into my eyes, unsure of what she should do. I gave her a gentle push forward, nodding, encouraging her to walk towards him fearlessly. And she did, one step at a time, careful but confident at the same time – curious.

I kept my distance; this was no place for me...

The Visioner eyed her thoughtfully as she gave him her hand without a second thought. Deep inside she was one of the most innocent and reckless creatures I'd ever met, maybe that was the reason she was always so reluctant, maybe because she knew herself to a certain extent; something, I found so appealing about her, even though I knew she was an unreachable temptation...

"What a beautiful soul..." he murmured, holding her hand in both palms, his deep blue eyes seemed mesmerized. Only then did I notice how unusually blue his eyes were, so deep and warm, unlike any blue I had ever seen. She just looked at him, in contained puzzlement; it looked like she recognized him. "I know you... You were at the hospital in St. George, when I visited my grandfather... It must be you..." she declared, with a significant amount of confusion and uncertainty.

He smiled. "You remember..." He confirmed her speculation and his eyes appeared to water, fill up with tears he couldn't control. "It's really you, you are here..." he told himself, in disbelief. The man fell down on his knees, overwhelmed by emotions. She kneeled down next to him, still holding his creased hand – they just looked at each other for a moment, eyed one another with amazing warmness and affection.

It must have been something so overpowering and intense for the Seventh Prophet. Finally holding the hand of the Chosen, someone he had been envisaging for millennium after millennium. He brought her hand to his lips and kissed it in awe, staring at the unique coloration of her eyes, staring right into her soul.

"Perfect..." he breathed, gazing her and then turning his eyes on me. It was almost shocking, how his eyes looked so young and deep, so out of place on his weathered body – she must have noticed that as well because she gazed at him so incomprehensibly, amazed by how timeless he seemed to be.

He examined me, looked into my eyes, into my soul.

"Sinner..." he exclaimed, not at all harshly or disdainfully like others, like most of Them; rather kindly and with a significant amount of understanding, like he knew the truth... like he knew I'd done it just to save myself, I'd done it instinctively, following the unwritten law of survival. Despite that, the understanding I found in his eyes, I still felt mortified and ashamed, because I didn't deserve something so perfect like her, that very moment she seemed even more out of reach.

That's how amazingly we matched. She was Perfect and I was the Sinner...

The Visioner suddenly stood up, so abruptly and nervously, like he was worried he would forget to do something of extreme importance, he let go of April's hand and started running into the darkness of the forest. "Follow me..." he ordered, his body language changed completely – from welcoming and friendly to oppressive and commanding.

April's pupils grew larger in just an instant. She grabbed my arm tightly, her fingers dug into my skin like talons and she wouldn't let go, she shook from head to toe, as though she had just discovered something so outrageous. "He is The Voices I've been hearing since that night you found me. I would recognize that sound from miles away..." She breathed staring right into my questioning eyes, so shocked.

The Voices?

I didn't know how to reply. I couldn't form an answer. The only thing I could focus on was that the Prophet's figure was moving away, fading into the woods. I just clutched her hand and dragged her with me after him. This was the only thing that mattered right now.

We followed in a sprint. He was moving fast.

I had no idea as to where we were going. I just followed his scent, the sound of his long, white dress-like piece of clothing as it swished between the ferns and the dense vegetation. He was out of sight, but I was sure we were close behind. There was almost no light in the woods now, the day was ending and I knew I had to hurry. I could only feel one thing.

Anxiety. Yes, something was about to go wrong and I was being very apprehensive.

"Where are you?!" I called out to him, a bit disorientated for a moment, I'd lost his scent.

"Over here!" he yelled back and suddenly he sounded as distressed as I was. What was going on? I was so sure he knew what was about to follow – he was a Visioner after all – and I was also sure it would be something bad; I just didn't know what exactly.

We were standing in front of him in just a heartbeat.

April was still panting, gasping but he didn't seem to care; he just grabbed her hand, turned it palm up and pressed his palm against hers closing his eyes in remarkable concentration – he was casting a spell. A blue light beamed through their joined fingers and nearly blinded me.

It looked like it took forever, but he finally removed his hand. There was something resting in her shaking palm.

This time my pupils were the ones that grew rapidly. A chill traveled down my spine at the sight of the object, a tool of darkness and evil rested in her palm. A palm of good and innocence. It infuriated me, scared me and made me realize how great my level of concern about her was and is.

She just looked at it curiously. Examined the fine, silver chain attached to the huge, black diamond, shaped as a rhombus. It shone incredibly although the amount of sunlight in the forest was insufficient. She gazed at it with amazing interest and wonder.

"It's beautiful..." she mouthed, not taking her eyes off of it.

Something inside me burned the instant those words came out of her lips. How could she think of something so wicked as something beautiful and worthy of admiration? But I forgot she was ignorant, that she still didn't know what it was or what it could do. It could save her or break her, that's how powerful it was...

"April..." I began trying to sound as composed as I could.

"Yes?"

"Do you know what that is...?" I asked her as calmly as I could manage.

"No," she replied, still unaware of the danger lying in her hands...

"That's the Locket of Hell..." I said rather bitterly, full of detest and repugnance.

She froze.

24. Cold

She turned her gaze on me; slowly. And just when I believed she had stopped quivering she started shaking again. She didn't know how to react, what to do or say. Her ignorance frightened her — I could see it in her eyes; the question, the enquiry for an explanation.

I grabbed the medallion by the chain and passed it over her head so that it hung down her neck. "It's okay; you need it, you can't capture the Core without it..." I told her trying to calm her down. I had terrified her, and that wasn't my intention; maybe not through words but through my posture or the fact that I was sweating or even my tight jaw or my hands that had immediately curled into fists.

The point was that she shouldn't fear it, if she feared it the game was over and it was certain that Life would be the one defeated. What she should do was to respect it — fearing power and respecting power are two completely different things, have a completely different value.

"Listen, April..." the Visioner interrupted, "... I have been protecting this from the Spirits for centuries; this belongs to you and only you are allowed to use it, and it mustn't fall into the wrong hands, guard it with your life," he told her, ordered her actually, holding her by the shoulders and staring right into her intelligent eyes. She nodded, realizing that this was no piece of jewelry and certainly no toy.

He eyed her gently and fatherly, and she felt that warmth, that genuine care and concern he felt for her. She had already become quite fond of him even though they had met only a few minutes ago. Then, he mysteriously started running into the woods as though he was being chased, suddenly terrified.

"Where is he going?" she wondered jogging behind him.

I put my hand on her shoulder — stopping her. "Let him go," I whispered and she obeyed, turned around submissively. Whatever was chasing him, it was better for him to deal with it instead of putting April in danger.

Because, in spite of April's cosmic power she still needed protection and I couldn't offer her any. And that Locket hanging down her neck was an invitation for trouble, the moment I passed that medallion over her head she was immediately made a target. Her fingers had curled around the black diamond protectively but she didn't really know the importance or the prestige of that charm, she didn't realize how many wanted it but most importantly, how many wanted to use it in order to serve the Spirits and the Demons.

The Core, Satan himself couldn't wait to lay his hands on it, and he was so desperate he would do anything in his own power to get it. And he didn't care about collateral damage, in fact, he sought to create extensive destruction and dead souls; that was the only way he ensured his ruling – through fear.

But what made him even more terrifying and unpredictable was the fact that he was a Spirit. He would possess creatures in order for them to serve his evil purposes, and his army of countless, soul-thirsty Demons would leave nothing but death in their path. These Devils were sly and devious creatures, they Claimed souls that weren't supposed to be claimed. Humans that weren't supposed to die at that particular period of time died and the dimensional world was out of balance.

Hopelessness overwhelmed the Life Commission; this distortion could not be balanced out by Them. Our last hope was April, the Chosen, someone with a soul so powerful and perfectly balanced that could not be harmed by the Spirits; someone with powers equivalent to the Core's. But unfortunately or fortunately, April had human blood running in her veins and that made her dangerous to the Side of Life – Our dimension.

She could betray us, she could be easily deceived by the Spirits because of her noble nature; something, I hated to think of because in my eyes she was the representation of light even though, I knew that that status could change in just four remaining days, until the Autumn Full Moon. From that point on, she would be left alone, all by herself in the darkness, coldness and hostility of the Spirits' Side where she would have to face her greatest fears. . .

"What am I supposed to do with this?" she questioned me, holding the precious stone in her palm, examining it. We were walking into the woods, walking back to the Life Commission building. I thought of my answer for a moment, I couldn't lie to her and I couldn't tell her the entire truth so I decided to say part of it. "It's your key to victory..." I said halfheartedly, not very convincingly.

"Oh..." she breathed. "And how am I going to win, how can I use it?" she asked me after a second, looking up to me, meeting the discomfort reflected in my eyes.

"You will be considered as victorious only when the Core is in the diamond," I explained as best as I could, instinctively avoiding her inquisitive gaze.

"And how am I going to get the Core in here?" she wondered, opening her palm, showing me the shining jewel, staring at me in expectancy.

"How do you usually use magic?" I questioned her, a bit rhetorically.

"Through thought?" she replied unsure of her answer. "Exactly," I reassured her. She nodded in comprehension.

I just had this terrible gut feeling and I couldn't stop myself from thinking about the Visioner, I couldn't get rid of the image of him running into the forest in total dread. Something was about to happen, I just knew it, the Prophet apparently was fully aware, he must've have had a vision of it the moment he was giving April the Locket of Hell. I simply wanted her out of the forest the soonest possible...

She stopped moving – utterly petrified in just a nanosecond, so abruptly and unexpectedly.

No sound was audible. No scent detectible. No sight visible. I knew I was panic-stricken, the moment I felt her eyes widen. She was so overwhelmed she didn't even tremble, she just stood still, wouldn't respond to anything other than what she had sensed...

"Pete..." She breathed cautiously, so soundlessly I wouldn't have heard if I were human.

"Yes..."

"Can you feel that...?"

"What?"

"The Cold..."

And the moment she mouthed that last word a great wave of coldness immobilized me too. A kind of cold that goes through your brain, stops your ability to think or act, prevents blood from flowing in your veins and your arteries, the kind of cold that turns you into nothing. Wave after wave of

ice hit us relentlessly, this was our nature as Life creatures warning us of what is awaiting us, warning us of the hazard ahead; this kind of reaction from our bodies could be blamed on just one particular kind of creature.
A creation of the Spiritual world. A creature of darkness.
A Demon.
But not just one, we wouldn't react so dramatically to just one Spirit, we were surrounded by myriads of them. We were trapped. And I knew exactly what they wanted; this wasn't an attack for souls, her soul was immortal and mine was a Sinner's, too bitter for Them to desire. What they wanted was the medallion resting on her chest. The medallion they feared so dearly but desired as much because with it they would find absolute rule.
"Can you feel it, Pete?" she asked me again. Her voice broke at my name; she was scared to the bone, clearly shocked by her body's response, she was considered an infant in Our World, everything was new to her...
"Yes," I replied weakly. I didn't know how to get ourselves out of this; we were at a dead end, so totally doomed.
"What is it?" she demanded, unable to control her nerves, once again her lack of knowledge outraged her. This time I couldn't tell her part of the truth, I couldn't present the situation in any mild way, I could only say it in one manner — raw.
"Demons."
Thud. Thud. Thud. Then, her heart stopped.
Silence and stillness, her breath was out of her lungs.
"Whatever happens, don't you give Them the diamond; guard it with every bit of you," I tell her, unintentionally sounding aggressive maybe due to my panic, or due to my desperation, my fear that she wouldn't make it.
I knew she wasn't prepared for this. But now she didn't really have a choice. This was her reason of existence, she was made for this; no one can refuse their own nature, no one has the right to, it's like disrespecting oneself...
I shout.
Something is pulling me away from her; it all happens so abruptly I can't even fight back, I turn my head around, trying to see what is holding me, and trying to identify the danger.
I see nothing, I try to move my body, to fight but I can't, I'm under a spell, I try to yell, to ask for help, but again, although my mouth is moving and I am using all the power I can find in my lungs, no sound comes out.

APRIL

"PETER!" I'm screaming, I'm screaming my heart out. I want to move my frozen body, to find him but I don't know which direction he has followed, there's no scent, no sound, there's nothing, it's like he has vanished – *magically*. I've never felt this kind of numbness before, I feel powerless, even lifting my chest to breathe feels like such a challenging thing to do. Blinking is painful. Gravity on my body is so strong I feel like I'm just two inches tall, it's like the earth is swallowing me and the *Cold* is the most torturous fact about the whole situation.

I can't describe it in any other way, it's just pure, raw *Cold* and it's abusing me, freezing me to non-existence. This charged scene keeps on replaying in my terrified mind.

"What is it?"

"A Demon."

A Demon. That word echoes in my head, bangs on the walls of my skull, makes me feel sick. My hand has frozen around the black diamond, the Visioner told me I should guard it with my life and so did Pete. I didn't need to be told to realize that this was something many desired, I could sense it, feel the real weight of that Locket.

I move; I make myself make a single step forward against the will of my body. There's nowhere to run and nowhere to hide, this is inevitable, and this time no one is here to help me or give me an explanation of the situation. This time, I have to find a solution on my own, this time I have to face things exclusively on my own. And this, would be my first taste of the reality awaiting me in four days.

"*It is quite remarkable; how powerful creatures like you can appear so puny and weak at moments like these…*"

A voice, and it's not Cassandra. This voice isn't just in my head, someone is talking to me. I turn around myself – slowly; attempt to find the direction from which the sound is coming, but I can't. It's like it's coming from everywhere.

"*I cannot believe I have to fear something as brittle as a human…*" A laugh followed, I now am sure this voice belongs to a male. It's deep and coarse, but what makes my hair stand on edge is how dark he sounds, the disdain he felt for me is so clear and perceptible. I think of answering, of replying but I choose not to – I don't know how to argue with *something* like this, with a creature I've never encountered before...

I hear a scream. Someone is screaming my name, someone is shouting in distress, telling me to leave, to run, so desperately; I know that voice.

"Peter!" I shout back. I look around once again, turn around myself futilely, my ear drums hurt – that's how loud he had yelled out to me; he's gone in just an instant, it's like he was never even here, it's as though he was never heard.

This time I can't handle my nerves, this time I bark.

"What did you do?!" I roar, the rage burning my insides is so great I cannot even describe it, fury mixed up with anxiety makes me lose even the slightest amount of composure. There is no room for composure, you fight madness with madness – I panic, and it's like I'm on fire.

"*Oh, nothing yet*," he replies indifferently, as though nothing is happening, as if everything is *perfect*. I didn't know where to look, where to focus my gaze on, my eyes swept across my surroundings, from the canopy to the forest's floor, repeatedly. Even though I can't see, hear or smell anything, I can feel *Them* watching me, monitoring my every move and reaction. I have no control over the situation and that is what makes me even angrier, the fact that I am in such a vulnerable position; I didn't even want to think about the possibility of Peter being tortured by *Them*, of the possibility of him losing his soul.

My heart throbbed ferociously in my chest.

This didn't even make sense. If this was about killing souls, why were *They* keeping Pete alive? Were *They* going to attack everyone in the Life Commission Building just a few heartbeats away from here? What happened if a Commissioner died? What happened to the Natural Balance if something like that occurred? Every little question joined to create one.

What do They want?

I try to open my mouth and say something, anything, just to show them that I'm not going to surrender; but my mouth is so dry no sound comes out. I swallow but there's no trace of saliva in my mouth; only then do I realize I have been panting reflexively.

"What do you want?!" I shout with every part of me, feeling my lungs so small in my chest, the oxygen in my body is inadequate, a wave of nausea suddenly hits me as tension becomes too much to bear.

"*I think you already know…*" he tells me, coldly, the sound of his voice enters my ears and cuts through them like poisonous razors, the sweat wetting my body is icy and a shiver rules my muscles.

I think. What does he mean "I already know"? I once again try to find the origin of the sound, but expectedly fail. *They're* closing in, I know because a new wave of frost engulfs me, the closer *They* come, the colder I feel. Every joint in me becomes stiff and this blanket of iciness wraps itself around me – I'm suffering, I involuntarily drop down on my knees, cling on the soil with my trembling fingers and scream. In pain. I can't even feel my wings.

What can He want? My mind is working frantically, going through everything in fast forward mode. Then, I tumble on something worth of my attention. It's the moment the Prophet has given me the Locket, that very short but significant sentence replays in my head once.

"*I have been protecting this from the Spirits for centuries.*"

My eyes are out of their sockets the moment I realize what I should have been protecting all along. My left hand is immediately out of the mud and around the diamond, I stand up as steadily as I can manage, it's so hard I grit my teeth and tighten my jaw, but I cannot stop the shriek of pain that escapes from the depths of my throat, so real and tangible.

I'm hyperventilating, uncontrollably.

"*Poor, little, thing, you Life creatures chose to be weak, I almost feel sorry for you…*" He was being ironic, mocked so successfully and so theatrically. I straighten my body as best as I can, I think of him being away, locked up in a cage, somewhere he cannot harm, because I know that that is his only intention, I can tell by the way he talks, by the way he moves between the shadows. He's malicious. I focus, concentrate; put all of myself in the spell I'm casting.

He laughs.

For the first time, my spell fails.

It actually *fails*.

"*You really thought your magic can be compared to mine? Do you even have the slightest idea about who you are talking to? I'm the strongest creature in the dimensional world and you, are just a human, a nothing.*" He howls at me aggressively, he sounds threatening, tries to terrify me even more than what I already am, but fortunately for my own sake, my level of horror has reached its climax – it can't move any further up, it has reached its final point.

The layer of slimy mud on my hands makes the crystal so hard to hold – but I cling on it.

I cast a different spell, if I want to guard the medallion I can *Shield* it. I think of a current of electricity surrounding the precious stone. I think of anyone else attempting to touch it, or take it dying at that very instant. I wasn't sure if it was going to work, I just hoped.

"*How smart... the shielding spell? Even an infant can do that...*" he said, in the same sarcastic manner.

This time, I replied. "Smart enough to keep you away from *It*," I spat out, thinking of Pete, so certain He was the reason of his disappearance.

I can now feel his anxiety, the uncomfortable position I have brought him in; I have the upper hand now and he hates that. He has underestimated me, thought that just because of my fright I would let him do what He wants. But I never did that, even when I was human; I never gave up.

"*If I can't take want I can still make everyone else hate you...*" he told me, with the same sourness and hatred.

"*Power is not fighting a battle for yourself, power is convincing someone else to fight the battle for you,*" he added, not losing a single bit of his confidence, his belief that he would leave crowned with a victory.

A moment of silence follows.
I blink once – slowly. Breathe in. Breathe out.
I open my eyes.
Peter is in front of me. Just a few feet away from where I am. He's standing in front of a tree, having his back pressed against it. He has lost his color, his limbs are hanging down, completely paralyzed, his head is facing the ground as well and strands of black hair cover his face. My gaze immediately falls on the wooden lance that has been passed through his chest and into the tree's trunk. He is drenched in blood, I can smell the raw flesh, and red liquid is still oozing around the gash.

At that point I lose myself, I can't think of anything else, I just run to him. My eyes water at the idea of him dying, leaving me. My hands tremble as I fumble the skin around the wooden pole that has been stuck into him in a way that is so barbaric and cruel, so brutal and monstrous. I take his face in my hand – he is unconscious, and no matter how loud I shout his name, no matter how loud I sob, he won't respond. A string around my neck is pulling tighter and tighter till I feel like I'm asphyxiating, like there's no air.

My picture of the world becomes obscure and blurred – I'm about to black out. I lose my balance and fall on to the Visioner who is in the same condition as Peter; with a spear stuck right through him, going right through the trunk of the eternal tree. I scream in desperation, holding my head in both hands, not wanting to accept this reality.

This is madness, insanity, it's sick.

Peter and the Visioner, side by side, with their backs against a tree, with a lance pushed through their chests, not responding, bleeding – *dead*.

"*They're not dead yet, April...*" he tells me; I don't want to hear that voice ever again, I just want to *kill* him, to strangle him to nothingness.

"*You decide whose soul I'm taking...*" he states, indifferently, it literally sounds like he is enjoying it, he sounds amused.

"STOP!" I cry with all of my remaining strength, my voice breaks, I'm pulling the hair out of my head, I cover my ears with my palms but still every sound is clear and defined.

"*What if I take both of them?*" He is manipulating me, playing with my charged emotions and my confusion. I don't even think about arguing with him, fighting back. I just know I can't let *Him* go.

That's how high my level of panic is.

"The Visioner! Take him!" I yelled terrified, too blinded by my sentiments to even realize I had just sentenced someone to death. The Prophet's hand reached out to me for the very last time, he grabbed me, and he looked at me with his set of tender, deep blue eyes and smiled at me parentally, as though he thanked me for what I'd just done to him.

Then, his eyes lost their color, turned into a vacant, light gray as his soul was being sucked out of him. After that, he was gone, empty.

Soulless.

I didn't even think about that at that particular instant; I just care about one thing and that is Pete. I try to pull myself together unsuccessfully, I tighten my bloody hands around the lance and yank it out of him in one move. His powerless body drops to the ground. I kneel down, in the pool of blood surrounding us. I hold his abused torso in my arms; I can see right through the opening on his chest and realize that it might be too late.

"April..." he breathes, and despite his ordeal, a microscopic smile forms on his lips.

"Don't talk..." I whisper, and it's hard not to feel relief, not to hope at the sound of his voice.

25. Tsunamis, waves, and emotional currents

I cannot relax. I still cannot breathe. My gaze falls on to the impressive size of Peter's injury; blood is streaming out of the huge cut and the scent is so strong I feel like throwing up, the sight is just so macabre and sickening that it's hard to look at.

I unbutton his shirt, take it off and use it as a cloth; he moans and whimpers as I touch him, as I wipe the blood around the wound fruitlessly – the bleeding won't stop and soon enough the cloth is soaked in blood; it's so wet I can squeeze blood out of it. I try to make myself think, to come up with some sort of plan so I can save him. I'm gasping, crying, shaking; and my state is not helping the situation at all.

I drop the cloth on the ground and take a step away from his mistreated body. I turn my back on him, close my eyes, not wanting to see or smell the blood covering me from head to toe. I try to even out my breathing and control my spasming muscles and just think.

"Calm down and think!" I order myself out loud, knowing that this is the only way he might have a chance of making it. Tension in me grows with every breath I take. His heartbeat is becoming weaker and weaker – I can barely hear it. My mind once again is working in a way that reminds of hysteria.

Magic. I was so oppressed by my fright that I forgot I possessed magic.

I ran back to him, with a flame of faith burning strong inside of me. I kneel down next to him and take him in my arms. He's spitting blood, choking on it. I try to hold him as up right as possible. I stare at his undressed upper body, the dark Marks spiraling around him, they're deep lines, wounds and some of them appear to be fresh – my brows join in wonder. But knowing that I do not have much time, I quickly place my palms on top of the humongous hole on his chest and press lightly in concentration. I can feel his body tighten, he instinctively wants to pull away, to avoid the pain but it's as if he knows that I'm trying to help him and forces himself to stay still.

This spell mustn't fail, not like the previous one. That terrifying possibility eats its way into my brain just like a filthy maggot and seizes me for a tiny moment; I thankfully manage to push it aside and just think of my spell. I think of him being healthy, I imagine flesh growing, closing the gap and then visualize skin pulling together, covering the gash. I think of the same things over and over again, being very dubious of my magic.

I lost record of time. I repeated the spell obsessively, out loud, having my eyes shut.

Then, he pulled away from me, sat up and turned around to face me. I removed my bloody hands from his chest and looked at my achievement carefully. There was no injury, not even a scar indicating that it had been there in the first place. I stared at him wide-eyed, impressed by what I'd managed to do.

He turned his head slightly to one side and spat out a few drops of blood that had been stuck on the walls of his mouth. He wiped his lips roughly on his arm and then gazed at me in a way I can't really describe. Was it gratitude? Surprise? Astonishment? I don't really know.

"Thank you," he said, and I could see it in his eyes – the real appreciation, something between thankfulness and admiration. It was so genuine and sincere; there was no joking and no theatricality – it made me want to kiss him.

"Anytime..." I mumbled out, feeling relieved, being able to breathe after what seemed like forever.

"The Life Commission!" He jumped on his feet, suddenly distressed, pulling me up with him.

"What? What happened?!" I asked, unsure, alarmed by his reaction.

"The Demons. *They* must've attacked already!" he whispered concerned, stretching his wings, preparing to take off.

"I thought the Commission was protected. You said no Spirit can enter..." I argued confused.

"I know; it's true. Someone must've let *Them* in..." he told me and I could hear the urgency in his voice.

"Who would do that?!" It surprised me, felt like a slap in the face – *We* were the "good guys." Weren't we?

"Someone *corrupted*, April..." he replied darkly, not wanting to accept the fact himself. "Someone that has literally sold his soul to the Devil," he added and darted up the sky faster than sound. I followed him close behind, not even thinking about the Visioner that was only centimeters away from me, still pinned on the tree with such atrocity. We left him unburied, left him to rot – something I regret to this day.

I regret killing him, but didn't think about what I had done at that time – it would be something that would torture me later on, the fact would hit with the ferocity of a wild tsunami, it would take me under, fill my lungs with water, the salt would burn my throat and I wouldn't find my way to the surface. I would twist and rotate underwater at the complete mercy of my guilt and my gratitude. Two contrasting emotions; I would feel grateful for saving the one I was now sure I loved enough to kill and would feel guilty for sentencing someone else to death.

I would drown because of these two powerful opposing currents – my thankfulness and my shame. Sometimes, you can't be a hero; you can't always be objective and just ignore your feelings and your thoughts. It's not possible. First, you always save the one you care about the most; everything, everyone else comes at second fate, that's how things work, that's what happens instinctively.

And as usual, even though I acknowledged that, I would still hate myself, I guess it's a part of my nature I can't control or overrule.

When we landed, piles and piles of dead bodies were there to greet us – it was a disturbing greeting. So revolting. My gaze fell on each and every corpse. Hundreds and hundreds of dead creatures of my kind? It sounded like a joke although it wasn't – I still didn't know what I was, couldn't name myself in the animal kingdom. So, too afraid to ask, or perhaps acknowledging the fact that no one would tell me, I thought of myself as a human hybrid, but I didn't know between what exactly – it just gave me a false feeling of identity.

What I still believe is the most terrifying thing about being soulless are the eyes. How the color fades away, how suddenly you're not yourself anymore, how nothing is reflected in your gaze, you just become another object, a material, a vacant body.

The number of corpses around us was so great, we couldn't see the ground; we had to step on them, something I couldn't get myself to do, so we decided to fly over them. From up there, the real magnitude of this destruction was apparent. There was nowhere we could land, every single bit of the Life Commission building was covered by a veil of bodies.

Suddenly, someone appeared in front of us out of nowhere – magically. I recognized him instantly; he had fought with Peter only a few days ago, right after my *Metamorphosis*.

Logan.

"Where are the Commissioners?!" Peter demanded, obviously startled by the enormity of this attack, so worried he thought there was no hope, no one to save.

"*They* took Mort with *Them*; we managed to save the four of them," he admitted bitterly, glancing at me briefly.

"What do you mean 'They took Mort'? There's no Life Commission without Mort!" he barked back, refusing to accept what his friend was telling him. Not wanting to be a part of this reality.

It was true, a terrifying truth. The Spirits had managed to take out a Life Commissioner. All of the Commissioners were of equal importance and value, if one of them "disappeared" then, there was no balance anymore. It would be like trying to find the edge of the horizon, the point where the land and the sky met; saving even a single soul seemed like something impossible at that very moment.

It was just a catastrophe, something unfixable, something of unfathomable consequences. And even I couldn't patch up that massive hole on the cloth of our dimensional world. What was I going to do in four days? Reality hit me at that instant, the moment I thought of what little time I had left. If the Natural Balance was entirely destroyed the second Mort was eliminated, saving the Sides seemed like an unreachable goal. It was very disheartening.

I had trouble breathing again, inhaling and exhaling properly after what I'd heard.

"Where are the four of them?" Peter asked again, still stunned by what had gone through his ears.

"Underground, in the Human world," Logan declared.

"What!? You know that humans aren't supposed to know about *Us*!" Peter just erupted, so furious and aware of the danger.

"I know! Of course I know! We didn't have another choice!" Logan yelled back at him, annoyed by the fact that he had thought he was so ignorant and unaware.

I wanted to go there immediately.

"Give me your hands," I ordered them, outstretching both of my palms towards them. They examined the level of seriousness mirrored in my eyes and understood I wasn't in the mood of arguing with anyone or anything. They both placed their palms in mine with a significant amount of unwillingness and thoughtfulness.

I closed my eyes forming a spell in my head, and I could feel them staring at me inquiringly. I thought of the Life Commission members, told myself I wanted to be wherever they were, I wanted the two guys to come with me. I concentrated for less than a nanosecond and found myself in an underground tunnel – I was getting so used to using my new skill, it almost happened instantly.

Pete and Logan let go of my hands and pulled away from me astonished.

The tunnel was dimly lit by a few candles. The smell of moist dirt overflowed around us, our feet sunk in thick mud and our eyes glowed in the darkness of this claustrophobic chamber. The boys and I, couldn't really see anything, we could only hear the heartbeats of the horrified Commissioners.

"Vie?" I enquired, as calmly as I could, walking closer to her scent. I heard crying, a sob she tried to compress to nonexistence futilely.

"It's gone, everything is over!" she said between her gasps, devastated, hopeless, admitting defeat.

I kneeled down on all fours and crawled towards her. She had her back against the wall, had brought her knees to her chest; had turned herself into a tight, shaking ball. There was nothing I could do or say to comfort her, to make her stop grieving and any attempt to that would be lame, because *We* all knew the truth. So I just put my arms around her, and allowed myself to cry with her.

Lost in an ocean of misery and desperation.

Drowning once again, my heart sunk in my chest like a rock.

26. Sleepless

Four days.

That's all I had. How did that happen? How did *everything* happen? How did ten days just pass by like that? So quickly and unnoticeably? It felt like a punch in my stomach, and it was hard not to be afraid especially now that Mort was out of the game.

I thankfully still had the diamond, and I knew it was the hope everyone needed to cling on to so badly.

When I showed it to Vie, she pulled away, both scared and satisfied. She looked at me like a mother, with considerable worry and contained optimism. "We might have a chance..." she breathed, wiping her eyes with her fingers.

"That's what I thought too..." I admitted, closing my palm around it – protectively, this was a piece of jewelry that I shouldn't lose.

Everyone's fate hung on my lips. One wrong word and everything would be over. And when I realized that, that I was the last tangible creature everybody counted on, it terrified me; I had hopes that perhaps the Life Commission would help me in some way the night of the Full Moon, and now, the Life Commission was powerless, almost did not exist anymore. Every expectation I had from them came crumbling down.

Once again, I felt alone.

I would've cried about that too, but didn't. This was serious; and I was in too deep to even think about swimming out of this situation, it wasn't a choice anymore – it had never been. I could only grit my teeth and deal with it. That was the ugly truth, a truth I could only confront.

No tears and no fears.

Not anymore.

We were underground in the Human Side for hours. A temptation burned my chest, I was *home* and I just wanted to jump out of this den, to leave all of this mess behind me – to just be human again. But it wasn't possible, if something like me walked around in the human world it could end up... let's say... in a lab, undergoing experiments, thought of as an alien.

It was better for the humans to be ignorant. In that way the Balance was kept safe. The Life Commission feared that if any human found out about the dimensions everything would be at huge risk of collapsing. It was no surprise that humans destroyed their own world, their own kind; what would stop them from ruining the Side of Life? The Commission thought that what they didn't know about, they couldn't harm.

Though I still felt human in a way, felt and still feel like a part of that world, I found logic in what they believed. Agreed with them; it was better for everybody.

We were all stuck on each other in that tiny hideout with the humidity making us sweat, making the hair glue to our skulls. Water was dripping from the ceiling and the amount of oxygen in there seemed so little; it felt like we were breathing in each others' exhales. And for some reason, I couldn't take my eyes off of Peter's shirtless torso. It wasn't because I thought of the Marks on his skin as ugly; I didn't even pay attention to that...

He looked so... beautiful.

"Stop doing that... We're not alone..." he said, so soundlessly, almost inaudibly; he could feel my gaze on him. I turned my face away in awkwardness and realized that everyone was watching me. I let my head tilt backwards and rest on the wall; I stared at the ceiling and allowed a loud exhale to come out of my lungs. I felt embarrassed, uncomfortable but at the same time thankful. I think I was just glad He was with me; I was trying to take in every part of him, his muscular physique, his broad shoulders I so badly wanted to hide in, his eyes, the way his hair folded into waves, the smell of his sweat, even the sound of his steady heartbeat.

I was too happy; it sounds ironic, but I felt happy, ecstatic just by looking at him.

I was scared, expected the Commissioners to ask me why I was covered in mud and blood, but they never did, didn't even open their mouths to talk to each other, as though they already knew exactly what had happened, or were just mourning for Mort's loss. I couldn't know; they just eyed me in a very weird way.

At some point, late at night, we were back at the Commission building. I needed to wash myself so I made the trip to the nearby lake. I left my clothes on the river bank and fell into the water completely naked. I wanted to wash every part of that day off of me, to get out clean – in every possible definition of the word.

I swam, the water was cold but I didn't mind, I actually liked it, it had a soothing effect on my tired muscles and joints. The Locket was safely around my neck, but I regularly checked my neckline with my hand, just to make sure the diamond was still there. I lost record of time and felt myself relaxing; I could breathe unbothered, calm. All I could hear was the sound of the water as it caressed the shore and all I could see was the reflection of the stars on the water's surface. I started feeling sleepy, felt my eyelids closing, but I didn't want to leave. It was beautiful. It was me and myself – nobody else, and I enjoyed that.

I ended up moving in the water having my eyes shut. It seemed like nothing could ruin this moment, it was simply too perfect to be destroyed – but as usual I expected too much. I suddenly bumped into something that appeared to be a log; I opened my eyes and jumped away at the sight of the dead body floating in front of me, out of breath – disgusted by the fact that I had touched it.

It was the corpse of a man, someone that had lost his soul.

Every little bit of tranquility I had battled to create burned into ashes, at that very instant. Every part of this day I had managed to push out of the corners of my mind found its way back in. I felt mad, confused, revolted. And as if that wasn't enough, I could now think of myself in a different way, I could use a new adjective.

Murderer.

I thought of what I'd done to the Visioner at that very second.

I ran out of the lake panic-stricken, thrown off of my feet, refusing to accept that. I slipped in my muddy, blood-stained clothes not even bothering to clean them, I ran away, sprinted to my room and locked myself in there, ripped my garments off of me, threw them out of my window and wrapped a blanket around myself. I shuddered – this person couldn't be me. I stared at myself in the mirror and didn't recognize me anymore.

I sat on the edge of my mattress, in my underwear, having my hands pressed between my knees – scared of me, staring into nothingness. I examined my room, checked for any kind of difference.

There was a clean pair of clothes right next to me. A blouse and Bermuda pants. I wore them. Then, I crawled in my bed, pulled the bed covers up to my nose and turned myself into a ball. And although I was just about to sleep seconds ago, I had to force my eyes shut with all of my strength. I lied to myself, whispered out loud that this was just a bad dream, that I would wake up in the morning and nothing of this would have happened. I repeated those words over and over again, but it didn't work. My entire body quivered, the hairs on my arms stood on edge, and I started sweating.

A constricting feeling squashed me around the chest – guilt. A feeling I had always hated. A feeling that overpowered me every time, even for the slightest mistake. But this wasn't a harmless mistake; I had the responsibility for someone's death.

It was a load I couldn't lift.

Then, I started thinking about all those bodies I'd seen surrounding the Commission building a few hours ago. Dozens of them; I was supposed to protect them; I was supposed to guard everybody. I had failed. I had failed to do that as well. I wasn't responsible just for the Visioner's death, but for everybody's death.

I felt I was suffocating. This responsibility swallowed me piece by piece; I felt like I was decaying, I felt filthy and dirty. I tossed and turned in my bed trying to convince myself to sleep, albeit I knew that wouldn't happen – it was a lost battle. My eyes watered. No matter how bad I felt, and in spite of my suffering and my huge feeling of remorse, I could not make myself feel regret and that made me worry; made me think I might be turning into a monster.

I didn't regret killing the Visioner and of course I didn't regret saving Pete. I did not. I actually thanked God he was still with me, thanked God for choosing everyone else instead of him. It was a sick and monstrous thought – I know, but that is the truth. Raw and unprocessed.

I stared out of my opened window, into the night sky. I could see the moon, bright and shining, it glimmered so beautifully and it was almost full. Goosebumps traveled up my spine. I stayed there for a while, crying, exhausted and confused, yearning for my simple, old, human life once more.

At some point, I decided to fly out of my room and just walk. I jumped out of the window and landed in a garden I had never been to before. There was nothing special about it; the ground was just dressed in grass and a few trees surrounded it in a perfect circle. Berry trees. I could hear the sound of water somewhere faraway. I lay down. A cool breeze made me shiver a little bit, forced me to fold my arms, to let my wings fall over my shoulders like a blanket.

I heard the sound of cracking grass behind me, someone's walking – I sat up responsively.

"What are you doing here?" Peter asked me, his eyes looked almost as tired as mine. I didn't need to be told to realize he was out here for the same reason as me.

"You can't sleep, can you?" I questioned, eyeing him weakly.

"Not really," he admitted, sitting right beside me. "Quite a day…" he murmured.

"Yeah." I breathed, close to inaudible.

"At least we got the medallion," he added, laying down, placing his hands behind his head so casually.

Silence from my side.

"I don't think you want to talk," he noticed, gazing at me tenderly.

"Not really…" I confessed and it honestly sounded like a whimper, a moan; I lay down as well, exhaled loudly, under pressure.

He passed his arm around me and pulled me closer to him so abruptly I almost lost my breath for a moment. He held me against his chest and kissed me softly but passionately, till I could think of nothing else.

"Sleep," he whispered in my ear, caressing my hair, tucking a strand behind my ear. I didn't think, half-hypnotized already, light-headed, absolutely paralyzed. I was surrounded by his warmth, his smell, his touch, it seemed like too much to handle. I clung on to the fabric of his shirt, having my head over his heart, *listening* to its strong beat I always found so comforting.

I closed my eyes and slept as if nothing had happened.

Unworried, at ease.

PART 3
The Battle

27. When the truth is not ugly but abusive

It's raining heavily. I can see and hear lightning; the clouds' color is close to black. It's dark and cold and a vicious wind is whipping me relentlessly. I look around disorientated, I'm in a valley and there isn't a single tree or flower standing. There's just mud and my feet are sinking in it. Everything around me appears to be so... dead.

My parents! I can see them floating above the ground with the grace of gods, extending their hands towards me, smiling at me. My automatic reaction is to reach out to them. Then, Peter appears in front of me, in the form of a human, puts his body between me and them and gives me a petrifying look.

They suck his soul out, his body is completely paralyzed, his green eyes lose their color, and his empty body falls to the ground. These are not my parents. I scream and try to fly. Only then do I realize I don't have wings and strands of chocolate brown hair hit my face because of the strong breeze – I'm human again. I'm a target. I run as fast as I can, but I'm too slow; my knees sink in the slush, my supernatural strength is gone. I panic.

I shout, and jump up in my bed. A Powerball flies out of my hand and hits the wall of my room, burning a hole through it. *A dream, it was just a dream*, I think to myself, gasping for air.

It was *just* a dream.

I couldn't control my magic anymore; it just came out of me involuntarily, even when I stood up to get out of my room. I opened the door and took the whole thing with me. I couldn't understand why that happened, why suddenly everything around me seemed so breakable and fragile; it felt like just a touch was enough to get things done. I had to pull back, to measure the strength even in the slightest of movement and action. If I did not do that I could do some serious damage, I could hurt someone.

I found myself walking absentmindedly in the Commission building, trying to shake off that nightmare I had seen. I was thirsty, so I got outside, in one of the numerous gardens available and stumbled on some kind of blooming bush I had never come across before and satisfied myself.

I struggled to follow Peter's advice – I didn't think much; or at least, tried to. I actually didn't want to think at all. I didn't want to know and I didn't want to learn. I believed that this was as bad as it could get and I was so sure that there was no way it could get any worse than this.

The final countdown had started. Three days to go. A huge burden pressed my chest, and at certain points made me feel like I couldn't breathe, made me feel as though a massive anaconda was squeezing the life out of me.

This weight I felt could only be the pressure – the pressure of everyone's expectation; their expectation and almost certainty that I would win. That I would restore The Balance. I guess they lied to themselves, desperate to find that hope that was so tiny and trivial they couldn't even see.

It was pathetic. It was the only word I could use to describe the situation.

Pathetic.

"Why did you do this?" a weak, female voice asked me. I turned around in search of the owner of that question. A woman sat under an Oak, her knees were pressed against her chest and her wings fell over her shoulders powerlessly, veiling her body like a blanket – all I could see were her swollen eyes.

She must've been crying for quite a while.

"Why did you let *Us die*?" she demanded with detectable bitterness. My heart tightened. I didn't know how to reply. I stood there for a second unsure of how I was supposed to react. Then, in discomfort I couldn't disguise, I made a few steps towards her and kneeled down. She pushed her back against the tree; it nearly looked like she was afraid of me and avoided my gaze.

"You have every right to hate me," I said, sitting on the ground, crossing my legs, facing her. There was no satisfactory excuse to reason what I had failed to do. I accepted the fact.

"That's all you have to say?" she wondered, surprised by my state of indirect remorse, curling her wings on her back.

"What do you want me to say?" I asked back, neutrally, mortified.

A long pause followed.

"*I just hope you don't betray Us like you did this time. If you leave Us for the Spirits...*" Her voice trailed off. What? What was she saying? "*We, along with the humans, have no chance of surviving. Everyone is praying you don't turn into a Demon.*" She finished and I could feel my jaw hanging open.

"What?" I breathed, more to myself, feeling my heart thudding in my chest in reaction to what I'd heard. Then, someone grabbed me, picked me off the ground and dragged me with him – outrageously fast.

Peter.

"What did she tell you?" he barked at me, anguished. We were in the arena. I just looked at him coldly, putting on a façade of fake composure. This time, I decided that I wouldn't scream and I wouldn't cry; it was the apogee of this madness called my life.

I tried so hard to hide my shock and my disgust that my entire body quivered, it shook and trembled uncontrollably. I felt anger; rage I had never felt so strongly.

Fury engulfed me.

"What do you think she told me?" I retorted slowly, tightening my hands into fists, so tightly, my fingernails cut through the skin of my palms. I gave him a lethal look and smiled toxically, feeling my chest burning with this new kind of soul-eating wrath I had felt for the very first time.

His gaze darkened in fear of me, fearing what I would do next, sensing my fury. The fury smoldering me, eating me piece by piece, until, all that was left from me was embers.

"April, I –" He breathed in an apologetic tone, but didn't find the words to continue. He knew it the moment he stared through my eyes – he couldn't reveal the truth in any mild way. I already knew.

"SHUT UP!" I growled, lashing out at him, putting my hands on his neck, pushing him against a wall, too blinded and overwhelmed by my wild emotions to even think that I was actually strangling him.

My perfect poker face had fallen off.

"April – I – can't – breathe –" He begged, panting, trying to get my hands off of him, attempting to curl his fingers around my hands unsuccessfully. I'm going to kill him. Only then does that fact register. I let go – even though I'm fuming, that is not my intention; instead, I slap him right in the face, exactly like a tennis player hits a backhand.

I'm using power, strength that can be fatal.

He's on the ground, holding his face in one hand and his neck in the other. His body is folding reflexively, bracing. This is the first time I feel something other than rage – I feel pity. I drop down on my knees and grab him by the collar of his shirt, confused, feeling something between anger and concern – I just don't know which feeling is dominant.

"WHY? WHY DID YOU DO THIS TO ME?" I yelled right into his ear, and felt my eyes water. There was a moment of silence, of absolute stillness.

"I was going to tell you… I swear…" he whispered grudgingly and timidly.

"WHEN? WHEN I WOULD ALREADY BE ONE OF THEM?" I howled, placing my hand under his jaw raising his face so that I could see his eyes.

"April, let me explain things to you. Calm down," he said rather assertively this time, surprising me, knowing that this aggression that had taken over me could only be translated into fear.

I gave up. Got my hands off of him. Suddenly so utterly powerless and unable, allowing the tears that had swollen up in my eyes to run down on my colorless cheeks. I fell down on my butt, immobilized; staring at something faraway, lost once again in a feeling of puzzlement I would never get accustomed to.

"*We* didn't tell you because we feared that you would leave…" he began, clearing his throat, sitting up, still trying to find his breath.

"And go where?" I whispered emotionlessly, staring at my sweat-drenched palms. He didn't say anything for a while, maybe realizing that what the Life Commission had decided to do was actually stupid and absurd.

Baseless.

"Because of your human nature, the Spirits can use you, if *They* see that they cannot fight you, *They* will try to deceive you. *They'll* promise you the heavens, anything that *They know* you desire so baldly, just to own your *power*. Your *mind*," he told me, looking at me this time. I noticed his right cheek was red – it was where I'd slapped him.

"How do *They know* what I desire?" I asked, meeting his gaze, alarmed by what I'd heard.

"*They're* powerful too, April…" he said. "The Core is the only thing that can be compared to you…" he added after a second. I felt my heart jumping in my chest exactly like a dying fish. I felt my lungs expand but, couldn't take in a single ounce of oxygen.

"If *They* manage to convince you –" he began, but I cut him mid-sentence.

"*They* won't," I exclaimed, moving my head from side to side neurotically, denying even the possibility of that happening.

"Let me finish…" He pleaded with me, placing his hand on the side of my face, attempting to calm me down fruitlessly.

"If *They* manage to convince you…" he paused for an instant and met my terrified gaze, "… *you will become a Demon.*"

A chill traveled up my spine and I felt everything I had eaten moving up my esophagus. I thankfully swallowed everything back down, stood up and walked away, tripping, so dizzy by what I'd heard – shocked.

"April…" He grabbed me by my arm, just when I was about to fall.

"Let me walk. I need to think…" I said pulling my arm out of his palm, knowing that he would try to prevent me from doing what I wanted, worried about me.

"But…" He tried to argue, outstretching his hand towards me, placing it on my waist.

"I SAID LET GO!" I barked so irritated, just wanting to be left alone. Suddenly, my hands were on fire and flames ate my fingers. I just pushed him away, still unaware of the fact that I had literally ignited. A sound of pain came out of him. In just one touch, I had managed to burn through the fabric of his shirt, to damage the skin on his shoulder and to make him bang on the arena's wall.

But I didn't care. At all. All I could hear was that phrase repeating in my head:

"*You will become a Demon.*" "*You will become a Demon.*" "*You will become a Demon.*"

I couldn't feel anything other than the heat, the rage and the desperation burning me. I broke into a run, trying to run away from the truth itself. I was crying, like a baby; I felt ill.

It all made sense now. This truth was surrounding me from the very first day. When everyone told me I should fight my human nature, because that nature of mine made me susceptible and vulnerable. I knew they were hiding something from me, but I could've never imagined something like this. This was just... too much. It was beyond the climax. There was no metric unit to calculate the level of this insanity.

It was just *too much*.

I cried till I actually threw up. Somewhere in the woods. Alone, exactly as I wanted to be. This truth wasn't just ugly, it abused you, it beat you mercilessly, up to the point where you thought you would pass out, and in fact, that's what you wished would happen so that the torture would stop, but it never did.

I lay down on the ground and lost record of time. I recoiled and allowed my wings to cover me – I suddenly felt cold. It was getting dark; there was just a weak twilight. I felt the vibrations of footsteps; someone was looking for me and only then did I understand that I had been out in the forest for the entire day.

I didn't move. I stayed there; I guess I didn't care, or perhaps I was just too exhausted to even bother. I closed my eyes, wanting to sleep, to forget, to feel safe once again.

I kept my eyes shut even when he picked me up in his arms. I didn't have to see him to recognize him, I could tell by his scent, by how careful he was when he held me, by the sound of

his breathing, his unique warmth and of course, by his heartbeat. That beautiful beat.
Peter.
In just a moment guilt leaked into me. I regretted what I had done to him; it wasn't his fault, he had no say.
"I'm sorry..." I squeaked almost inaudibly, smelling the burnt flesh, touching the blistered and bloody skin of his shoulder, healing it routinely.
"Shhh, it's okay..." he reassured me, and kissed me on my forehead.
I was horrified, shook like a leaf in the wind.
I knew I was condemned.

28. Granted

This truth I had become aware of so unexpectedly and abruptly had startled me to an inconceivable point. I thought I was on the verge of madness. Everything was out of order and out of plan. I thought I knew I was on my own when Mort was taken out by the Demons, but after this final piece of the puzzle I felt isolated.

Why?

I could think of nothing else other than that same question made out of just one syllable.

Why?

Why had they done this to me? Why had they kept me in the dark? Why should *The End* be *tomorrow*? Why should it be me? Why? Why?

I was the last pawn on this chessboard and in fact the most weak and vulnerable of all. The king. Because even though the king is thought of as the one with all the strength and rule, it is actually the most unable and incapable pawn. You can only move a king one square at a time. And my move needed to be a winning one, which was impossible in my eyes.

The odds were against me.

I had to pull myself together; to grit my teeth and tighten my heart and just get it over with. That was my perception of the situation. I had to get it over with. What was meant to happen would happen. I had no control over that. It was the first time I realized that in spite of my power, of my mind; of my ability to do and have anything I wanted and desired I was actually defenseless. Nothing.

It was that fact that made me even angrier.

"Are you still mad at me?" he asked me, walking with me, across the river bank.

"I'm not mad at you, Pete," I said quietly. "That's not physically possible," I added trying to joke about what had taken place the other day. I felt him smile. Crookedly. He tried to grab my hand, but pulled away the moment his skin touched mine.

"You're hot," he exclaimed, placing his index finger on his lips, licking it, afraid the skin would blister.

"I'll take that as a compliment of my good looks." I mocked feeling a bit uncomfortable. I didn't need to tell him why my entire body burned, why I was soaked in sweat constantly. He knew it was magic, my anxiety and agony coming to the surface.

"I told you that the hardest part is to control it," he told me, suddenly serious. "And that slap... was quite something..." he said, trying to tease about it in vain, remembering that in awe, moving his hand from his lips to the side of his face.

His cheek was almost entirely covered by a big, purple bruise, and it seemed to pain him.

I healed it automatically, in just a breath.

"You fixed me, didn't you?" He questioned me, surprised by the fact he didn't feel his face sting, or hurt at his touch. I nodded once. He smiled. "I kind of fear you whenever you do that. Naturally; as if it's nothing worth attention," he stated.

I remained silent.

"I have a question," I began. "What... What do Demons look like?" It was the only thing I didn't know, and something I needed to know.

He hesitated for a moment, unsure of what to tell me. He stopped walking and held me by the shoulders, ignoring my insanely high body temperature. "Demons are spirits; they don't look like anything..." he told me.

My eyebrows pulled together immediately, he continued just when I was about to argue, to doubt what he was telling me. "Demons... cannot be killed, even when the Core is in the Locket," he informed me, pointing at the medallion around my neck. He stopped for a second, forming his next sentence; thinking of the words he should use. "They just fall into some kind of lethargy," he explained.

"But what if they attack me? How can I defend myself?" I bombarded him, agonized for some reason, feeling as though I didn't know enough.

"They can't attack you, April. At least not physically…" He tried to reassure me.

"But?" I wanted to know, just so badly.

"They'll just play with your head, your thoughts, your emotions; they'll 'illusion' you maybe…" He just said it as if it was something insignificant, of trivial or even no importance.

"And you think that's okay?!" I retorted in disbelief, stunned by how easily and unresponsively he had mouthed it.

"That's not what I said." He disagreed, staring right into my eyes. "Just…" He needed time to think of how he should continue. "Just keep in mind, that they're sly, canny creatures. Okay?" He shook me once, with all the force he could find in his hands, gazing at me in a way that reminded me of hopelessness. Terror.

I nodded, feeling his horror being transmitted into me through his tight fingers. I didn't need to be told to know that he feared for me. For my *End*.

"How do I get to *Their* side?" I enquired, feeling tension.

He smiled, astonishing me, eyeing me in a way I thought could only be translated as sympathy. "When will you realize you can do anything, just by using your mind?" he asked me rhetorically.

I shook my head and said, "I guess I'll never get used to it."

"It's good you don't take things for granted," he commented.

My gaze fell to the ground, in reaction to what he had just expressed. "I'm not to be taken for granted," I muttered lamely, thinking that tomorrow I would stop being myself; I would turn into some sort of Spirit and just run around sucking souls. I would be an ally of the Demons, of the Core himself. I would be capable of killing my own parents; I would lose my own will and my own judgment. They would manage to brainwash me, convince me into becoming some kind of merciless, brainless monster.

I would stop being April.

That phrase I had mouthed was my pathetic apology. I apologized to him so sure I would betray him. I apologized fearing that indeed, deep inside, I had a dark side that would become dominant.

His hands fell off of my shoulders, and I could feel him gawking at me, but I didn't have the guts to stare back at him, so instead, I chose to look at my feet. He inhaled deeply and exhaled loudly. "Having an attitude suits you better than pitying yourself," he whispered. "And only by having an attitude you may have a chance of surviving this, oh, and don't look at me like that; helplessly, you're anything but helpless. You're admitting defeat, before you've even given battle. And don't you think, I haven't noticed that," he said, and walked away, obviously infuriated by my state of mind.

His words had a resentful effect. I ran after him.

"I didn't ask for this..." I breathed, clinging on the sleeve of his shirt, feeling my legs wobble, letting my eyes water.

He just stared at me; at the despair reflected in my eyes. "I didn't ask for this either..." he whispered back, pushing the collar of his shirt with his finger, down enough for me to see the *Marked* skin. "But sometimes, things happen to us and we can only deal with them," he said, a bit more understanding this time, then placed his palm on the back of my skull and kissed me on my forehead. He then curled his fingers around mine and forced me to let go of the fabric of his top.

He paced away.

And as the sound of his heartbeat faded, I sank in this ocean I had been in from the start of these two torturous weeks. With the only difference that now, I had a complete picture of this vastness. Initially, I was being given pieces for me to put together, and I now suddenly realized that I had a finished puzzle in front of me. It was a wave of astonishment that hit me forcefully.

There was just one little but very important piece missing – the end, the finale. And that's when I understood, for good, that I had no way of getting out of this intricate situation other than confronting my obstacles, my fears, my emotions and ultimately, myself.

29. A suffering of the mind

You can never be ready. No matter how much effort you've put into preparing yourself, into trying to put your emotions in order, into evening out your shaky and unstable breathing – you can never be ready.

You are never ready.

The sun had set. It was today, tonight – the End. I formed the word with my lips but didn't give it sound; I did not allow myself to. It was enough to give me chills though, to immobilize me for a long second. I was on the roof of the Commission building, hundreds and hundreds of feet above the ground, staring at some faraway mountains, waiting for the autumn full moon to climb up the night sky and signal the beginning of my cosmic task.

I felt tired, exhausted, worn. All of this time of mental and physical unrest had such a massive impact on me. The pressure, the pressure was the worst thing about this whole experience, the one I hated the most. I felt like Atlas himself, as if I carried the weight of the world on my shoulders – and that was true in so many ways. At least, after this night everything would come to an end – a happy one or a sad one, it didn't matter which one, I just wanted this story to reach its ending.

I wanted to *breathe* again – a real, normal breath; and I didn't care if this breath I would take in would be a breath of relief or frustration. I simply thought that that was unimportant.

I saw it; the first ray of moonlight. My eyes glared hypnotized by some strong, primitive instinct that left me absolutely blank in just a fragment of a moment. This was a different kind of moonlight; it had a peculiar and unnatural effect, a paralyzing one. It disabled you, made every single thought drain out of your brain. It ordered you to do one thing.

To follow it.

And that's what I did, I ran after the arousing moon exactly like a blinded and unintelligent moth. I couldn't think or feel; I just followed at an astounding speed. I felt a unique kind of euphoria and ecstasy I had never experienced before. I guess the kind of feeling you feel when you're sure of your every move, of your every breath, when you feel that your destiny is this. A sense of who you really are, of what you are, of where you actually belong.

It was sunshine before the hurricane. A deception. A mistake of your intuition.

Somehow, the moon told me to stop, to come to a halt. I turned my wide eyes towards the night sky, in a way that reminded me of an animal crazed by rabies. Then, I suddenly fell down on the ground, released by that mysterious spell, fully conscious and aware of the world around me.

My fingers curled around the black diamond hanging down my neck immediately, with maternal protectiveness. I looked around, through my glowing, unblinking eyes. *Where am I?* I thought to myself. I was surrounded by trees, planted in a perfect circle.

It was time. I knew it was time to go to *Their* Side the moment I felt the moon's glow caressing my skin so tenderly but harshly at the same time. The instant I felt it shining on me with the power of a spotlight.

It chose me. I was the Chosen.

I knew it because I felt it; everything suddenly made so much more... sense. All the confusion and bewilderment I had been feeling just burned into ashes, in that meaningful instant. It was like a single, breathtaking goose bump rising up your spine. It hit me with such force and almost brutality that it made my heart stop and made my eyes pop; I froze completely. My hair stood on edge and I could feel drops of sweat wetting my temples already.

I started focusing, casting the spell that would take me to the Spirits' Side. I was going against my will to stay, knowing that by doing so, I would not only be the one responsible for the Visioner's death but for the death of an entire dimension.

I close my eyes, still on my knees, feeling the moon shining on me. I think of *It*, though I don't really know what it looks like; I imagine it's dark, empty, hostile – *dead*. I remain in that position for quite a while, tightening the black diamond in my palm hoping to find reassurance, and when I finally open my eyes what I see is far worse than what I have created in my head.

Macabre, and gruesome; I'm wordless. I can't believe what my senses are telling me to believe. I'm afraid to accept that this is a tangible fact. A reality.

The first thing I see are the bodies. Naked, abused human bodies. From innocent, tiny infants to wrinkly elders, eaten by this acidic, flesh feasting mud they're soaked in. Acres and acres covered in corpses, I can hear the sizzling sound of that toxic sludge as it burns through them. I can smell the roasted blood and the smoldered skin. Their mouths are hanging open but they're not breathing and their eyes are just a clear white – they're *soulless*.

I feel any kind of food I had managed to eat through the day rising up my throat in an instant of nausea and disgust. True sickness. I swallow so hard, I think I'm pushing down my tongue too. I inhale and taste the blood in my mouth. The scent is so strong I feel like the oxygen around me is inadequate.

Why are they here? The humans? It's not their Side... I think to myself, surprised to find creatures of my kind – well, of my ex – kind, if you can say that. Though, I still feel connected to them in so many ways; I can imagine their vulnerability and frailty, their terror, their inability to run or hide; their pain. And for the first time, I'm glad I'm not one of them. This sight left a very bitter taste in my mouth and aggrieved me inconceivably.

I stand up cautiously knowing that *They* can't be very far away from here.

I scan my surroundings, taking every little detail in. First, I throw my gaze on the sky, it is a gray so dark, you can call it black, I can hear distant thunder and lightning. I would soon learn that there is no sun in this world; it is a world of constant darkness and gloom. There is absolutely *nothing*, an empty sky and a stripped ground.

No plant, no animal, no sign of life.

I feel my feet sinking in the mud, in the same poisonous slush that is eating away the dead in front of me. It wraps itself around the ankles of my bare feet, tries to burn through me repeatedly but it cannot and the only thing I feel is a gentle, rather pleasant and harmless touch. I smile in satisfaction, at its incapability.

I'm immortal, that's why... I tell myself, somehow reluctant; it was a fact I had not yet accepted. And only then did I become aware of the fact that what was actually protecting me was the Locket. The diamond glowed so otherworldly, so beautifully, sending white beams towards every direction through my tight fingers still clinging on it.

I let go mesmerized and it just levitates for a moment, then, it lands smoothly on my chest again.

"APRIL! APRIL!"

A scream, someone screams out my name, so desperately, in a pitch so high, in such distress, I almost do not recognize the so familiar to me, owner of it.

My mother.

Oh God... Is the only thing I can think of; *no, it cannot be her, they can't have her, it's... it's impossible...* "Mom?!" I yell out, unsure of where to run, which direction to follow, I'm lost, I look around disorientated.

"APRIL!"

She shrieks again and now I'm certain it's her, *They* have her; I can listen to her cry, to the painful sobbing – to her torture, a mixture of shouts and hurtful moans. "MOM!" I bark in fear, fearing that something might have happened to her. My hands fly to the sides of my face, in a gesture of undisputable panic. I sprint forward, tripping on the half-eaten bodies, overwhelmed by this sudden tsunami of fright.

I can't think clearly, and I have forgotten something basic.

I'm still between the burnt carcasses, I stop. "WHERE ARE YOU?!" I call out with all of the power I can find in my tired lungs.

The second I shout that, I feel my blood run cold.

I can feel *Them*. I'm surrounded by *Them*, *Cold*. I can just feel the *Cold* and suddenly I'm immobilized, I'm as stiff as a statue. I close my eyes in realization of what has actually happened. One, sour tear slides out of my lid, on to my eyelashes and runs down my pale cheek – the feeling of repulsion is almost immediate.

It's a trap.

I'm trapped, I know I'm trapped, I'm at *Their* mercy and it's all my fault. It was one of their brain-games, they deceived me, played with my head, exactly like Peter had warned me. This iciness I feel is constricting me now, my body is warning me, although now, it's too late.

For some reason, I feel this human urge to grab someone and strangle him, to beat someone up, to exterminate in the way humans do. But *They're* Spirits, *They* can be the air I breathe in, *They* can be the murk itself, I cannot catch *Them*, I can't kill *Them*, because *They* simply do not exist in the way I know and am familiar with.

That acknowledgement is enough to make me feel powerless. *Nothing* compared to *Them*.

My heart is banging against my ribs with such ferocity I think it is going to jolt out of my chest and a knot has tied itself around my throat, pulling tighter by the second. I stand there motionlessly, unable to feel my limbs, so totally helpless.

Even breathing is painful, hard to do. I feel like a hammer is battering on my head, on my skull over and over again, continuously. I know *They*'ll attack, maybe not in a physical manner but a mental one and that's what I'm afraid of the most. Perhaps, I can handle a physical torture better than a torture of the mind – that, I might not be able to bear.

I'm shaking, my entire body is spasming; I'm waiting for it, I'm just waiting for it because there is nothing else I can do now. I don't try to prepare myself for it; I know that that is something impossible and unachievable. I'm fully aware of the fact that it is simply going to happen and I just know that I'll have to bear it, to stand it.

And it happens.

They attack.

30. Pandemonium

Pandemonium.
Just that.
A series of images, sounds, scents, tastes and textures crazes me. Every scene gives way to the next one rapidly, so fast you don't have time to process it, as though everything is on fast forward. It doesn't just confuse you; it makes you dizzy; it makes you trip and fall down on your knees surrendering to that mental tornado in your head.

A tornado that destroys your little, personal world, the kind of tornado that shatters everything and leaves you blank and vacant – with absolutely no control over anything, not even over your own mind. And that is a cruel thing. That means you're insane, mad – but most importantly, you are weak. When you lose the ability to think and act you immediately turn into something frail and fragile. Like a flower – utterly powerless, at the complete mercy of others.

First, I'm in a bright, shining room with my grandfather. I stand up, and pull myself out of the mud, which I'm not aware of, so hypnotized, deceived by what *They* are creating in my head, by what *They* are making me see, by what *They* are making me believe.

I reach out to him, smiling – my whole face is glowing.

'*He's not in a coma; He's alive, he's with you!*'

That's what they're telling me, in a voice that is so sweet and melodic – so incredibly persuasive. I can see him; he is still in a blue hospital robe but he is standing right in front of me, gazing at me emptily. He's alive; my grandfather, someone I perhaps loved more than my own parents.

I run to him, but when I try to put my arms around him, I realize that I'm actually embracing myself. My eyes open wide, and my head moves around spastically as I'm trying to understand what has really happened.

I'm not confused, I'm panicking as I now am in a sea, drowning, fighting with wild currents that disorient me and I can't differentiate the up from the down. In reality though, I'm just battling with the mud I'm soaked in, hitting on the bodies surrounding me, which through my deceptive eyes I see as massive rocks. I have now reached the sea bed and I feel like I cannot breathe, as though my lungs are indeed swollen due to water. I can taste the salt, I can feel it burning my throat; and just when I'm convinced my heart will stop beating I find myself in a valley.

I'm still panting and coughing, lying down in crispy, untrimmed grass, my facial expression turns from miserable to happy automatically, unnaturally fast. I'm facing the sky, and it's dark. Then, abruptly snow starts falling down the sky so violently I can feel it battering on my body. But truly, what is hitting my body with such brutality is water – a strong, dense downpour of *Their* world. I feel pain, but this time it's not just the hail, I feel the *Cold* – and it's the first time I'm in touch with reality after a long while of living in a world that existed exclusively in my head, in my possessed mind.

That happens for just a minuscule fragment of a second, but it's enough, enough for me to *almost* realize what is actually happening, it is enough for me to doubt what my untrustworthy, delusional eyes are demanding me to believe.

The Spirits are conscious of that fact, of the fact that I might have become aware of even the slightest of detail about the torture *They're* inflicting on me. So *They* hit me in another, vigorous wave, and everything *They* have creates replays in my bewildered mind.

I experience everything from beginning to end, time after time, but still whenever I find myself in that valley, I can feel the *Cold*, again and again. There's this little part of my mind that has been awakened, that is alert, a part of myself that has managed to overrule *Their* spell. I know everything is a lie, nothing of it is real, but yet, I can't fight back – I react to every single vision and hallucination *They* create.

Every time I attempt to think, I realize that I'm trapped in my own head – just resisting, making the effort to comprehend makes *Them* nervous and causes *Them* agony and I can tell that, because each time I try to find my way from insanity to sanity, *They* attack me in the same, identical way, as if *They* have no back up plan, as if this is *Their* only option and strategy.

I'm in that ocean again; I can feel the water surrounding me and engulfing me, but in spite of the fact that I feel terrified, I kneel down and hold my head in my hands, bending over into my own lap, screaming in frustration – refusing to accept what my distorted senses are forcing me to accept.

After that very crucial moment, I can think – with extreme difficulty, but I can *think*. I try to ignore, to push aside, every false and fake scent, sound and image *They* insist on bombarding me with so persistently and with such discipline.

And for the first time, after what seemed like an eternity, I unfold my trembling body and open my tear-stung eyes to view the real world.

I can think, I own my mind, so I have *power*.

What can They want? What can They desire? I ask myself, tightening my temples as the Spirits try to interfere in my thoughts once again. Futilely and vainly. I instantaneously built a unique mental wall between *Them* and me, I shut *Them* out pulling myself out of the mud that has almost eaten the clothes off of my body, but is incapable of moving past my skin and flesh.

I can now use my brain's full potential and supernatural capability.

What are They looking for?

I question myself repetitively in anguish, using the exact same inquiry, not even changing a single comma.

I knew they wanted something, but being so overwhelmed did not allow me to think of the apparent. I was trying to be logical, to think and come to conclusions after taking every aspect of the situation into account. The first thing that could not be doubted and I was sure of, was that *They* couldn't possibly desire my soul – my soul could not be taken by Demons, my soul was and is immortal. The second fact I could also be confident about was that *They* certainly weren't trying to defend themselves — *They* may be powerful creatures, and I admit that, but *They* are dumb, *They* don't think, *They* act based on *Their* desire for souls or according to the Core's orders.

The *Core*.

It suddenly started making sense. But what could the Core want, what could that so insanely strong spirit fear? What could stop *It*?

The answer lay around my neck, in the beautiful jewel resting on my chest.

The Locket.

My fingers curl around the diamond spontaneously in realization of just how precious it is, in understanding of the fact that without it even the slightest chance of me winning this battle will vanish. The fact that it is desired by so many registers. I tighten my fingers around it so hard, that the stone's sharp edge cuts and wounds my palm. I feel blood dripping out of my hand but I don't let go — I'd rather hurt a little bit than to leave the medallion out of my sight or my touch.

A wave of adrenaline revitalizes me. *They're* around me, I still feel *Their* presence but *They've* stopped trying to get into my head in any way, but yet I'm very cautious; I won't victimize myself by giving *Them* the opportunity to harm me. So I make sure, that that mental wall I've created stays in place.

I think of what I should do next. The only thing that comes in my mind is that I should find the Core. That's all that matters. Nothing else. Demons themselves could never really damage me, what had happened a few seconds ago was just a lame display of power that could only be interpreted as fear.

They indeed feared for *Their* end in the exact same way I feared for mine — and it just made me a bit understanding for a moment. I thought of it from *Their* perspective; this would be the fall of *Their* great empire, the death of *Their* prestige and authority, the end of *Their* rule.

That was a bitter thought for both the Side of Life and the Spirits' Side, the feeling was identical. And once again, I felt jealous of the Humans, jealous of their ignorance. It was the only thing I used to daydream about; I imagined myself being human, I *envied* their unawareness and their lack of knowledge – and I had never been the kind of person that envies; that is jealous, that hates himself. And that's what had happened to me; I ended up hating myself – my new self. I detested who I was unimaginably.

I unfold my wings; I stretch them and flap them in spite of the fact I still feel numb. I know that being on foot isn't a good thing; I can't have a complete picture of this world, a proper panoramic view. That's what I need to do; I need to map my surroundings, to orient myself towards some direction...

I ascend in great difficulty, there's a fierce, bone-snapping wind attacking me relentlessly, and water almost zeroes my visibility. I'm as wet as it gets, I try to fly as steadily as I can manage, struggling with the extreme weather conditions. I'm slow, these circumstances do not allow me to speed up and even my powerful senses are having trouble forming a picture.

But I don't stop, I move slowly but progressively, gritting my teeth, tightening my jaw, and narrowing my eyes – every bit of me is engrossed in this task, in this struggle. When I finally fall down to the ground, I realize that it's not due to my exertion but due to someone else's spell – someone has pulled me down.

I freeze.

Suddenly, I cannot feel any exhaustion or weariness. It's like I'm being electrocuted. It's like pieces of glass are being pushed into my flesh so inhumanly and murderously. My breath catches, and I can't inhale again; the shock is so impressive I swear I felt my brain moving in my skull.

Then, the shuddering began.

This I could not call *Cold* – it was beyond that. Beyond anything I have ever experienced. I'm on my knees again, silently begging for mercy. I feel as though I'm in an ice cube, so immobilized and unable to do anything. Blood has frozen in my veins and arteries; I can feel *His* presence so deeply and so vividly; in every tissue, in every nerve, and in every capillary.

I can *taste Him* on the tip of my tongue.

It's *Him*.

That so special, inconceivably strong Spirit.

Their leader.

The *Core*.

I correct myself; I correct my original thought. I haven't found *Him*. *He* has found me. I could've never imagined anything like this. Unfathomable power. It hit you like an infrared ray, like radiation kills you from the inside out. *He* was just lethal. Toxic to me, to my nature as a Life Creature; every instinct I possessed told me to leave, to run – but I couldn't find my feet; and that's when I realized that I was too deep in this, to back out now.

I don't dare to doubt that – his authority, his unquestionable and undeniable rule over me and over everything and anything. This is my rival; I've just met my match.

This is the moment of truth. Everything leads to this.

The *End*.

31. I can give you what you've always wanted...

I'm clenching my teeth. I tighten my grip around the diamond so much, its ends cut through my tissue, till they hit my finger bones. But I can't feel pain; I can't feel a thing, so overwhelmed, so absorbed into that very moment. I look around.
Where is He? Where can He be?
The fact that I am still able to think surprises me. I thought I was too *frozen* to even breathe – that is just a sensation though, it isn't real, it's just a warning; nothing has happened yet; I find comfort in that thought, it gives me a false feeling of courage. I push my shoulders backwards and arch my back, trying to make as much room as possible for me to inflate my lungs to their full potential – resisting my own reflexes and instincts isn't just hard, it's painful – literally. I find incredible resistance, it's as though I'm in a clamp and it's squeezing the vigor out of me by the nanosecond.
I inhale.
I exhale.
I swallow, but there is no way I can push down that huge, imaginary lump in my esophagus. My heart accelerates in expectation of what will follow, even though at that particular instant I didn't know what exactly. I can now breathe somehow but my body is still paralyzed – I'm overruled, overpowered by *Him*.
Where are you?! Where are you?!
I'm screaming in my head, I'm on the verge of hysteria, mad at my incapability and vulnerability, so infuriated by my weak and irrevocable position. I let go of the Locket of Hell, abruptly and clumsily, fighting against my nature in an even more vicious manner. I raise my hand to the level of my face to view my severely gashed palm.
The sight is just appalling.

My skin hangs lifelessly attached to my sliced and chopped flesh, I can see straight through, at my bones, I've also slit my blood vessels and blood is streaming out of me as though it's just water, gallon by gallon. Only then do I become conscious of the unspeakable amount of strength with which I had been clinging on the diamond for so long and although the sight itself sends goosebumps up my spine, I cannot feel pain.

None at all. And that's what horrifies me the most.

I tighten both of my hands into two, shaking fists, desperately trying to turn my terror into fury. Fury, I could always handle better than terror, it was a feeling I preferred. This time I decide to shout out loud, to release all that anger and excruciating fright twisting my guts.

"COME ON! FINISH ME OFF!"

Tears sting my eyes the moment those words slip out of my mouth. Words soaked in hopelessness and fragility – misery. My voice echoes, once, twice, three times, four times...

Walking, I can hear someone approaching; I still can't see anything other than the darkness and the gloom, but I know it's *Him*, because as he comes closer, the colder I feel, the sicker I feel...

I can smell Him. The scent of the body *He* has taken over.

A scent I think is rather familiar to me, the fragrance of someone I know...

I root on spot, shocked, refusing to believe that this is actually happening, that I'm about to meet my *foe*.

My *End*.

A long pause follows, I can't hear anything once again, and a creepy silence spreads around me.

Then, suddenly; just so unexpectedly and unpredictably a reply reaches my eardrums.

"*I could never finish you off... you're too useful; it would be a shame...*"

He exclaims so confidently, so sure of *His* superiority. My heart is beating so forcefully, my pulse is visible on my temples. Bang, Bang, Bang – it pumps blood to my limbs with such ferociousness, as though someone is stabbing me relentlessly, time after time, beat after beat and it hurts indescribably.

He laughs, amused by my lame and pitiful state. Every chuckle makes every single hair on my body stand as if electricity is being passed through me. *He's* so close I can hear the sound of *His* breathing; I can hear the inaudible clatter of his eyelids as *He* blinks.

"*Oh, April...*" He tries to continue but still can't control his chortling and stops once again. He despises me; he hates me so deep – and I can tell that by the way he said my name; by the way he pronounced it.

All I'm trying to do is to not allow a single tear to slide down my terror-stricken face. Even though I'm weak and immobilized just *by His presence* I won't give *Him* the satisfaction of seeing me in such a condition of emotional turbulence. Albeit *He* knows exactly what is going on inside my head, I won't let *Him* see it on the outside – just to show *Him* that he doesn't own me, just to show *Him* that my resistance isn't over yet. If it's for me to go down, it's better to go down fighting...

"*I never really understood you, you life creatures...*" *He* utters, suddenly transforming from laughing to being dead serious – I can't even find a trace of irony or sarcasm in *His* dark, melodic voice. A voice bound to persuade; a voice bound to convince.

"*What can Life offer you that I can't?*" *He* demands, in a thundering, chilling tone. I don't answer, focusing on how I can get my body to respond, to move, trying to feel my fingertips.

"WHERE ARE YOU?" I scream out in frustration; it's as if he's everywhere. I look around, just by moving my eyeballs – my neck is too stiff for me to twist it even a tiny bit. It's as though his voice is coming from every direction I throw my gaze on to, I can sense him so clearly; he is just so painfully close...

I hate that feeling and I've always hated it – vulnerability. I have no target and that makes me a target automatically.

"At least have the guts to face me!" I spit out with discernible bitterness and unbelievable loathing. "*Coward*," I add, and my contempt cocktails with rage.

I need to know where he is – I must know. That can probably explain my provocative and impulsive behavior. You don't insult or even think of challenging the strongest creature on earth. But I can't see that aspect of my actions; I'm too blinded by my desperation and my inexplicable anger. Anger that literally consumes me and suddenly once again, flames cover every inch of my body – I'm burning, from the inside out – my feelings of disdain and disgust are so powerful my body reacts to them.

An ominous silence follows; perhaps he's shocked, perhaps I've caught him off guard. He certainly didn't expect me to act in such a jeopardous way; I pushed my luck, I was being reckless.

Step one.

Step two.

Step three.

I can see *Him*; *He* has roused from the shadows...

My blood solidifies in my veins, my pupils widen exactly like a feline's, not because I'm lamely trying to seem threatening but because I'm so numb, so astonished by what I am witnessing.

I'm staring at a tall, well built man, *His* face is unshaven and *His* black hair frames *His* triangular face. Then, I meet his intimidating gaze; *His* huge eyes, glimmer like two polished diamonds empowered by undisputable dismay. I notice the Life Commission suit *He's* wearing and I immediately lose my breath, the sense of my lungs actually...

A feeling of betrayal brings tears to my eyes, and these tears I cannot control... *How is this possible? He was on my Side, on Our Side, the Side of Life... How can He be one of them? The strongest Demon in existence? How?*

I don't want to believe it, to accept the fact that this individual I knew so well, this individual I was supposed to trust and thought of as my ally had always been the real enemy...

The corrupted...

But it's true.

I am staring at the Life Commissioner we lost on the day of the Demon attack... Someone, I instinctively disliked for some reason from the very first day of my arrival in this multi-dimensional, magical world... And now I knew the reason.

I form his name on my lips, too breathless to give sound to my declaration...
Mort.

I can't.
I can't take this... It's too *much*; I can't describe it otherwise... it's just too *much*. Big tears, big lies... And this *Lie* was right in front of me from the very first minute. I'm terrified but I'm not sobbing, I just allow my teardrops to soak my blank face one after the other feeling so stupid, blaming my innocence and ignorance for this...

"*What? I'm not as impressive as you expected me to be?*" He questions me rhetorically and ironically – I can see the pleasure in his eyes, the satisfaction he feels viewing my suffering. I'm quivering from head to toe... my level of pain has reached its apogee – I want to scream...

"*Don't fight me... It's not to your benefit...*" he tells me, giving his voice a hypnotizing shade... he comes closer and closer until he is just a few centimeters away from me, hovering over me. Right now, I feel like I'm in a car compression machine... Graviational forces are so strong on me I'm being squashed to nonexistence.

He kneels down and leans into my ear – I moan and whimper and I cannot blink. I can feel his icy breath on my shoulder and my heart stops beating in anticipation of what he is about to do. "*Look at you...*" he states in contempt, theatrically trying to sound compassionate, and pushes a strand of hair behind my ear. He touched me; and my body stopped functioning, I froze – my head was just seconds from exploding.

"*Weakened by my presence... just by my touch...*" He continues, in the same disapproving tone, and almost touches my ear with his lips. I want to pull away, to run but I'm petrified – truly. I cannot even move my eyeballs and just stare vacantly into the night. "*What an irony...*" he goes on, and smiles poisonously...

running his long fingers through my hair, amused by my grimace of torment.

"*I have to fear something as puny and negligible as a Human...*" He breathes in annoyance; the fire that had once covered me has gone out so long ago. Time seems to tick by so slowly and lazily – torturously. "*April... I know you don't want this...*" he murmurs, so bittersweet, so unemotionally and neutrally. I'm bathing in my own sweat and blood, unable to respire.

"*I know you hate this...*" And once more, his voice takes that seducing color... I'm pressing my mouth shut and I know that if I do not do so, I will scream; my lips tremor...

"*I know you too well...*" He stops for a second. "*I know you well enough, to know what you love, what you hate, how you think, but most importantly... What you **want**...*" He mouths in a way that I am drawn to so sickeningly and masochistically...

It pains me so deeply but I *like* it.

"*And I can give you what you've always wanted...*" he whispers so demonically and soullessly. Then, pulls his hand out of my hair, rolls on to his feet and paces – just a few feet away.

An impressive exhale comes out of me and I let my shaking torso fall in front, into the mud, in relief and I support my weight on my elbows. I'm panting; my system has been starved of oxygen... As I move my head slightly to one side, I see that my hair is not green or blue but a chocolate brown.

An alarm rings inside my head instantly.

I immediately search for my wings, but I don't have any. I pull up timidly, so shocked – in disbelief and stare right into *His* aggressive eyes.

It's astounding and astonishing – so *tempting*.

I'm a human again.

32. My Only Power

I'm dead! I must be dead by now. I can't sense *Him*! I can't feel that sensation of *Cold* that is so torturous but vital to me – that's how I know I'm actually a *Homo sapiens* again. Really and literally. My supernatural senses have transformed into useless human ones. My bone-snapping physical strength, speed and mental sharpness have all abandoned me. I can now feel pain – insufferable pain – I try to push my half naked body out of the flesh feasting muck that is now burning my skin; making me a bloody, blistered entity. I scream, heartbreakingly. I howl; lost in a world I could officially call *Hell*.

I'm a human, something I should find so irresistible under other circumstances. It's everything I ever asked for. A life much simpler than this, a life lacking exhausting detail and illogical facts. A life in ignorance. Everything I had ever desired was within reach, but I'd rather disintegrate in that blood thirsty slush than choose that kind of living; I already knew too much to leave. It was a matter of pride and ethics. If I chose what I *wanted*, what I honestly and truly yearned for...

There's nothing to go back to... if I betray everyone and choose to be human, there will be no *Human Side* to return to... No matter what I do, what has happened is irreversible and permanent... And once I've sorted that out in my confused, overwhelmed *mind* I realize that that indeed is the only thing I am left with.

My thoughts. A power no one can take from me, a power we're all born with.

"NO!" I shout pulling my smoldered self up, on to my feet – I stagger towards *Him*, feeling indescribable pain with every step I take. *He* is leaning against some kind of old wall, something that looks like a destroyed building and is staring at me so apathetically having his arms crossed unbothered and undisturbed by me – I knew, from the very first moment, just how much he loathed me.

I reach for the medallion hanging around my neck with my almost functionless fingers.

His eyes shine.

I can think of just one thing, I repeat it in my head over and over again.

In the Diamond, In the Diamond, In the Diamond. I can't even form a complete sentence. But before I can even get my hand on this so important jewel, *He* is holding it in his hand, having the chain wrapped around his index finger ostentatiously, letting the precious stone swing around. "*Beautiful, isn't it?*" he stated hypocritically. "You forgot something basic... we're playing the same game..." he tells me and smiles so evilly.

My comprehension is so slow, so inadequate. I lose details; small little things that I know do exist, but I just can't detect. I can hear thunder, something that I would normally react to so intensely, as though a spear is pushed into my ears, but now I am nearly unaffected by it. Perhaps that was to my benefit... I couldn't feel that iciness, that *Cold* and that helped me function in a better way, leaving out all my severe physical injuries.

I imagined his fingers burning off and instantly – just like that – his whole hand was on fire. I could still use magic! Having a human form did not affect my ability to cast spells! A tiny wave of hope revitalized my terrified mind. I saw his fingers falling to the ground one by one, while he was shrieking, staring at his own cremated hand. It gave me satisfaction – I have to admit; he was getting a taste of his own medicine.

And with his hand, fell the diamond, on the solid, stone floor he was standing on. I dragged myself there, and out of the slime that continued to eat away the tissue around my ankles. But as soon as I do so, he leans down and grabs the Locket in his other hand so incomparably fast to my human abilities. *He* wears the glimmering crystal, picks me up by the neck and throws me down on to the ground with force I cannot find words to describe. My skull cracks with a breathtaking snapping sound and I swear my brain moved inside my head.

My perception of the world blurs and obscures in just a fragment of a second. I cannot possibly express the pain, the feeling of that kind of slow death... And then *He* did it again, lifted me up and banged me on to the ground with monstrous ferociousness. I knew what he was trying to do – he was trying to stop me from *thinking*, because as long as I could think, I could win *Him*. He was trying to eliminate my last, only power.

This time, I felt my hair soaking in blood.

He let go of my neck, stood up and stared down at me – his black eyes blazed with disdain and something else he couldn't disguise but was so apparent – fear. He spat on me – a gesture that although I was in a state where I couldn't respond in any way, aggravated me so deeply.

He had just stained my *dignity*.

"How dare you?" I breathe so dimly, not staring at anything in particular, my eyes can't focus. I'm struggling to respire, inhaling and exhaling is excruciating.

He kneels down next to me and grabs my wrist. "*Shhh... you won't be with us for long...*" he whispers so self-satisfied and places his arm on top of my mouth and nose – he has no hand; I burnt it. He presses hard and my heart races demanding more oxygen I cannot provide it with.

His grip around my wrist tightens and I feel the gashes on my palm extending, traveling up the inner side of my arm – I can hear at the slitting, tearing sound of my skin and flesh – he has cut blood vessels and fountains of blood create a pool around me.

My muffled screams accompany my slaughter and the huge cut is climbing up my shoulder. I can see the black diamond; it's just a breath away, resting on his chest.

"*You won't stop me,*" he murmurs in my ear. "*No human can do that,*" he adds revoltingly, so sickeningly and wickedly. In a way that reminds me of a bewildered animal...

He is too blinded by his victory to notice that fatal mistake he has made...

I visualize in difficulty, using the very last amount of air left in my body. I picture Him, the Spirit leaving the body it has taken over and entering the walls of the diamond. I imagine it and think of it as vividly and realistically as I can – I want it with every bit of me, even if it's to be the very last thing I will ever think of.

And just when the cut reached the edge of my chin I saw *It*.

The Core leaving the body it had been in and entering the Diamond in the form of a dark shadow. The soulless, unoccupied corpse fell down on me, still wearing the medallion.

I wasn't even holding it – the Locket – but yet, I was the only one who could use it.

I breathed.

I won.

Game over.

33. Something about green...

It's over. I just can't believe it's over.
Although I am beyond a wreck, destroyed beyond description, and in spite of the fact I almost cannot breathe anymore a microscopic smile pulls the edges of my lips. It must've been such a bittersweet sight; the winner is bound to die with the defeated; it is a victory no one will ever know or learn about, no one of the two will survive to tell the story – such a tragedy.
I kind of realized that – that I would die. I relived my entire life through an intense flashback that took me back to when I was a toddler, I saw my parents, my grandpa, my friends, my cousins and Peter. It surprised me, I only knew him for so little and yet it seemed as though everything orbited around him.
He was the center of my universe.
He was the reason I had chosen to do what I'd done – just because I didn't want to disappoint him or betray him; I didn't want him to feel ashamed of me; being the supporter, friend and lover of the Chosen whom betrayed Life itself.
Even if I died I still wanted him to feel proud of me, to walk with his head held up high because I would have passed away for something *Good*, for the benefit of everybody else.

Every single atom in my make up felt dead – already. I was so completely ravaged. With virtually no meat around my ankles, with a ribcage crushed into so many pieces it could not support me, with an arm ripped and slit just like a fish fillet, with open wounds and stinging burns all over my exposed body and a skull so unutterably damaged I lost the sense of my surroundings, of time and myself.
And as if that wasn't enough, it started raining – hard – something I expected to be rather relieving, but instead, was so unbearable.

It was raining acid, a substance so toxic and lethal I assumed I was being skinned alive. My voice passed the pitch or intensity of screaming and this sounded like the screech of a car's wheels. Each venomous drop of that killing liquid hit my body with the force of a sharpened blade sinking into me.

But, even in that helpless and hopeless state my instincts told me to fight, to defend my fading self. I kept my eyes closed – afraid that poisonous solution would smolder my eyeballs. I pulled Mort's cold, lifeless body on top of me, in a desperate attempt to shield myself. I started fumbling his corpse with my nearly useless fingers, searching for that thin, silver chain around his neck which was attached to the Diamond.

The *Diamond*. My breath caught in realization of something – my very last chance of surviving this. I grabbed it – the large stone, then felt my way up the chain and pulled it off of *Him*.

I weakly and sluggishly pushed the carcass in the mud a few centimeters below me and heard the ravenous slime feasting on Him – consuming His skeleton as well. I held the prestigious crystal in my hand just above my chest and some kind of transparent bubble formed around me at once – something I could only think of as a *regeneration capsule*.

The Locket protected me. Sheltered me.

I kept my eyes shut; if it were for me to die – so be it. If it were for me to live – so be it. Yet the odds of me leaving this world were greater, I now felt hope. I felt it.

Safe, in this artificial, magical womb I was rejuvenated. I didn't have to order myself to do anything, I couldn't think anyway… it was just a natural reaction of self-repair. Proof I indeed was immortal, which was a part of my nature I only then accepted. Skin pulled together and chunks of muscle and flesh grew from where they had been torn off but I couldn't really feel anything in this lethargy I'd been in from the very beginning of my rebirth.

I could respire without pain, effortlessly; that's when I opened my eyes; to see the blood-red raindrops banging on to the clear, see through "cocoon" which was the only thing between me and my breakup. My shattered bones still needed time to join but once the hurting stopped, I could *think*, clearly and there was only one thing I could *think* of.

A set of glowing green eyes.

It was the first image that came in my mind.

And I found myself in his arms. He appeared to be shocked, perhaps in disbelief. I was now out of that nourishing bubble. He muttered all sorts of stuff which I didn't pay attention to in unspeakable silent exuberance, just because I could feel his heart thudding against my ear; just because I could smell his scent again.

Just because I could feel that pair of glimmering, lime-green eyes staring at me.

I allowed my half opened eyes to close completely, still clinging on to the lifesaving medallion.

"Take it. I don't wanna see it ever again." I breathed half asleep, giving him the diamond clumsily and fuzzily.

He moved abruptly, grabbed it before it hit the ground. He smiled – I felt him smile, heard the sound of his lips brushing the outer surface of his teeth as they formed a smile.

"It's okay now…" he muttered almost inaudibly and I hid even deeper in his broad chest, feeling so light, so weightless, so unbelievably reassured and satisfied.

Happy.

I was almost unconscious when I thought of the last thing I wanted to know, the only thing left concerning me. I turned my face towards him, gripping tightly on the fabric of his clothing and asked him in a whisper.

"Pete… *what am I?*"

He smiled even wider and answered in a gentle, smooth voice. "You're a fairy, April… you're a *fairy…*"

A fairy. What a beautiful thing to be… A grin stretched my mouth instantly – I finally knew. I knew.

I know.

Then, I drifted away in a world of dreams…

34. Guilty, Guiltier, Guiltiest

PETER

No one could have possibly imagined this outcome. The chances of her resisting were so minuscule you could easily say they were nonexistent; but yet she got out of there intact.

In one piece. In the form of a human.

And what made a human so powerful? This was the only thing I could not grasp or understand. It just was so fascinating; it changed Our way of thinking of humans, of that so weak and imperfect species. They created heroes, something so unexpected and impossible to Our comprehension. Maybe they weren't that stupid, or selfish, or inconsiderate, or insensitive after all. Maybe, there was hope for them too.

But human or not, powerful or weak, in my eyes she seemed the same. Equally important. Equally necessary. Equally needed. To me.

Now, she certainly was closer to my reach, at least I was allowed to be drawn to her.

At least. But I didn't want to destroy her...

Yes, that would be the worst of my crimes.

She had been out for three days straight. Hibernating. She looked damaged – physically. Only poison could do that, some sort of venom had been injected into her and magic needs time to fix that. But I did not worry; she couldn't die in any way. For that, I was sure.

It just angered me; who could possibly hurt a creature like her? Who could have had such a sick and wicked mind to do that? My muscles tensed; I felt my hands tightening into fists in response to that infuriating thought. I felt like an idiot, I just wished I could've protected her from that – instinctively.

Yes, I admit I wasn't just drawn to her. I loved her. She was the only thing I was left with.

I watched her as she breathed, covered in shiny, white satin, all washed and clean from mud and blood, her silky brown hair was spread on her pillow combed and cared for. She was in a state of total tranquility and serenity – I had never seen her so calm or peaceful in these two weeks – I felt satisfied, pleased; she deserved it.

The fact she was still in the form of a human mystified me though. As it all turned out, she could transform whenever she wanted. She had the power to. She was equally as human as the Chosen, no part of her had ever been lost – that is not naturally possible. She started squirming in her bed and interrupted my thoughts. I stared through the transparent curtains surrounding her and realized she was finally waking up.

I stood up and walked towards her soundlessly.

APRIL

I sat up in my bed rubbing my eyes. He reached out, pulled the curtain to one side and sat on my mattress. I looked at him for a moment.

"How long?" I asked; so sure he would understand.

"Three days," he replied. I paused for a moment, yawned once, ran my fingers through my brown hair – it surprised me, I kind of got used to that electric blue…

"You didn't believe I would make it, did you?" I questioned him, narrowing my eyes trying to read his expression accurately – somehow, my senses had come back. Even though it was tiring at some points, I loved having such a vivid and perfect perception of my surroundings; I didn't want to miss anything.

"No," he answered so sincerely – something I loved about him, he never tried to dress and cover the truth; he was always honest.

I noticed he kept on staring at my eyes; he wouldn't stop as though he was witnessing something so amazing. "What's the matter?" I enquired, raising one eyebrow.

"Your eyes… they're brown. I haven't seen anything like that before… I didn't know it was possible…" he muttered, still gazing at me intensely.

I chuckled.

"Are you trying to change subject?" I asked him smiling.

"No, not really... What was our subject again?" he wondered crookedly. His face pulled theatrically and I just couldn't avoid laughing. He did too.

I knew what it was coming out of both of us – relief. It was almost like a spastic, neurotic giggle; we were either going to cry or laugh our hearts out. We chose the second.

I kissed him. Just like that, in one second, all at once, without warning, while he was still chuckling.

"That's a nice a way to make me stop..." he whispered – I smiled and pulled away.

"Make you stop what?" I retorted.

"Anything," he murmured keeping his eyes on me, something giving me indescribable satisfaction. I climbed out of my bed and paced to the center of my room.

"You know you can go back to your family, right?" he told me; a somewhat rhetorical question.

"I noticed that," I said, twisting a strand of my hair around my index finger – examining it in controlled awe.

"Well you can either stay here, or live between the two *Sides*... you choose; at least that's what the Commission told me to tell you," he informed me.

I remained silent for a while.

"Can you do that?" he asked me, trying to read my blank face, while I was still playing with my hair.

I looked at him. "I think so..." I replied timidly, untying that little piece of hair. Should I feel happy? Sad? I didn't know what I was *supposed* to feel. Under other conditions, I would've ran away with just a single word – back to my parents, to normality, but now something pulled me into this world I originally thought of as crazy; and it wasn't just Peter. It was that I had a responsibility I would carry for the rest of my life. I was obliged to return and live between these two stunningly opposite worlds – and I did, because I was the Chosen, because I am the Chosen yet I did not choose anything of this.

It was my purpose in Life.

"We'll keep on seeing each other, right?" I questioned as calmly as I could, the idea I wouldn't see him again caused me unease — just the idea itself. This was the only thing I was actually concerned about.

"Yes. We can arrange something like that." He tried to reassure me, but I could see the discomfort in his eyes. The hate. He loathed the idea…

"Go," he added abruptly, just after a breath, standing up. "Go, don't think about it too much, just *go*," he said, clearly and loudly, in a way I could not find the courage to argue — that prestigiously.

I just nodded.

I hate a lot of things. But guilt — I just can't bear it. And can you feel guilty when you've actually saved *everyone*?

Can you?

Because I did; when I walked through the snow, in my home state Wisconsin, when I felt that bone-chilling winter wind whipping my body, when I moved through the forest of Saint George, just by Lake Michigan, when I smelled the scent of cypress and pine and frozen dirt.

It was like I'd stepped into a different world — my understanding of my surroundings was so different, so much more improved I felt like this was a world I didn't know. Of course, I had to act as normal as I could, as human as I could, I shouldn't use much strength or speed and it was hard, so hard to pretend you're unconscious of all of that life around you.

But I had to. Period.

I felt guilty because I had always thought of the Human Side as such a plain and empty world — it was such a great misinterpretation. A massive mistake.

And no words can describe the guilt I felt when I saw my mom pulling in our driveway, in her red Golf, looking so pale and sick and restless. My stomach tied into a knot.

That's when I felt as though I was a criminal. I felt ashamed.

I walked slowly, noiselessly towards her. She didn't notice me at first, locking our car. Then she looked up and I stood absolutely still, just a short distance away from her. She froze for a moment, stared at me, in my short sleeves. She walked towards me nearly tripping on the way, and wrapped her arms around me. Somehow from standing we found ourselves kneeling in the snow and she held me even tighter. She cried; sobbed loudly, pressing my face against her chest, my head was tucked under her tear-dripping chin. I hugged her back.

"I'm sorry," I said, in a tremor, feeling my eyes starting to water too; so happy I still had that mothering love and protection I could have never possibly forgotten. Feeling her heartbeat made me feel like an infant again.

I cried with her.

The next two months were terrible. Trying to convince my parents I had not been attacked or raped or abducted in any way was so difficult. They just thought of the worst – naturally. The police had told them the chances of me being alive after all that time I'd been away were tiny. The fact I had returned seemed like a miracle to them; and to me too – in many different ways and meanings.

I did not lie to them; I could never lie and I never did, but I could not tell them the truth either – it was a law of the Side of Life I could not overlook or ignore. I told them part of the truth. I told them I ran away because I needed to rethink a lot of things about life and myself and that there was a part of me that was yet to be discovered.

It sounded so poetic, right? But the chief of our town's police department came to the conclusion I had been so deeply traumatized from whatever had happened to me, that I actually had psychological problems and suicidal behavior.

I had to go to a therapist twice a week, where I acted so normal – or at least tried to avoid paying attention to all of those details and facts surrounding me twenty-four-seven. I did not talk or answer to any of his questions. I could see the frustration in his eyes, his blood pressure rose and his heart accelerated, he perspired and I could smell it. I detected and discerned everything in a very subtle and clever way, slyly, in a manner that was not obvious to the human eye or the human senses in general.

I pretended. Everything I did was pretend, even the way I breathed.

But the most challenging thing was to control my paranormal strength. I once tried to open the door of my room and instead pulled the whole thing out of its place. Holding a pen at school demanded a lot of self-control. I restrained myself; I could not move abruptly or react to a sound or a scent in the same way I could in the Side of Life.

My Life back in the Human world was full of restrictions and limitations; it was a life of hypocrisy. I could not consume any food; I could and can only drink pollen, even my mom's blueberry muffins unsettled my stomach. What I would do was that I would eat in front of them, of my parents and family and then walk up the stairs to my room and kneel over the toilet seat where my body would naturally make me vomit.

That's when they thought that apart from my "weird" behavior, I had an eating disorder.

I was now, officially, a real, problematic teenager in their eyes.

"What happened, April?" my mom would ask at least three times a day.

And my answer, every, single, time, would be: "Nothing. I'm fine, Mom." But she would never be convinced. Ever.

That was the one thing I hated and loathed with every bit of my soul. The fact that I could not trust anyone in this dimension, not even my own parents. I despised it, because I made everybody around me miserable. And somehow this became my routine. I would wake up and go to bed with that one feeling I could never stand, but had now become accustomed to.

Guilt.

JANUARY

FEBRUARY

MARCH

APRIL

35. Whispers of Demonized Souls

We all want a perfect life, don't we? We're all greedy and unsatisfied creatures – by nature. It is the only human trait I haven't managed to get rid of and I will never get rid of; it doesn't really bother me though, it makes me feel like there's still a part of me that belongs in this world, my home world. And this was the only reason why I didn't decide to live exclusively in the Side of Life; I felt and knew that there was a part of me that couldn't do without the humans. So my life was in constant turmoil as I tried to balance out my need to be in two utterly different dimensions simultaneously.

"Relax, April," Peter whispered, stroking my hair, running his fingers through them and down my spinal cord. He could see it too – I was shaking, I wanted to let my wings spring out of me so desperately; but I knew it was prohibited; any display of magic in the Human Side would result in the Ultimate Punishment.

Automatically.

"It's okay; you can let your wings out," he told me.

"No. it's not okay!" I snapped at him.

"Trust me, even if you do, *They* can't *Punish* you in any way, first you're above *Them* and second you're immortal..." he stated keeping his temper.

"And is that an excuse?" I asked him in a rhetorical question, so sure he wouldn't answer, and he didn't. "Should I take advantage of *Them*? Of everyone?" I questioned, and got no reply.

A long moment of silence followed.

I looked around me, at the fresh, crispy grass covering the surface of the meadow, at the countless flowers swaying around us; I could smell them in the spring wind, and I could taste them on my tongue. I reached out and cut one diligently, I pressed my back against the trunk of the ageless pine tree we were underneath and stared at the afternoon light as it passed through the dense canopy. I felt calm, nature always calmed me down even when I was a human, I would often visit this little clearing I quite ironically thought of as *magical* all along.

I closed my eyes and brought that bright red poppy to my lips. I licked it once, but then allowed it to drop to the ground; for some mysterious reason I'd lost my appetite. I let my head rest on Pete's shoulder who was also resting his back against the tree.

"Do you know the myth about the *Whispers*?" he asked me, in a very tranquil manner.

"No, what is it about?" I questioned curious, but didn't move from my position.

"It's about the *Demonized souls*; they say, *They Whisper*..."

I didn't say anything, I waited for him to continue, his heart raced, this conversation caused him anxiety – I could sense it.

"When a soul is taken by a Demon, it's demonized, which means that the darkest side of someone's character becomes dominant," he explained.

"But what if someone doesn't have a dark side?" I enquired subtly, trying not to pressure him.

"*You* are the only creature on earth that doesn't have a dark side..." he informed me, honestly shocking me. "There's just *inferno* for the rest of us, April..." he said, trying to chuckle once, without success.

"That's not fair, I mean don't we deserve anything better?" I wondered out loud.

"Life is a gift itself, demanding for more is being greedy, we will never live forever. That's the truth," he stated, indifferently.

I thought of my next question carefully, formed it in my mind.

"What are the *Whispers* about?"

"That's different, the *Whispers* occur only when a soul is taken while it's still alive..." he explained.

"Like... like what happened to the Visioner?" I asked reluctantly. That memory still caused me nausea.

"Yes. Exactly like that..." His voice trailed off. "And that's what happened to my parents..." he added in a nearly inaudible murmur.

For some reason, I froze. His parents and their murder were a subject I never dared to touch.

"*You see a few years ago the Demons attacked the Side of Life. The Spirits would not only take living souls, but they would also possess bodies. Even when the attack came to an end, even when They left I had suspicions of my parents' bodies hosting Demons, so I decided to kill them. Don't ask me how I managed that... I don't know, I guess that when you feel threatened you can do anything... It's an instinct.*" He stopped suddenly. I stared at him, feeling my jaw hanging open.

Silence.

"*As it all turned out my parents had never been taken over by any kind of Spirit but even so I was not granted with the Ultimate Punishment by the Life Commission because I claimed I had killed them in my defense. Instead, I was Marked by the Mirrorers; and I will remain Marked for the rest of my Life...*" he added, aware of my disbelief and total astonishment.

Another torturous moment of stillness followed.

"*I didn't tell you because I thought you would hate me... Most creatures hate me, that's what the Marks are for, so that every living thing in this dimensional universe knows I am a criminal...*" he whispered so deeply and obviously mortified.

I still didn't know what to say.

"But you don't seem to care... *do you?*" He looked at me, he just appeared to be in search of one thing – acceptance.

I smiled approvingly. "No I don't... I think you're brave," I answered. His face lightened exactly like a little child's.

We remained quiet for a few seconds.

"The *Whispers of the Demonized Souls* are about creatures like the Visioner and my parents, souls that weren't supposed to die at that particular moment in time and now want to return from the dead, so what we hear as whispers are Their desperate screams..." he told me gently, passing his arm around my waist.

"I know it's probably untrue, but it just creates the illusion that they're still with me, that maybe they have forgiven me..." he muttered in a way that reminded of unspeakable heartache.

"Okay, let's try to listen..." I breathed, allowing my head to rest on his wide, muscular chest once again, feeling a mothering need to calm him down, to reassure him, to protect him. I placed my palm on top of his hand, holding him tightly appreciating his trust so deeply and soulfully.

I closed my eyes, trying to focus, trying to distinguish that sound he had described as a whisper. I ignored the swishing sound of the wind as it passed through the leaves of the trees, as it bent the grass around us, as it made the flowers and blossoms surrounding us dance to its rhythm. I overlooked the beautiful singing of the birds, the sound of the waters of the lake a few kilometers away.

I could've sworn I heard something.

A sound so weak and trivial, no human could possibly detect it. A sound close to mute, overruled by everything and yet, I had managed to break up any other kind of noise and to listen to it carefully – yes, they were whispers indeed.

I squeezed his hand in mine; perhaps it was not just a myth.

We could hear the Whispers of the Demonized Souls...

Rate this book on our website!

www.novum-publishing.co.uk

The author

Born in Cyprus, fifteen year old Antonia Kattos is the daughter of an Australian-born Greek mother and a Greek-Cypriot father. Whispers of Demonized Souls is her debut novel which she hopes will be the first of many. When not writing, Kattos enjoys composing and performing music, loves drama, ballet and spending time with her cats. She also cherishes long and lively discussions with her twin sister Irene.

novum 🟥 PUBLISHER FOR NEW AUTHORS

The publisher

> **Whoever stops getting better, will in time stop being good.**

This is the motto of novum publishing, and our focus is on finding new manuscripts, publishing them and offering long-term support to the authors.
Our publishing house was founded in 1997, and since then it has become THE expert for new authors and has won numerous awards.

Our editorial team will peruse each manuscript within a few weeks free of charge and without obligation.

You will find more information about
novum publishing and our books on the internet:

www.novum-publishing.co.uk